SLAMMED

SAN AMARO SINGLES 3

KELLY JAMIESON

This book is a work of fiction. The names, characters, places, and incidents are products of the writer's imagination or have been used fictitiously and are not to be construed as real. Any resemblance to persons, living or dead, actual events, locale or organizations is entirely coincidental.

Slammed

ISBN: 978-1-988600-34-5

Cover by Mayhem Cover Creations
Print Formatting by Stacey Price

PRAISE FOR THE NOVELS OF KELLY JAMIESON

"Kelly Jamieson delivers a blazing passionate read that tugs at the heartstrings!"

~ Carly Phillips, *New York Times* Bestselling Author

"seductive and bewitching from the very start… Softly romantic and wickedly provocative"

~ *RT Book Reviews* on Rule of Three

"Kelly Jamieson now has a permanent place on my keeper shelf and I can't wait to see what she writes next."

~ Joyfully Reviewed

"…I love Kelly Jamieson's books and the way that she depicts her characters…"

~ Sizzling Hot Book Reviews

1

Stand up as best man at Matt and Corey's wedding? Jesus, he'd rather take a longboard in the nuts.

Dylan gave his cell phone a black look and then held it back up to his ear. His best buddy Matt had emailed him about this, but now he was on the phone pressing for an answer. "Yeah, thanks and all, but I don't see how I can get back there for the wedding."

"We planned it for September because we knew you'd be back then for the Jackson Cole Pro," Matt said. "You're going to be here anyway."

Huh. Dylan ran his tongue over his teeth and stared out at the blinding turquoise of the South Pacific lagoon from the deck of his thatched bungalow over the water. Fuck. He couldn't miss that competition, even though he knew he'd likely have to see Matt and Corey when he was back for it.

"The wedding's the weekend before the competition," Matt added. "That gives you time to get here from Tahiti."

Yeah. True. Having just finished the Rip Tide Open in Tahiti, his next stop on the tour was San Amaro, California.

"We want you here, man. Seriously. It would mean a lot to us."

Best man? What a joke! Seeing as the bride-to-be had picked another man, Dylan hardly felt like the "best man".

He drew in a long breath and let it out. "I don't know. I don't know if I can swing it."

He looked up as Lexi emerged from the bungalow onto the deck, completely naked. Her tanned body gleamed in the sunlight and she shook back her long blonde hair, giving him an impatient what-the-hell-are-you-doing look. He smiled.

"Look, I can try to make the wedding. But I can't commit to being best man if I don't know if I'll be there for sure."

He heard Matt's sigh of frustration. "Dylan. We gotta talk about this."

"Talk about what? You know I'm stoked for you and Corey." His insides twisted as he said that. Lexi sauntered across the deck toward him and he let his gaze run up and down her stunning body. Sadly, he was too rattled by the phone call from Matt to be aroused by her. She lowered herself onto his lap and wrapped her arms around his shoulders, nuzzling the ear not occupied by the phone.

"Then come home and help us celebrate this."

Dylan gritted his teeth. He was being cornered into this. He couldn't make many more excuses. "Can I let you know? Give me a day or two, okay?"

After a brief pause, Matt said, "Okay. Fair enough."

"I'll see what I can do," Dylan promised.

Yeah, he'd see what he could do about finding a reason not to be there.

He ended the call and tossed the phone onto the small table.

"Come back to bed," Lexi murmured. "We're waiting for you."

He grinned, thinking of Suri inside, with her smooth bronze body and long black hair. "Yeah. Sorry. Had to deal with that."

He stood, lifting Lexi with him, and strode back into the bungalow. Suri was stretched out on the white sheets of the four-poster bed. The wooden blinds had been closed, filtering the sunlight and making the room cool and dim. The ceiling fan circled lazily above them, the slight breeze from it fluttering the sheer white fabric draped from each of the bed posts.

Two hot and willing women in his bed would take his mind off that phone call and all the things he didn't want to think about.

"How about a trip to Tahiti?"

Brooke stared at her boss across the table in his office where their PR team had gathered for a meeting. "Tahiti?"

Barrett nodded, his steel-colored hair gleaming beneath the small pot lights of his office. He looked at her over the black-framed reading glasses perched on his prominent nose. "Yeah. All expenses paid."

She frowned. "I don't get it."

"We have a little problem. With Dylan Schell."

Oh God. Not again. She sighed. "Now what?"

"He's out of control. We can't have one of our athletes running around the beaches in Tahiti naked, having orgies, drunk and high pretty much all the damn time."

"Sounds like a good time to me." Her co-worker Tim gave an envious sigh.

Brooke pursed her lips to stop her smile, then gave Tim a reproving look.

"Kidding," Tim said. "Sort of. I know, I know, this is a PR nightmare."

Brooke swallowed a sigh. "He did well in the competition there last week, didn't he?"

"Yes," Barrett said. "He came in second place and now he's ranked third. He has a great chance to win the Jackson Cole Pro if he can beat Heath Marlow. But the better he does, the wilder his behavior gets. We're trying to sell a wholesome image to all those kids who're buying our gear. This isn't cutting it."

Brooke bit her lip. It had been her idea to sponsor Dylan

Schell about a year and a half ago. His pro surfing career had been on the rise and the fact that he was a local boy made him perfect to help sell their casual clothing. She'd pushed hard to get them to agree. She recalled telling them how Dylan Schell was one of the most progressive and exciting surfers in the sport, with good looks and charisma that made him super popular with the fans. Then he'd had that accident, and a broken foot had kept him out of competition for a couple of months. That had been bad luck and crappy timing. He'd gotten back to it with a slow start, looking like he'd lost his edge, and they'd all been biting their nails to see if he was going to live up to their expectations. He'd started winning again, but the next sign of trouble had been when he'd lost a big competition after a spectacular wipeout and had then told the media, with a shit-eating grin, that he knew he shouldn't have had group sex the night before. He'd gone on to win a few more competitions but had then caused an uproar when he'd been drunk on a flight, which had to turn around and return to Sydney. Apparently he'd been trying to convince some of the female flight attendants to join the mile high club with him.

"Why do *I* have to go to Tahiti?" Tahiti was nice, but that would involve flying. On a plane.

"He needs someone to keep him out of trouble," Barrett said.

Brooke snorted. "You think *I* can do that?"

Barrett gave her a cool look. "You wanted us to sponsor him."

She firmed her lips and met his eyes. "Yes. I did." She'd take responsibility for her actions and defend her decision. Even though Dylan Schell was making it difficult. "I still think he's a good choice."

"No," Barrett said. "He is not a good choice. We're spending a ton of money on him and we're not getting the return on our investment that we need. With profit margins as slim as they are, every dollar we invest in an athlete should propel sales ten to twenty times that investment."

"Realistically, that's never going to happen," Tim pointed out. "With anyone."

"I don't give a shit," Barrett said. "It's not happening with him and it's not even close."

"You want to cancel his contract?" Brooke leaned forward. "That will cost a lot too. We signed him for three years."

"I know. That's why we're not doing it now. We're willing to give him one more chance. The Jackson Cole Pro is coming up. We want you to go get him."

"I think we should talk to his agent first."

"I did. Holden's wife just had a baby. He's a little preoccupied and isn't going to be flying to Tahiti. But he says he's with us one hundred percent on this and will work with us when we get Schell back here. Which is great, but not good enough. We need to get him back here and keep him out of trouble."

She swallowed. "How am I going to do that?"

"We're going to set up some things to keep him busy. You're going to stick to him like shit on a shoe."

"Things like what?"

"I don't know! Find something for him. Do some talks to kids about staying off drugs, some motivational crap about finishing school, yadda yadda. We haven't worked out the details of what we'll get him involved in. That'll be your job. Yours and Tim's. You know what I want. Now make it so."

"You want me to babysit him."

"Call it what you want. You're going to have to lay it on the line for him. He either does this or he's in breach of his contract with us and he's done."

She nodded slowly, processing what he'd just told her. "I'm still not sure I'm the best one to do this."

A trip to Tahiti sounded amazing, other than the fact she had to fly to get there, but going to deliver a top pro athlete a lecture on his bad behavior, give him a hard line ultimatum and then make sure he acted like a good boy, did *not* sound like fun. They needed someone with a lot more—ahem—balls than she had to do something like that.

"You've said you're interested in moving up in the company."

Barrett narrowed his eyes at her. "You've told us you're willing to do whatever it takes. You've said you're willing to take on any projects to demonstrate your abilities."

Yup, she'd said those things. She was so screwed. "Okay." Her stomach clenched hard. "I'll go."

"You're the one who pushed for him," he reminded her again. "If we can't turn this around, upper management is going to want someone to take the fall for this."

She kept her face carefully composed as she glanced at Tim, whose mouth had fallen open a little. Barrett's comment didn't really surprise her. She'd seen this happen before. When things were going well, Barrett was the first to take the credit, but when things went wrong, he was only too happy to let someone else take the blame. If Dylan Schell continued to screw up, the message was clear—she'd be the one to pay the price.

"I'm not sure if Brooke has the stones to play hardball with him," Tim said.

Brooke's back teeth ground together and she curled her fingers around the armrests of the chair she was sitting in. But Tim was only trying to help. The truth was, she wasn't sure she had the stones to play hardball with Dylan Schell either.

"I can do it." She firmed her lips. Okay, yeah, she got it. She had a choice. Either drag Dylan Schell back here, keeping him out of trouble, or Dylan wouldn't be the only one out on his ass—she'd be out of a job too.

Shnippits! She'd been busting her butt at Jackson Cole for three years now. She was doing a good job. Could they really fire her over one bad decision? And it hadn't even been her decision. She didn't have the power to decide who they sponsored, she just made recommendations. She picked at the loose cuticle on her thumb as her mind whirled.

Yeah, they probably could fire her. She loved her job there and had ambitions for moving up in the company, but she had no illusions that this was a business, and she had no illusions about the type of boss Barrett was.

"When do I leave?"

"As soon as you can. You and Tim have some work to do to get things planned. I want every minute of Schell's time filled while he's here, and not with parties and drunken orgies."

She met Tim's eyes.

He lifted his eyebrows and gave her a small smile. "Sure. We can do that. Let's get started, Brooke."

Three days and a fifteen-hour flight later, Brooke landed at Tahiti Faa'a Airport in Papeete. Tired, grouchy and grungy, she was also ready to kiss the ground once off the plane. God, she hated flying. She'd almost been willing to fill the prescription her doctor had given her the last time she'd had to travel, but she hated to resort to drugs. Surely she had guts enough to make it through a flight on her own. So she'd spent most of the flight in a heightened state of anxiety instead of sleeping like she should have been, and now she was exhausted. Relieved, but exhausted.

She located a taxi to drive her to L'Auberge Pacifique, where Dylan Schell was apparently staying. She should be thrilled to be in such a beautiful, exotic location, but instead she was irritable and on edge. She tried not to take it out on the front desk clerk who checked her in, or the smiling young man who carried her suitcase up to her room for her.

The hotel was amazing, sleek and modern with shiny dark wood floors and white furniture arranged in the lobby in casual seating areas. They passed by a coffee shop, a long white leather banquet that curved into a half-circle with small dark wood tables and bright orange leather chairs, then a lounge with dark wood stools pulled up to a sleek metallic bar and funky wicker chairs grouped around low glass tables.

God, she wanted to lie down. She rubbed at gritty eyes and shoved a hand through hair that felt lank and greasy.

She tipped the smiling bellhop and tried to smile in return, then let the door to her room slowly shut behind her. The room was small, but she wasn't going to be there long. She grimaced at the thought of flying halfway around the world for what would probably be two days.

She walked across the white tile floor toward floor-to-ceiling windows, the dark drapes pulled to the sides, windows which were actually sliding doors onto a small balcony. Outside the sun shone down on lush green foliage, palm trees waving gently in the breeze.

She turned to the bed, covered in a pristine white duvet. Oh yeah. That was what she wanted. She eyed it hungrily, but she had to focus on business first. She needed to track down Dylan Schell and arrange a meeting.

She sat on the bed and called the front desk, asking to be put through to Dylan Schell's room. The phone rang and rang but there was no answer. When voicemail picked up, she hung up and bit her lip. Okay. She tried the cell phone number they had for him. Also no answer. Hmm. What to do now?

She could go looking for him. Apparently he was staying in one of the little thatched bungalows over the water, from the word they'd gotten about his recent activities there. She was curious to see those luxury accommodations. Dylan must be doing okay in the prize money department if he could afford to stay there.

With a last longing look at the bed, she rose and picked up her purse.

Outside in the hotel grounds, the sun seared her retinas and she rummaged in her purse for sunglasses. She slid stylish Jackson Cole shades onto her nose and started down a path that curved past lush lawns, carefully trimmed shrubs, bright flowers and of course more palm trees. Warm humid air caressed her skin and soon she was sticky and sweaty in her black pants and white shirt.

Damn, she should have changed before she came out here. She was used to warm weather living in California, but San Amaro right on the coast never really got that hot, and off-shore breezes kept it comfortable. This was tropical with a temperature near ninety degrees, and the scorching sun made her black pants feel like a sauna.

She dug into her bag for an elastic band and pulled her hair back into a ponytail, which helped marginally.

Definitely beautiful here though. She passed by tennis courts and then a sparkling turquoise pool and her feet slowed and halted as she took it in—turquoise water lapped on white sand. This was the *pool*? Holy crap!

She shielded her eyes and followed the path. Up ahead she spied more blue water. That must be the lagoon and hopefully where the bungalows were.

Indeed. Again she stopped to take in the sight of the wooden deck that stretched out into the lagoon and the quaint thatched roofs of the huts on either side of it. She sighed. Unless Dylan Schell was outside it wasn't going to be easy to find him.

She stepped onto the beach, strolling past the small stone wall that separated sand from grassy area. Dammit, these ballet flats weren't meant for this. Sand inside them scraped uncomfortably on her feet. She stopped and slipped them off, picked them up then continued toward the dock, her feet sinking into silky pale sand. She'd give anything to get out of these clothes and into a swimsuit. But that wasn't exactly professional attire for an important business meeting, even if this was French Polynesia.

Women in tiny bikinis and sarongs wrapped around their hips strolled along the deck, men in flowered board shorts with some of them. She regarded their casual attire enviously. A family with several small children squealing with excitement headed toward the pool. Brooke studied people, looking for Dylan.

She hadn't seen him in person for years but she was pretty sure she'd recognize him. They'd gone to the same high school in San Amaro, but that had been ten years ago. She'd seen recent PR photos though, the ones on his website, the ones they used to help market their apparel and other ones on the Internet about the Association of Surfing Professionals World Tour surfers. He hadn't changed much since high school, according to those photographs. He still had longish dark hair that hung over his forehead and he still had those amazing silvery-gray eyes fringed with thick dark lashes, still had that sexy smile that beamed white in his tanned face.

She wandered down the deck, glancing at the bungalows, unsure which was his. Perhaps she should have left a voicemail. But she had a feeling he wasn't going to return a phone call from someone from Jackson Cole wanting to arrange a business meeting.

Drunk. High. Orgies. Her stomach clenched thinking about Dylan's activities lately. He'd always been a bit of a bad boy, even in high school, with girls after him all the time. He probably wouldn't even remember her. She'd never been one of those lucky girls who'd attracted his attention. Not that she'd wanted his attention. Okay, well, she couldn't say she would've turned him down if he'd noticed her, but really, that was so far outside the realm of possibility she hadn't even entertained that as a fantasy. He'd been a jock, a surfer, athletic and talented, someone everyone knew was going to make it big. He'd been fearless and exciting, charming and fun.

She blew out a breath. She'd lost patience with this. She returned to the front desk. "Hi." She smiled. "I need to know where Dylan Schell is staying."

"I'm sorry," the young woman said, as expected. "I can't give out that information."

"You can give it to me." Brooke made her smile businesslike. She pushed her card across the desk toward the other woman. "I'm with Jackson Cole, one of Dylan's sponsors. We need to meet with him urgently about some business matters."

"Oh." The woman looked at the card, then back at Brooke, taking in her attire, so different from the casual clothing everyone else there wore. Also taking in her lack of makeup, lank hair and sweaty face. Clearly she wasn't a beach bunny trying to get with a pro surfer. "Jackson Cole. Really?"

She no doubt recognized the name as one of Dylan's biggest

sponsors. They were well known in California and getting more known in the US, maybe even this far away. After all, the ASP event had just happened there; probably everyone had been aware of the surfers and the big sponsors and all the media who'd been there covering the event.

"Yes." Brooke kept her smile in face. "It's pretty important for his career."

"I could put you through to his room."

"I tried that already." Brooke leaned closer. "He didn't answer and…not that I'm worried…but I hope he's okay. Apparently he's been pretty…um…busy lately."

The girl nodded and lowered her eyes. "Er. Yes. He has."

Flerkinschmidt. She knew it because she'd been with him. Brooke resisted an eye roll.

The girl lifted her eyes and Brooke saw the ire there. Oh damn. The other woman was pissed at Dylan. No doubt he'd blown her off for other girls.

"He's in bungalow eighteen."

Yes! "Thank you so much." Brooke slid a U.S. twenty dollar bill across the counter.

She hurried back outside, retracing her steps through the grounds, past the pool, across the beach and down the wooden dock where the bungalows were. Sixteen…seventeen…eighteen. Yes.

She approached the small structure. The door was closed but unlocked. She gave a rap on it then stepped inside. "Hello! Dylan? Dylan Schell?"

She shoved her sunglasses up on top of her head. Even so, it took a moment for her eyes to adjust to the dimmer light inside the bungalow. She blinked a few times, looking around. Her eyes fell on the big four-poster bed and spotted a dark head there, a stark contrast against white pillows. His eyes appeared closed. He was in bed? At this time of the afternoon?

"Yeah, baby, suck me, just like that…" Dylan's hoarse words reached her ears, but before she could turn and get the hell out of there, his eyes flickered open and met hers. The bedcovers started moving and Brooke's gaze moved over the shapes beneath the duvet. Oh dear God…

A head emerged from beneath the bedcovers, a woman with long blonde hair, kissing her way up Dylan's chest, and then another woman emerged, this one with long dark hair.

Heat swept up from Brooke's chest into her face, scorching her cheeks.

"Hello, sweetheart," Dylan drawled, his white smile flashing in the dim room. "Have you come to join us?"

2

Pretty, but way overdressed. Dylan smiled across the dim bungalow at the woman standing in his door. Her pulled-back dark hair revealed a perfect oval face with big dark eyes and a small mouth. That mouth was now parted in surprise, her eyes going wide enough for her eyeballs to pop out and roll across the floor.

Hell. She apparently wasn't there to make the threesome a foursome.

"Oh God." Then she straightened her shoulders and pressed those pretty lips together. "No, I'm not here to join you." Her gaze flickered to Suri and Lexi. "I'm here on business. And you need to get out of bed and get dressed."

He narrowed his eyes at her. Who the hell was this? Jesus. This day was going from bad to worse. First Matt called and got him riled up by asking him to be best man at his wedding, the last wedding in the world he wanted to be at, then he'd been so rattled he'd actually had a hard time getting it up with two hot chicks.

"I don't think so, sweetheart." He pulled Suri and Lexi back down. "We're a little busy, if you hadn't noticed."

"I noticed. And you'll have to finish your little ménage à trois later…like maybe in a year and a half when your contract with Jackson Cole expires."

"Huh?" Jackson Cole?

"I'm Brooke Lowry, Assistant Manager, Marketing and PR. And we have important business to discuss. If you want to keep your lucrative contract with Jackson Cole."

Annoyance and a quick shiver of fear ran through him. "We can talk later," he told Brooke Lowry, Assistant Manager, Marketing and PR. Suri went to slide out of bed, and he caught her wrist. "Hey babe, don't go."

"I think we'd better." Suri slanted him an apologetic glance. He watched in dismay as both girls walked over to the dresser where they'd left their bikinis. Apparently being naked in front of a stranger didn't bother them one bit, and they donned their suits and retrieved sunglasses, flip flops and their big beach bags. Then Brooke stepped aside as they exited the bungalow with cheery waves.

"Catch you later, Dylan," Lexi called.

Well, he didn't give a shit about being naked in front of a stranger either, and this uptight Marketing and PR manager needed to loosen up a little. He threw back the covers and swung his legs over the side of the bed, then stood. Brooke's eyes dropped briefly to his junk, went wide again and even in the dim bungalow he could see the pink flush that tinted her cheeks.

She half-turned away and folded her arms across her chest. "Put some clothes on. Please."

"Meh." He sauntered over to the bar in the corner and grabbed a beer out of the fridge. He had no problem being naked. "I'm good. Would you like one?" He held up the cold bottle.

She glanced over at him, then did that little straighten of her slender shoulders again and turned to face him, although keeping her eyes on his face. "No thanks."

He leaned casually against the bar and guzzled down half the bottle of icy cold brew. Damn, that was good. "So what's up, buttercup?" He hoisted one eyebrow.

Her mouth tightened. "I really think this conversation is one you want to have with your clothes on."

Alarm bells went off in his head. "What conversation is that, sweetheart?"

"Please don't call me sweetheart. This is business. Fine, if you want to do this here and now, let's do it." She drew in a breath and looked up at the ceiling briefly. "Head office sent me to talk to you about your recent conduct."

"My conduct?" His insides contracted.

"Yes. Your exploits have made it into the news, which has gotten back to the executives at Jackson Cole. They are not pleased, to put it mildly."

He kept his face neutral. He hoped. "What 'exploits' would those be?" he asked, his voice bland.

"Things like group sex in the middle of the afternoon."

He narrowed his eyes at her again and lifted the bottle. "Hey. We were in the privacy of my bungalow and *you* came barging in. What I do on my own time in my own bedroom is my business."

Her cheeks pinkened again and those dark eyes flashed sparks. He wanted to grin. Yet somehow he knew this wasn't going to be funny.

"Other things then. The drunken partying. The orgies that people *do* know about. The dope-smoking and nudity on the beach. We've managed to smooth things over with the media on some of the other things you've done, not the least of which was being arrested for that Quantas Flight having to turn back to Sydney."

His back teeth ground together a little at the mention of that. Yeah, that hadn't been one of his more epic moments, even he had to admit. It had all just been in fun, a little flirting with the flight attendants, and yeah, he'd had a few beers, but Jesus, they'd totally overreacted by turning the plane around. It wasn't as if he was dangerous, for fuck's sake.

Suddenly being naked didn't feel quite so comfortable, and he set down the beer on the bar and reached for the board shorts draped over the nearby chair. He stepped into them and quickly tied them loose and low on his hips.

Brooke's gaze dropped briefly once more, tracking over his abs and the shorts, then jerked back up to his face. "For God's sake, take those off," she snapped.

"Uh..." He gave his head a little shake. "Okay, sure sweetheart, but I thought you wanted me dressed."

"Those are Billabong shorts! You can't be seen wearing the competition! Do you have some kind of death wish, or what?"

Her words made his insides leap and he stared at her.

"Where did you get those anyway? Why would you even *have* them?"

He looked down at them blankly. "I don't know where I got them," he said shortly, fingers fumbling with the ties. He let them drop to the floor, kicked them aside and strode over to the dresser. He yanked open the top drawer and grabbed a pair of shorts. He had a fucking hundred pairs of them and he was pretty sure most of them were Jackson Cole. He stepped into the shorts, this pair a black and white flowered pattern. He picked up the offending garment and held it over the waste basket, catching her eye and then dropping it in.

"That's better. Geez."

"My deepest apologies," he said in a dry voice. "I didn't mean to offend you. Who knew my nudity would be less offensive than a pair of board shorts made by the competition." He held out a hand to the small sofa and chair. "Have a seat. Sure you don't want a drink? I have water, pop..."

"No thanks." She did move toward the sofa and took a seat, perching stiffly on the edge.

He took a seat too, on the chair adjacent, and gave her one of his most charming smiles. "So, I'm in trouble."

She eyed him for a few seconds then jerked her chin. "Yes, Dylan. You're in trouble."

Great. Just fucking great. "Is Jackson Cole pulling the plug on me?" He leaned back, trying to appear casual, but his heart had started to beat a little faster.

"Not right now. But you have to turn this around or they will be. One more chance."

He frowned. "What does that mean?"

"It means, they sent me here to get you and bring you back to San Amaro. Next stop on the tour, right?"

"Right."

"Our PR team has some things lined up to keep you busy over the next few weeks. Some charity events and good causes for you to work at. We'll make sure the media sees you at these events. We are going to polish your image all up and put a halo on your head. And then you are going to surf your ass off and win that competition."

He studied her, sitting there with her hands on her knees, her spine straight. "Hey. Don't I know you? Brooke Lowry!"

She tipped her head to one side, lips pursed. "Took you long enough."

"Man! Pacific Heights High School! I can't believe it. Now you work for Jackson Cole?"

"That's right."

"What a coincidence!"

He really only vaguely remembered her from high school. She'd hung out with a different crowd, the kind of crowd that had intimidated him—smart and yet not geeky, they were the kids who'd run the student council, the social committee and probably a dozen other things he didn't remember. He'd never been that much into school. He hated sitting still for any length of time and the only thing that had gotten him through had been Matt's tutoring. He couldn't help but remember that with fond gratitude toward Matt, even though the bastard had ended up with Corey.

He wasn't going to think about that right now.

"I guess it is." She shifted on the couch and dropped her gaze. "Long time no see."

"For sure!" Maybe being old friends would soften her toward

him a bit. Except they'd never really been friends. And clearly she already knew who he was when she'd arrived there and she hadn't exactly been...soft on him. Shit.

He kept his smile firmly in place. "So. Tell me what you've been doing for the last...uh...ten years."

She waved a hand. "That's not what I'm here for. We're here to talk about you."

"Oh. Yeah." His smile faded. "Look, things can't be that bad. I've been having a little fun celebrating my wins, that's all. I'm a surfer, people expect us to do those things."

She gave a heavy, long-suffering sigh. "Unfortunately, that's true. That surfer counter-culture holds some appeal for certain people. However, your sponsors—or I suppose I can only speak for one right now—do not. Jackson Cole has been expanding our brands, trying to enhance our image. We don't want a drunken stoner representing our products."

"That's not me!" He gaped at her, but heat washed over him as he recalled the wild parties over the last few days. Again, shit.

"We're booking you on the next flight back to the States," she said firmly. "With me. And then we have work to do."

"The next flight." He frowned. "Back to San Amaro."

"That's right."

His gut cramped, but he pulled his mouth into a smile again and sat back, crossing one ankle over the other knee. "No can do, sweetheart."

"What?" Now it was her turn to gape.

He shook his head and pushed his hair out of his eyes. "No can do. I can't go back to San Amaro right now."

Brooke's fingers dug into her knees through the black pants that were still baking her alive. God, she envied Dylan's loose, cool shorts. Or nudity. Although the sight of his naked body was doing alarming things to her pulse and respiration. And other parts of her.

Holy guacamole, he was gorgeous. His tanned, athletic body was honed to perfection, lean enough to show off every single one of those perfectly cut muscles. Ripped didn't even begin to describe him. His chest was smooth and hairless, his abs mouth-wateringly defined, his arms strong. He walked around the small bungalow on long legs, his thick thighs and strong calf muscles flexing as he moved, his butt muscular and his back as defined as his abs. And geez Lord his package…she'd gulped at the sight of his thick, half-hard penis resting on his testicles, surrounded by a thatch of black hair.

There was something to be said for the athlete's body. What would he be like in bed? The sex would no doubt be athletic too, and her mind started heading off down an inappropriate path. She had to give herself a mental slap to bring herself back to reality.

"What do you mean you can't go back to San Amaro now? Why not?"

His beautiful lips pressed together and he dropped his gaze. "I just can't."

He looked like a sullen little boy, which should have annoyed her but instead made her heart flutter. "Either you tell me a good reason why you can't—and it better be a good business reason—or we're on that plane tomorrow."

"I can't tell you." He lifted his head and the pleading look in his silvery-gray eyes had her going soft inside. "Could you just take my word for it? It's not a business reason, it's personal."

Oh for the love of cheese…she could only imagine the "personal" reasons that would make him not want to go back to San Amaro. A woman. Or women, no doubt. She closed her eyes and rubbed her forehead. "Somehow I knew this wasn't going to be easy."

"I'm sorry, Brooke. It's nothing personal against you."

She met his eyes, softened even more by his apology. "I know. But I have a job to do."

His mouth tightened and he nodded. "Sure. But I'm still not going."

"You sound like a two-year-old. And you've been acting like one too."

"I have not." Their eyes met and he burst out laughing, then shook his head ruefully. She couldn't help the smile that tugged at her lips. "I guess that didn't convince you I'm not acting like a two-year-old. But seriously. Two? I don't think so." She caught the carnal gleam in his eye. "Sixteen, maybe," he added, and she rolled her eyes and repressed another smile.

"Let me lay this out for you." She leaned forward. "Do you know how much Jackson Cole is paying you? Or does your agent deal with all that for you?"

"I know," he muttered.

"Good. Then you know what exactly is at stake here."

He sighed.

"I know you have other sponsors. But I'm still thinking that losing this one would be a hard hit. Am I right?"

He pursed his lips and gave her a baleful look.

"You know, you should be nicer to me. I could turn around and go home alone and tell them I couldn't convince you."

He tipped his head to one side and regarded her thoughtfully. "Go right ahead."

Shit! He'd called her bluff. She couldn't do that because her own effing job was on the line. "I'm booking our flights." She reached for her purse. She dug her phone out of her purse as he glared at her, found the airline information and made the call. "We leave tomorrow night at eleven forty-five," she told him when she ended the call. She sat back in the chair. Okay. What were they going to do for the next…uh…twenty-nine hours? She rubbed her index finger over the ragged cuticle of her thumb.

"Great." He slumped lower in the armchair. "I need another beer."

"How many have you had today?"

He squinted at her. "Really? You're going to monitor my alcohol intake?"

"You bet I am."

"This is my second beer."

"Bullshit."

He sat forward, elbows on his knees and fixed her with an intense silvery look. "I may be acting immature and irresponsible and whatever else you want to accuse me of, but *never* call me a liar," he said very softly.

A shiver worked its way down her spine. "I'm sorry."

He held her gaze.

"Fine. Have another beer. But you're not leaving my sight until we're on that plane tomorrow night."

He smiled slowly. "Really. You're moving in here with me then? There's only one bed." He cocked an eyebrow and let his gaze roam over her body. "I'm up for it though."

Her fingers curled into her palms, nails digging into her flesh and she took in a long, deep breath. "No, I'm not moving in here. Okay, I didn't mean I need to watch you sleep. I just meant, I'm keeping you out of trouble. So I'm sorry, but your friends will have to do without you. No more threesomes, no more partying."

He dipped his chin and gave her a look through eyelashes. "Oh come on. Partying is fun. You can't tell me you came all this way to spend one night here, and you're going to pass the time sitting watching TV or something? Nuh-uh."

"I'm sure there are other things to do that don't involve getting drunk and taking our clothes off."

"Well, sure," he drawled. "But those don't sound nearly as fun." He lifted his chin, smiling. "Admit it."

Her insides quivered and heat washed down over her. She glanced at her watch. "We'll go have dinner. In the hotel restaurant. After that we'll see."

"After that we'll see if I can get you drunk and naked?"

She gritted her teeth. And it wasn't just out of annoyance at him. She was annoyed at her own hot reaction to the idea of getting naked with him. Geez, what was wrong with her? He'd just rolled out of bed with two other women, two centerfold-worthy women with whom she could never compete. He was nothing but a…a…man slut. Why on earth was she even thinking about what sex with him would be like? "Dylan. You can't talk to me like that. We're…business colleagues."

That sexy lift of his eyebrow had her melting a little bit. "No we're not."

"Yes. We are. I'm here to deliver a strong message to you and basically give you a choice. Either you shape up or you're going to be in breach of your contract. Not only will you not get paid the remainder of the fees, it's highly possible Jackson Cole would sue you."

His smile disappeared. "I need to talk to Holden."

His agent. "Go right ahead. We already talked to him. He would have come here himself if he and his wife hadn't had a baby four days ago. He knows all about this and he's on board with the plans. My team is working with him back home, while I'm here."

"San Amaro isn't home," he muttered.

She wanted to roll her eyes, but his refusal to go back to San Amaro and now this comment triggered something inside her that made her curious about what was going on for him.

"Well you may not live there now, but you grew up there and everyone still thinks of you as the hometown boy who made it big. We're going to capitalize on that in the media as soon as we get back."

He dropped his head, looking at the floor between his knees and for a moment he looked so defeated and vulnerable, she wanted to go over to him, drop onto her knees beside him and rub his back, comfort him… Oh for God's sake. *Get a grip, Brooke.*

"Okay." He stood. "Let me change and then we can go grab some dinner."

3

"I need to change too, before we go for dinner." Brooke looked down at herself. "And shower."

"Sure. How about we meet in the restaurant in an hour? Is that enough time to beautify yourself?"

"I'm not going to beautify myself. I just want to wash the travel off me and change into something cooler."

He eyed her clothing. "Yeah. Don't blame you."

She rolled her lips in. "Gee, thanks."

"We can meet at La Terrasse." She blinked at his perfect French pronunciation. "Tonight there's dancing—Tamure."

"Tamure?"

"Tahiti's national dance. You'll enjoy it. And since you're only here for a day you should see some Tahitian culture. Did I mention how insane that is to fly this far for one day?"

"No, you didn't." She hesitated before leaving. "You'll stay out of trouble for the next hour?"

"I'm going to call Lexi and Suri back for a quickie." He shrugged. Then he caught her eye. "Kidding! Jesus. I'll be fine."

"And you'll show up at the restaurant?" She fixed her sternest gaze on him.

He sighed. "Yes."

"Okay. One hour. See you then."

She wasn't sure if she entirely trusted him, but how much trouble could he get into in one hour? Although part of the trust issue was doubting that he'd actually show up. What would keep him from taking off across the island somewhere with his surfing buddies? She bit her lip.

"Brooke. I said I'll be there."

He held her gaze steadily and her doubts faded somewhat. He seemed sincere. "Okay."

She hurried along the wooden deck that linked the thatched bungalows together. It was nearly six o'clock and the sun was setting already, tinting clouds that lined the horizon peach and lavender, turning the lagoon to liquid silver. She spared a glance for the beauty of it, her footsteps slowing as she paused beside a palm tree and let the low fronds frame the sunset. A sigh escaped her. This was a stunning place, and she had the next twenty-some hours to enjoy it. When she wasn't arguing with Dylan Schell.

Frack, she'd walked in on him and two other women. How frickin' embarrassing was that. He hadn't seemed embarrassed. Oh no, not at all. Probably because he did things like that every day. God.

She let herself into her room, now dark, and flicked on the light. She hadn't unpacked a thing, and she quickly unzipped her suitcase and found her toiletry bag. In the bathroom, the shower felt like paradise. She used some of the body wash provided by the hotel, scented with pineapple and papaya and passion fruit, inhaling the sweet fruity fragrance. She washed her hair with similarly scented shampoo, then stood there and let the water from the soaker head pour down over her like rainfall. God, that felt good.

Strangely she wasn't as tired as she'd been earlier. Her little match with Dylan had given her a shot of adrenaline or something. After blow drying her hair, she wrapped a towel around her body and strolled into her room to find something to wear. She'd packed more than enough clothes for one day. She actually hadn't been sure how long she'd be there, depending on how long it took her to track Dylan down and convince him to come back with her. She still wasn't sure if he was going to be on that plane with her tomorrow night. He'd told her when he said he'd do something, he did it, and it was true, they'd never had any issues with unreliability. He did manage to show up for events that he was supposed to. But even though she'd booked the tickets, he still hadn't said he'd come home to San Amaro with her.

She pulled out a sundress which she hoped would be suitable for the restaurant. The resort seemed very casual despite the luxuriousness. She slipped on the bright orange halter-style cotton dress then returned to the bathroom to add a little makeup. She eyed her reflection in the full wall of mirror above the marble vanity. She'd thought she had a nice bit of color after the summer but compared to people there in Tahiti, including Dylan with his bronzed skin, she looked pasty. Whatever. Too much sun was bad for the skin.

She brushed a little color on her cheeks, added a few swipes of mascara to her lashes and then used a peachy lip gloss. Good enough. Now to find the restaurant.

She perused the directory in her room and located La Terrasse on the main floor, to the right of the reception desk. She could find that.

Dylan stood at the entrance to the restaurant, waiting for her. She took in his beige pants, the fitted white shirt that he wore untucked with the cuffs turned back on his strong forearms. He turned as she approached, his dark hair falling across his forehead, his hands in his pockets. She caught the flash of surprise on his face when he saw her.

"What was that look for?" She looked down at herself. "Am I dressed okay for here?"

"Yeah." He blinked. "Hell yeah. You look gorgeous." He frowned. "I don't remember you being gorgeous in high school."

She rolled her eyes. "You sweet talker, you."

"I didn't mean to be insulting! I just mean, why didn't I notice you more in high school?"

"You were too busy fending off all the other girls who were after you."

"Oh. Well, yeah, there is that."

She shook her head, smiling reluctantly.

"I guess you weren't one of those girls."

"As if." He would never have noticed her.

His mouth tightened a little, but he set a hand on the small of her back to guide her into the restaurant.

"Good evening, Mr. Schell." The hostess smiled at him, but flicked her eyes at Brooke. "We have your table ready."

"Your table?" Brooke murmured, following the hostess.

"I called and booked one for us. It gets busy here the nights the show is on."

They were seated at a table for two near the stage, which currently was dark and quiet. Soft music filled the room along with a hushed murmur of voices and clinking cutlery. Strategic lighting provided an atmosphere of intimacy despite the size of the restaurant.

"Very nice." She pulled her chair in.

"The food's amazing too."

"You've been here before, obviously."

He lifted a shoulder. "I come here a few times a year, for the last…shiz, I don't know how many years. Yeah, I've been here before."

She looked around, took in the smiling, laughing guests, all of them dressed similarly to her and Dylan, casually but yet with an air of affluence. This was a little out of her league, but she kind of liked it. She picked up her menu and opened it.

"Is there anything you recommend?" She scanned the selections.

"Hmm. Well I'm pretty partial to red meat, myself, so I'll probably go for the Black Angus sirloin. But if you like fish or seafood, I'd suggest the mahi mahi."

She nodded and read from the menu. "Mahi mahi with sweet vanilla sauce and pureed sweet potatoes. Vanilla sauce?" She lifted questioning eyes to him. "On fish?"

"It's awesome. Try it."

"Okay." She looked over the appetizers and desserts too. When their server approached, Dylan ordered a bottle of a New Zealand Sauvignon Blanc.

"You're pretty sophisticated for a surfer dude, aren't you?" she commented once he'd ordered.

He grinned. "You pick up a few things when you travel around the world constantly. Even though you may think all I do is smoke dope and party."

"I didn't say that's all you do." She fiddled with her cutlery. "But you have attracted a little attention lately by doing that."

"Whatever, dude."

Her gaze snapped up to his face. "No, not 'whatever, dude'," she said, exaggerating his surfer drawl. "This is serious business, Dylan."

"I surf for a living. How serious can that be?"

She stared at him in frustration. Was he serious? This was how he earned his living. This wasn't a game or a party or a joke. This was big business. Millions of dollars big.

But then she saw the way the corners of his mouth dipped down, the shadow that crossed his eyes as he looked away from her. She nibbled her bottom lip.

The server returned with their wine. Brooke studied Dylan as the server uncorked and poured the wine.

"You folks just arrive here?" the young man asked.

"Yes," Brooke said.

"Nah," Dylan replied.

The server's forehead creased but he smiled. "Well, hope you're not leaving soon."

"Why's that?" Brooke asked.

"Big storm coming."

She blinked. "Oh. Really?"

"Yeah. They're saying it should hit tomorrow. Could be a Category One hurricane."

"Oh Lord." She looked at Dylan with wide eyes. "Did you know about this?"

"No." He grimaced.

Oh yeah, apparently he'd been partying too hard to pay attention to the weather.

"The brunt of it may miss us," the server said cheerfully, setting the wine into the wine bucket. "It'll probably hit more north of here, but we're still going to get some weather."

Brooke picked up her wine glass and took a gulp. "What does that mean?"

Dylan shrugged. "Who knows? If it's expected to be really bad, they'll tell us."

He was so laid back about it. A freakin' hurricane? Dear sweet Jesus.

"Can't do anything about it." He leaned back in his seat, once more smiling and relaxed. "So who's paying for this dinner?"

"Jackson Cole."

He grinned. "Great. Maybe I'll have a lobster tail too."

She dipped her chin to look up at him through her eyelashes. "I don't think they'll question my expense account for this trip."

"Killer. We can go into Papeete later and hit some clubs…"

She held up a hand. "Okay, they *might* question my expense account."

"Darn," he drawled.

"Are you ready to order?"

Brooke looked up at their server with a smile. "I think we are." She ordered the Asian salad with shrimps, soy bean sprouts and peanut and coriander vinaigrette sauce, and the mahi mahi. Dylan requested the same salad and the sirloin steak. No lobster.

"Have you ever seen Tamure?"

"No." She shook her head. "I've never been to the South Pacific at all. Not even Hawaii."

"Oh man." He gave her a sorrowful look. "Some of the best waves in the world."

She smirked. "Not San Amaro?"

"Well, I do have a soft spot for Breaker Beach."

"You did well here."

He grinned. "Hella good. I was frothing. The waves here are killer."

"I've watched videos of you surfing. You're pretty amazing." She hated to stroke his already inflated ego, but it was the truth.

To her surprise he looked a little embarrassed. "Thanks."

"You get to travel a lot, don't you?"

"Yeah." Then he actually sighed. "Sometimes it gets kind of old. I mean, it's fun, and I love surfing, more than anything. Really, I'm lucky I've been to some amazing places. Brazil, Portugal, Australia, Brazil."

"I'd love to be able to travel more. I spent time in Europe after college, but now I never seem to have the time."

He eyed her. "Workaholic?"

She made a face. "Pretty much, yeah." She was also a bit of a homebody. She'd missed her hometown and all her friends and family so much when she'd been away at college, all she'd wanted was to go home.

"So maybe now you'll tell me what you've been up to for the last ten years."

She smiled crookedly. "Sure. Why not? We have all night, right?"

"If you say so, babe."

It was like he couldn't turn it off, couldn't help that sexy flirting that came so easily. Sadly, she was apparently as susceptible to it as every other beach bunny that hung out with the pro tour. He probably didn't mean a word of it, but it sure seemed like he did, like he looked at her and found her attractive, like he really did want to…oh God. He made her melt inside. He made her—dammit—like him.

"After I graduated, I went away to college."

"Where?"

She repressed a smile. "Phoenix. I got my MBA in Marketing. I missed San Amaro a lot, so I came home to find a job after I graduated. I ended up in San Diego. I got a few years experience and then an opportunity came up at Jackson Cole. Their home office is right outside San Amaro and it was the perfect chance to move back. That was three years ago."

"You like your job there?"

She looked down at her wine glass. "I do. I really like the work and I love the company. My boss is a bit…difficult." She looked up and smiled. "But that happens to everyone at some point, right? I work with a good group, and the company itself is amazing. They're doing some great things and I've learned a lot."

"That's good. I was really happy when they wanted to sponsor me. I liked the idea that we were both from San Amaro."

She nodded. That was one of the things she'd used to sell him when they'd been considering the sponsorship.

"So I gather you're not married." He glanced meaningfully at her bare left hand.

"No."

"Boyfriend?"

"Eh…no. I was seeing someone for a while, but it kind of fizzled out."

"Fizzled out?" He lifted one eyebrow. "Couldn't have been that great, then."

"It was okay. He was nice."

"Nice. Huh. Sounds boring."

She frowned. "He wasn't boring. He was nice. He was…you know, comfortable."

"Oh, babe." He leaned forward, those silver-gray eyes gleaming like moonlight. "Comfortable is boring."

She shivered with little ripples of excitement. No one would ever call Dylan Schell comfortable. Or boring.

"So if you've been with Jackson Cole three years, why didn't I meet you when they signed me?"

She pursed her lips. "I was just a junior Marketing Assistant at that time. Very much behind the scenes."

"And look at you now. In the big time, baby, traveling all the way to Tahiti."

She snorted. "Hardly. I'm now an Assistant Manager, but that's not even close to the big time." She didn't tell him how much she wanted to manage her own marketing unit, not only for the additional responsibility, which she knew she was ready for, and not only because of all the ideas she had for innovative ways to market their products, but because then she'd report to the Head of Cross-Channel Marketing, instead of to Barrett.

"So what exactly do you do?"

"Lots of things. I manage day-to-day relationships with external PR agencies, I do online media monitoring and crisis management. My department creates communication strategies, in collaboration with store operations, of course. We also work with legal, finance, merchant and marketing teams. I develop relationships with journalists, bloggers and PR agencies, respond to media and blogger inquiries and work on developing written materials like marketing briefs, press releases, corporate messaging. That kind of stuff."

"Huh." He looked thoughtful. "So it was media inquiries about me that started this whole thing?"

"Yes." She held his gaze.

Their salads arrived and they chatted more throughout the dinner, Dylan telling her surfing stories and things about Tahiti, reminiscing a little about San Amaro.

"When was the last time you were back there?" she asked.

"About a year ago. I spent some time there when I was out with my broken foot."

"Oh that's right. That must have been tough."

He shrugged and laid his cutlery on his plate to indicate he'd finished. "I survived. How was your fish?"

"It was amazing. Your steak was good?"

"Bitchin'."

She grinned.

"Do you have room for dessert?"

"I don't think so. You go ahead."

"Nah. I don't do sweets."

"Oh." She blinked. "You follow a special diet?"

"As much as I can. Traveling makes it hard sometimes. Mostly I do high protein, low carb. I haven't worked out the last couple of days since the competition, so better not do dessert. And…" he made a face, "…I've had a few digestive problems lately. Some kind of acid reflux thing. Christ, that makes me sound like an old geezer."

He was an athlete, she had to remind herself. His discipline with his eating seemed at odds with the hedonistic lifestyle he lived. "Of course it doesn't. It's good that you manage it. It sounds like you're very disciplined."

He met her eyes. "With some things," he drawled.

Um. Yeah.

The show started, so when their table was cleared they both shifted chairs to face the stage, which brought them closer together. The lights dimmed and spotlights illuminated the stage as seductive drumming music began. Tribal and insistently throbbing, it set off an echoing pulse inside Brooke's body.

Dancers filled the stage, moving to the drum beats, girls dressed in swaying skirts and bikini tops with flower wreaths around their necks and on their heads. Their arms moved in fluid lines, their bare feet graceful on the stage. At first Brooke thought it similar to hula dancing as the rhythm alternated between smaller, faster drums and deeper, thudding drums, the girls shaking their hips in perfect unison. Then the tempo picked up speed, the girls' hips moving so incredibly fast yet in perfect rhythm, the dancing became almost frenzied.

The girls were so beautiful with their dark hair and eyes, lots of smooth skin, the costumes revealing toned midriffs and bare arms and legs. The dancing was sensuous and suggestive. She snuck a glance at Dylan from time to time, his face illuminated red then gold in the stage lights, his attention focused on the dancing, even though he'd likely seen it many times. Then as she looked at him, he turned his head and met her eyes and smiled. "Enjoying the show?" He leaned closer to speak into her ear.

His scent rose to her nostrils, a fresh clean scent, like wind and water, warm and male. She breathed it in and it filled her head. She nodded with a quick smile for him, then turned back to the stage. Aware of his big body near hers, his big dark hands lying on the white table cloth then lifting to applaud at various times, the flash of his white smile at the entertainment. At one point, one of the dancers smiled back at him, holding his gaze and he lifted his wine glass in a subtle acknowledgement. Brooke slanted a glance sideways at him. Did he know her? Oh what was she thinking—he probably knew *every* dancer up there. Intimately. Her insides clenched at the thought.

Another woman came on stage to perform a solo dance to the beat of a single bongo-type drum. Her long, black hair hung to her waist and shimmered in the spotlights. She wore a red flower over one ear, a red bandeau bikini top and a wrapped skirt rolled at her hips. She began to sway to the music and again the tempo picked up, the drummer playing faster and faster, the woman's graceful arms waving and her hips shimmying. When she turned her back to the audience, her skirt twitched and swung as she rotated her hips with jaw-dropping speed. Brooke couldn't take her eyes off the way she moved, the sexuality in her motion.

When the show ended, she turned to Dylan. "That was amazing!"

"I thought you'd like it."

"I wish I could move my hips like those girls!" Their grace and control amazed her.

"You could learn."

She laughed. "I don't think so. That's mind boggling how they move like that."

He leaned closer. "When missionaries arrived on these islands, they were horrified by how suggestive the dances—and how naked the dancers—were. They thought it was sexual and sinful, so they banned it."

"Um. It is pretty suggestive." That sounded prudish. "Not that I don't like sex." *Oh my God.* She'd obviously had too much wine at dinner. "I mean, those girls are beautiful and sexy." Heat swept over her face. She turned to the breeze that drifted into the restaurant through large opened windows, letting it blow her hair back and cool her hot cheeks.

"Hey, don't worry, you're just as sexy as they are."

"I wasn't worried." She shifted back from him.

"Well, good. So…what now?"

"Um…"

"Do we call it a night?"

"I guess so." Fatigue rolled back over her. "I'm really tired. That was a long flight and I didn't sleep much."

"Okay." He rose and held her chair for her as she stood too. "So. Your place or mine?"

4

Brooke gazed back at him. "When Barrett said to stick to you like…um, well to stick close to you, I don't think he meant we had to share a hotel room."

Dylan grinned and lifted a hand to ease back a strand of dark hair that had blown across her face. The wind was really picking up outside. How bad was this storm going to be? He glanced out into the dark night, at the palm fronds tossing in the wind, then mentally shrugged and turned his attention back to the beautiful woman in front of him.

She'd surprised him when she'd appeared outside the restaurant. Earlier, when she'd interrupted his sexytimes with Lexi and Suri, she'd seemed so buttoned-up and tight-assed, hair scraped back off her face, dressed in business clothes that seemed so out of place in the exotic paradise. Then she'd arrived wearing this tropical-orange halter dress that showed off an amazing body, including killer legs from what he could see of them from the just-above-the-knee hem. Her hair hung down past her shoulders in loose waves and curls, and with shiny lips and a little color in her cheeks, she was…hot.

The sexy, half-nekkid dancing, although he'd seen it many

times, always stirred up a little heat inside him. Maybe that was making him see Brooke as hotter than she was. Maybe that was making him say stupid suggestive things like "your room or mine" when he didn't mean it.

Oh hell, who was he kidding? He totally meant it. He'd do her in a heartbeat.

"You never know what trouble I could get into overnight," he murmured.

More color flooded her pretty cheeks and her long eyelashes fluttered. "Hmm. That's true."

His heart skipped a beat. "I only have one bed," he reminded her.

"Me too." She sighed. Then she patted his cheek. "We'll just have to go with the separate rooms, I guess."

"Damn." He smiled into her eyes and she held his gaze, and holy shiz, heat flared up sizzling hot between them. He was pretty sure it wasn't one-sided either. "I'll walk you to your room."

"That's okay. It's not far from here."

But he took her hand and led her out of the nearly empty restaurant. They passed through the spacious lobby, still buzzing with people after the show, then up the elevator to her second floor room.

"You don't have a view of the lagoon," he said when they turned right after emerging from the elevator.

"No. It's a garden view, or something. It's still pretty and I didn't come to sit and look at the view."

They paused outside her door and he noted the room number. She fished her key card out of her little purse then paused. She turned her head up and looked at him over her shoulder. "Thank you for a lovely evening. I actually enjoyed it."

He laughed. "You sound surprised."

"Well, I didn't really expect to enjoy this trip. I pictured myself chasing you with a big stick, trying to get you on the plane."

"You haven't got me on the plane yet."

She turned her body more toward him, her forehead creasing.

"You are going to come back with me, aren't you? Didn't I convince you how serious this is?"

He smoothed back a strand of hair again. She had really nice hair, long and shiny and silky. He wanted to wrap it around his hands. "Sure. But I also told you I don't want to go back this soon."

"When did you plan to show up in San Amaro?" she asked with a touch of exasperation.

"I usually get to a competition a few days ahead of time."

She slumped against her door. "Not this time, Dylan. We have plans."

"Maybe I have other plans."

She turned and let her forehead drop against the door with a thunk. And then did it again.

"Hey." He pulled her back. "Don't do that."

"You're frustrating me. And I'm too tired to deal with this right now."

He blew out a breath. "It's late. Let's meet up for breakfast. No, brunch. You need sleep. Call me when you're up."

"Fine." The word came out between clenched teeth, which amused him. She slipped the card in and out and then opened her door and stepped inside. "Good night, Dylan. Behave."

"Yes, ma'am. I will."

He watched her door swing closed with a click, then turned and headed down the hall. Behave. Fuck. He was going back to his bungalow, alone and sober. Two things he did not like to be lately. Alone and sober he started thinking about crap, thinking about things like tanking in the water, things like being pounded by a wave, and things like Matt and Corey getting married.

As he passed the bar, he cast a longing look inside. He saw a few familiar faces. Most of the guys had left Tahiti and headed home or off to their next competition. He could go in and have a drink and shoot the breeze with whoever was there who wanted to talk. Probably there'd be some beach bunny in there who'd be eager to go sheet surfing back at his bungalow with a champion surfer.

Then Brooke's face appeared in his mind. He shook his head. If she made him go back to San Amaro, he'd have no excuse for not going to Matt and Corey's wedding. He'd have to be Matt's best man. Christ, he couldn't do that!

Tension gripping his body, he passed by the bar and headed out the back exit into the hotel grounds. The winds had picked up even more, bending palm trees and blowing leaves around. He picked up his pace into long strides until he reached his bungalow, let himself in and then leaned against the door for a moment. Going to bed—alone, dammit—was about all he could do.

He awoke after a restless sleep full of frustrating dreams about tanking and being pushed to the bottom of the ocean, interspersed with sex dreams involving… Christ, no, not Brooke. After he'd left San Amaro, he'd dreamt a lot about Corey, but only now did he realize that hadn't happened for a while. But Jesus, he'd just met Brooke yesterday. Well, technically he'd met her about ten or twelve years ago, but that didn't really count.

He ordered coffee from room service then walked out onto the deck overlooking the lagoon. Holy crap. The dark sky loomed close to the ground, wind churning up the water of the lagoon into foamy waves. Down at Teahapoo, the waves were probably eight or ten footers, but with the wind and rain, there would be no surfing. Thank God the competition had wound up earlier in the week.

Trade winds whipped the palm trees back and forth, some of the more slender trunks bending under the pressure. A few drops of rain splattered him and he headed back inside, closing the doors he usually left open.

He showered, drank coffee, watched a little television, waiting for Brooke to call him. He was starving. He checked his cell phone for the time. Shiz, nearly noon. Was she still sleeping?

A knock at the door had his head whipping around and he jumped to answer it, expecting Brooke. Instead it was hotel staff.

"My apologies for disturbing you, Mr. Schell. But we're moving everyone out of the bungalows because of the storm."

"What?" He leaned against the doorjamb.

"The full impact of the storm is expected to hit here tonight. We need to move everyone to the main hotel building for safety. I'm very sorry, but we'll find you alternate accommodations for tonight, or longer if necessary."

"You're kidding me."

"No, I'm sorry. If you need any help packing your belongings, I'd be happy to send someone to assist you."

"No, no. I don't need any help. When do we need to move?"

"As soon as possible. As you can see, the winds are really picking up and it's beginning to rain. If this does turn into a Category One cyclone, these bungalows will be at risk."

"Yeah. I guess so. Sure." The man nodded and turned away.

Dylan closed the door and surveyed the bungalow. He'd been here a while and had his shit all spread out, but he always traveled pretty light, other than his boards. He sighed as he began to throw stuff into his bags.

Once packed, he headed out, shaking his head at all the others exiting their bungalows with worried expressions on their faces, loaded down with their luggage. What was he supposed to do now? Go to the front desk, probably, and find out where they were going to put him for the night.

But the hotel lobby was pandemonium with guests and suitcases everywhere, kids screaming and running around, anxious parents trying to control them while they lined up at the front desk. Jesus. Dylan paused and rubbed at the faint burning feeling in his chest, then sighed and bypassed the lobby and went to the elevator. He rode up to Brooke's floor and hauled his stuff down the hall to her room.

When she didn't immediately answer his first knock, he frowned again. Had she gotten up and gone for breakfast without calling him? He raised his hand to knock again and the door opened.

She stood there, hair mussed, eyes sleepy, dressed in a pink tank top and a pair of pink-and-white polka dotted shorts. His eyes immediately went to her braless breasts, soft beneath the top, nipples clearly visible. His groin tightened and he swallowed.

"God, what time is it? You woke me up."

"It's past noon. You slept for twelve hours."

"Oh wow." She rubbed her eyes and blinked at him. Then her eyes fell on his luggage and she frowned. "What are you doing? Did you check out already?"

"Er, no. Bad news about the storm. They made me evacuate the bungalow."

"What?" She shoved her hands through her hair. "Come in. I'm not awake yet and I'm confused." She stepped back and he followed her in, bringing his belongings with him. The room was black, with the curtains drawn across the windows and no lights on. She obviously wasn't aware of what was going on outside.

He crossed to the windows and drew the curtains. Watery light spilled in, but here, away from the ocean, looking into a courtyard of sorts, the effect wasn't so obvious. The palm fronds whipped back and forth and a gust of wind blasted rain against the glass doors. "The storm is hitting hard. They're worried about the bungalows so they made us all leave. They're going to find other rooms for us, but it was gnarly down there in the lobby so I came up here."

"Well, we're leaving tonight anyway," she pointed out, staring out the window.

"Um. Doubtful. The airport is likely closed."

"What?"

He gave her a big smile. "Sorry, sweetheart. It's not my fault."

"Well, you don't know that for sure, do you?"

"No. But I'm fairly certain."

"I'll phone and check." As she moved to the desk where her phone was charging, he admired her legs. Yup, killer. She was probably only on the high end of average height, but her legs were long. Long, slender and smooth, making him want to run his hands up and down them. His dick twitched in his loose shorts.

She made the call but didn't say a word, so she must have gotten a recording. Then she stabbed a button on the phone and dropped it to the desk. "Shit. I can't believe this." She turned to him. "It is closed. All flights in and out are canceled."

He lifted one shoulder and smiled. "I figured. You wouldn't want to be on a plane trying to take off in a cyclone."

"Cyclone!" Her eyes went wide.

"Yep." He moved back to the window to look outside. "I guess we're safe here."

"Oh my God. I can't believe this."

"I'm starving. Get dressed so we can go find some food."

She stood there, her fingertips of both hands resting on her jaw. "Food. Okay." She looked around the room as if still half asleep.

"Or we could just go back to bed." He glanced at the queen-sized bed with rumpled white sheets, pictured her naked there, with those long legs wrapped around him. Oh hell, now he was really hard.

She snorted. "As if."

Well, that had gotten her moving. She poked around in a suitcase and pulled out another sundress. With a glance his way, she then found what looked to be the skimpiest little pink panties in the world and then…he watched…a strapless bra. She disappeared into the bathroom to dress, closing the door firmly behind her.

His bottom lip pushed out in an amused pout. Then he smiled.

Heh, this was kind of funny, actually. Not that he wanted to be in the middle of a cyclone, but at least they weren't headed back to San Amaro tonight. This wasn't going to last forever though. Even the worst storm would probably only shut things down for a few days. He sighed. It bought him a little time, but she seemed pretty determined to get him back there. And he reluctantly had to admit he didn't have a helluva lot of choice.

He had other sponsors, but they were small peanuts compared to Jackson Cole. Yeah, he'd just won big prize money, but if he wanted to keep going, if he wanted to win it all, he needed money and he needed sponsors. He wasn't stupid. He knew if one sponsor dumped him because of bad behavior, it would be next to impossible to find another one.

The last year had been rough, with more losses than wins, meaning he wasn't exactly rolling in dough. It had also been rough mentally. Losing wasn't something he particularly liked. He had goals. He was going to be the best. He was going to win it all. He loved surfing. It was the only thing he was any good at, and last year when he'd come *that* close to losing it, it had totally fucked with his mind. If he didn't have surfing, he didn't have anything, and *that* was enough to pucker his asshole.

Brooke emerged from the bathroom, still a little heavy-eyed, which was bitchin' sexy. She shoved her pajamas into the case then brushed the skirt of her pink-and-white flowered sundress down over her hips. "Okay. Let's go. We can see if we can find out more about the storm. Maybe the airport will reopen later."

Yeah, not likely. But he didn't say that.

Down in the lobby, she surveyed the chaos with a crease between her eyebrows. "Whoa."

"Don't worry about it right now. Luckily you have a room. Let's grind."

She made a face at him that didn't hide her amusement and followed him to the coffee shop. When he ordered eggs and fruit, she shrugged and requested the same. They waited as the server filled their coffee cups.

"What do you know about the storm?" Dylan asked the young Tahitian girl.

"Tropical cyclone Joyce." She smiled. "It hit Bora Bora last night and is slated to hit here later today. The center is about two hundred miles west-northwest of here."

"How bad at Bora Bora?" Dylan picked up his coffee.

"Gale-force gusts and bursts of torrential rain. There are trees down, power's out. If it turns more south it could be worse here, but they don't think that will happen." She smiled again, seemingly taking it all in stride.

She left and Dylan met Brooke's worried eyes. "Are we safe?" she asked in a near-whisper.

"Yes. Of course." He reached out and covered one of her hands in a gentle squeeze.

"What if there's a tsunami?"

He laughed. "That would happen after an earthquake. It's just a tropical storm."

"It has a *name*. They only name *big* storms."

He laughed again. "True. It's a big storm. It could cause some damage, but they're used to it here. It happens. We're safe here in the hotel. Though it would be hectic out on the waves."

She gasped. "Don't even think of that!"

He grinned. "I'm kidding. Sort of. I'm not stupid. Well, sometimes a little reckless. But no, I'm not going surfing today."

"I guess not." She sipped her coffee, looking a little more bright-eyed. "What are we going to do today?"

"Good question. I thought you might want to see some of the sights, but I guess we're not going anywhere today."

She pouted a little. "I get one day in a tropical paradise and a freakin' cyclone hits. That is so not fair."

"True." He sent her a sympathetic smile. "But you'll probably get more than one day now."

"Damn. I need to get home. I have work to do. I left Tim with a whole list of things to work on to get in place for you when we get back."

He curled his lip. "Oh yeah. Okay, tell me what you've got in mind for polishing up my image." As if there was anything wrong with his image. People loved him. Didn't they?

"I contacted an organization in San Diego that deals with kids in disadvantaged neighborhoods. We're planning to bus a group of kids in so you can teach them how to surf. We think we can make it a regular thing. Of course you won't always be there, but maybe we can find someone else to keep it going."

He sat back in his chair. "Huh. Okay. I like kids."

"Good. That's good. How do you feel about the environment?"

He gazed at her blankly. "I'm in favor of it."

She laughed. "Also good. There are a lot of environmental groups who work to preserve oceans. I thought that might be something important to you, seeing as you spend so much time in the ocean."

He nodded slowly. "Yeah. True. I guess I'm not that up on the problems there are."

She leaned forward. "I found a group called Oceans Alive that's implementing programs to reduce urban runoff and preserve the environmental integrity of southern California's beaches and coastal waters. They're really keen to hook up with you and use your star power to further their cause."

"I don't know anything about urban runoff. But I do despise fudge tunnels."

She gave him a blank stare.

"When you're in a tunnel that's all brown and yellow because of the pollution. That's sick."

"Fudge tunnel. Um, yeah. So, good. In the next few weeks you'll be learning all about runoff and pollution, as well as learning about the challenges those kids face. You'll be talking to people about the importance of preserving the ocean and coastline around San Amaro and all of southern California."

He rubbed his face. "You make it sound like I'm going back to school." Bleh.

"Well, we'll try to make it as fun and interactive as possible, but you'll have some reading to do. In fact, I brought some materials with me, thinking that the long plane ride home might be an opportunity to get started. Maybe we could do that today."

"Sounds like fun." *Not.* Although he was kind of intrigued by her ideas. Last summer when he'd been back in San Amaro he'd hooked up with a couple of sisters who ran a surfing school that taught mostly kids how to surf. He hadn't been in the water with them because of his broken foot, but he'd spent some time with them and it had been kind of fun.

"There are a whole range of things we could do." Her voice warmed and her hands moved as she talked. "There are a lot of environmental groups, there are skin cancer foundations—"

"Skin cancer!"

"Yes. Because you spend so much time outdoors and in the sun, it's something you should be aware of for yourself, and promoting sun safety would be a good link."

"Uh huh."

"But we thought it's probably best to pick a couple of key things and focus on those, rather than spread yourself too thin."

He shoved a hand through his hair as their waitress appeared with their meals. They waited as she set plates in front of them then refilled their coffee cups. He pulled a pill out of his shorts pocket and downed it with his orange juice, then looked up to find her staring at him. "What?"

She blinked. "What was that?"

He rolled his eyes. "Just some medication for the acid reflux thing. Don't worry, Brooke, I'm not popping illicit drugs at breakfast."

She bit her lip. "Oh. Sorry."

"Okay. So no skin cancer stuff?"

"Well if you feel really strongly about it, we could…"

"No. No, that's okay. Kids and the environment sound good."

She frowned a little, picking up her fork. "You have to come across as sincere about these things, for this to be really effective. We need passion and commitment from you."

"Passion and commitment." He stared down at his plate. Well. Passion he understood. He had it for surfing, lots of it. And commitment too, he supposed, although that word did always make him clench up a little. He definitely liked his freedom. Being tied down to anything gave him the willies. He looked back up at her. "You do know that once the competition is over, I'm out of there? I don't live in San Amaro anymore and I can't stay."

She picked up some of her scrambled eggs and he watched her mouth open to pop them in. She chewed and swallowed. "Yes. I do know that. We hoped you might stick around for a while after, but we know you have your surfing to concentrate on. That's your first priority and we recognize that."

"Okay. Good."

"What is it with San Amaro? You don't want to spend any more time there than you have to, do you?"

5

Dylan shrugged, again dropping his gaze to his food as he cut a piece of pineapple and stabbed it with his fork. "Nothing. It's just…there's nothing there for me anymore. I don't need to spend time there."

Once again, a tingle of intuition told her there was more to it than what he was saying. She didn't want to push him but geez, if she knew what was bothering him, maybe she could help him get past that and then this wouldn't be so painful for everyone involved. She'd anticipated some resistance when she came here, because he was probably having fun living a wild party life and probably didn't want to be dragged back to reality and working for the sponsorship money Jackson Cole was paying him. But she hadn't anticipated *this* much resistance, and it was clearly because of going back to San Amaro.

"Do you still have family in San Amaro?" She already knew he didn't, but this could be a starting point to finding out what the problem was.

"Nah. My parents split up years ago and they both moved away."

"Was that a tough time for you?"

He blinked at her across the table. "What? My parents splitting up?"

"Yes."

He snorted. "Not hardly. They never got along. Fought all the time, made everyone miserable. Ending their marriage was the best thing they could've done." He shrugged. "Anyway, it happened after I'd left home. I guess they probably stayed together because of me, and then when I started traveling and surfing, there was no reason to stick it out any more."

"Do you have bad memories about their fighting? From when you were a kid?"

He narrowed his eyes at her. "What is this? Some kind of counseling session?"

She smiled, trying to appear relaxed and conversational. "Just talking."

"My life wasn't that bad. I had friends. And surfing. I had a lot of fun."

"Yeah, you seemed like a guy who had a lot of fun in high school."

"I wasn't exactly a serious student."

"No. But we all have different talents."

"True."

Well, that had gotten her exactly nowhere. "Do you keep in touch with friends there? Who did you hang out with? Oh, I remember…Matt Ferber. Wasn't he your best friend?"

The flicker in his eyes told her she might have hit on something. "Yeah. That's right. And yeah, I keep in touch with him. Some. Haven't seen him a lot since high school, since I'm traveling so much."

"But you were back last year, you must have seen him then."

"Yeah, I stayed with him." He set his cutlery down on the empty plate and pushed it away from him. "I'm done. How about you?"

"Mmm." She picked up the last piece of sweet and juicy papaya and popped it into her mouth. "This fruit is so good."

"I think I'll hit the hotel gym and work out." He pulled out a wallet and drew out money to pay the bill.

"Hey, I'll get this. It's a business trip."

"You got dinner last night. No worries." He tossed the money on the table. "Let's go."

Well. Just when she thought she might be getting somewhere, he changed the subject and now he was bolting.

"I should work out too." She pushed back her chair and followed him out of the restaurant and into the lobby, still crowded with displaced guests. Through the front doors and windows, rain poured down in gray sheets, wind tossing it at the window where it beaded and ran in silvery rivulets. "Wow, look at that."

"Storm's picking up."

"When do you think it will be over?"

With unspoken accord, they began walking toward the elevator.

"No idea. I guess we could check on that."

"I should call the office and let them know what's happening. We weren't sure how long I'd be here, but yesterday I sent them an email telling them I'd be back Tuesday."

"Guess that's not going to happen."

"Guess not."

She pulled out her phone as they stepped out of the elevator but frowned at the small screen. "No service, dammit."

He peered at her phone. "Nope. I guess the storm's interfering with cell service."

"Shit. Well, I can try the room phone."

But once in her room, she discovered the phone lines were down too. "Oh man." She sank onto the side of the bed with a sigh. "This is awful."

"At least we still have power."

The lights flickered ominously. She glanced around. "You're jinxing us."

He grinned. "Don't use the elevators any more today."

She bent her head. "Jesus. Wouldn't that be perfect, getting stuck in an elevator?"

He started unbuttoning the loose, brightly printed shirt he wore.

"What are you doing?"

"Changing. To go to the gym."

"Oh. Um…"

"They said they'd find me another room, but apparently that's not going so smoothly down there." He shrugged out of the shirt, revealing that chest she remembered so well from yesterday. She gulped, remembering how much of his body she'd seen yesterday. And how much she was apparently about to see again. "So I may as well stay here with you."

"What?" Her mouth fell open. "You can't stay here with me."

"Why not? I have to stay somewhere. Do you want me sleeping on the floor of the lobby?" He sent her that sexy grin as he flicked open the button of the knee-length shorts he wore then unzipped them. She averted her eyes. He apparently felt no need to duck into the bathroom to change as she had earlier. But then yesterday he'd had no problem walking around and having a conversation with her while completely nude.

She almost sighed. If she had an incredible body like that she probably wouldn't mind showing it off either.

"I don't want you sleeping on the floor. But I'm sure they can find another room for you."

He walked over to the bags he brought in with him earlier and unzipped one. She snuck a peek at him. He was wearing a pair of black boxer briefs that hugged his round butt and muscular thighs. Her heart fluttered in her chest and she forgot to breathe, watching him crouch there, his thighs flexing and the muscles in his back rippling as he rummaged around then pulled out a pair of black athletic shorts and a white T-shirt.

She sucked in badly needed air and quickly looked away as he rose.

"Well. I can check later after I work out, but I don't have patience for standing around in line down there, I gotta tell you."

She didn't blame him. She wouldn't be too happy about that either.

"You coming?" She risked a look at him as he pulled the T-shirt over his head and swallowed a sigh. "You said you could work out too."

Maybe that would be a good thing to do. She could run on a treadmill or something and burn off this…excitement. Or whatever. "I'll meet you down there," she croaked.

He grinned. "Clucked, aren't you?"

"Uh…what?"

"Clucked. Chicken. Afraid. You don't want to change in front of me."

Heat swept from her hairline to her toes. "I have no intention of undressing in front of you," she said coolly. She made no move from the bed and waved her hand in a "go on" gesture.

Still smiling, he shoved his feet into a pair of Nikes and strode for the door. "See you down there."

When the door closed behind him, she fell back onto the bed and stared at the ceiling. Dear sweet Jesus. The man was having too much of an effect on her girl parts. And her heart, which was pumping as if she'd already done a few miles on the treadmill. She blew out a long breath.

After another peek outside at the raging storm, she sighed and pulled her workout gear from her suitcase. She'd optimistically packed it but hadn't really thought she'd need it. Once changed into the snug black shorts, sky blue tank top and her own running shoes, she grabbed her iPod and key card and left the room.

She found the gym and Dylan there, alone, on his back on a weight bench, pressing huge weights.

"Something seems wrong about working out when there's a natural disaster occurring outside," she said to him as she climbed on the treadmill and studied the buttons.

"What are we going to do about it?"

She could easily sit and worry and fret in an effort to control the weather. But he made a good point. She couldn't really control it.

She poked at a button. Nothing happened. Then another. The belt started moving. She adjusted the speed until she was at a comfortable pace. She worked out regularly at the gym in San Amaro. Staying fit was important to her. Not as important as it was to a professional athlete, obviously.

Funny, before this she hadn't really made that "athlete" connection. It sounded stupid, because of course she knew he was a professional athlete, but "surfer" didn't sound the same as "Olympic athlete" or even pro football player or hockey player. Why was that?

She knew only too well how big pro surfing was. She'd grown up in San Amaro, a surfing city that hosted a major pro surfing event every year. She'd done the research when they were signing Dylan. She lived in a city where surfing was a major pastime and she'd done it herself, many times, though she was far from accomplished at it. So why hadn't she taken his athleticism seriously?

Seeing him go through his workout, which she was sure was somewhat adapted to the hotel gym facilities, made her appreciate the work he must put into staying in shape. She watched him finish the chest presses with the dumbbells, then do some jump squats, a further series of one-armed dumbbell exercises, more squats on one leg, biceps curls—done while sitting on a large stability ball—some triceps presses and then a series of demanding crunches that made her own abs ache.

He said something to her. She pulled the earbuds out and let them hang. "Sorry, what?"

He grinned. "Sorry. I said how often do you work out?"

"I go to the gym a couple of times a week, and I run a couple of times a week. And swim."

"Cool. Which gym?"

"Power House."

"Ha. That's where I worked out last year when I was there."

"It's a good place. How about you? How often do you work out?"

"I work out six days and then take a day off. I do some pretty intense circuits, but I change it up a lot so I challenge myself and don't get bored. For cardio, I run, bike, swim or paddle."

"Paddle?"

"Standing on a surfboard and paddling."

"Oh yeah, I've done that at the beach. Wouldn't that be kind of easy for you?"

He grinned. "It helps me work on my balance. And variety is good. And on top of all that, I try to surf seven days a week, if I can." He grimaced. After a few more crunches, he said, "You surf?"

"Sure. I'm not that great."

"Like I am." He grinned and relaxed onto the mat, hands behind his head.

She rolled her eyes. "Yeah, not like you, Mr. Modesty."

"Oh come on. I know I'm good. I wouldn't be here if I wasn't."

She had to chuckle, the twinkle in his eye making light of his boasting. "I suppose."

"I'm sure you're good at your job too."

"Yes. Yes, I am." If only Barrett would acknowledge that. Oh well. "I'm glad to hear you say that actually."

"What? That you're good at your job?"

"You said, 'at your job *too*'. Which means you consider surfing your job."

"Of course it's my job."

Breathing was getting harder, but she continued. "Yes, it is. And that's why you need to be more serious about it. Obviously, you take the physical part of it seriously." She gave a short gesture to the gym. "You take your workouts seriously and you try to eat right."

"Yeah." He lifted his head and eyed her. "I do take it seriously."

"You need to take the business part of it seriously too, though."

"Fuuuuuck. Another lecture." His head fell back to the mat.

She couldn't help but laugh. "Sorry."

He began to stretch and they finished their workouts amiably, but when they returned to her room together, she suddenly realized that she needed a shower, and probably so did he. And he had no room to go back to. Shit.

Inside her room, he appeared to have the same realization. He'd already stripped his damp T-shirt over his head when he paused. "Uh…you going to let me use your shower?"

She held back her smile. "You'll owe me."

He gave a slow sexy smile in return. "Oh yeah? Owe you what?" He moved closer.

"No more pushback about going back to San Amaro. As soon as the airport opens."

He rolled his eyes. "That wasn't what I had in mind."

"I know. Go on."

"Wanna come too? We could be efficient…conserve water…"

She laughed. "No."

"Fine." He disappeared into the bathroom and she heard the shower start. She turned on the television to try to check for some kind of weather update, but all she got was a blank screen. Great. No TV now either. They'd have to go down to the lobby and check with hotel staff about what was happening with the storm.

He emerged from the bathroom a short time later in a cloud of steam, a towel wrapped around his lean hips, dangerously low and not concealing the bulge at his groin. She dragged her gaze away and bolted into the bathroom for her own shower, locking the door behind her. How on earth had this happened? Here she was sharing a hotel room with Dylan Schell. This was nuts.

Her eyes fell on the small black toiletry bag sitting unzipped on the counter. With one finger, she tugged it open and peeked inside. Razor, antiperspirant, hairbrush…and a small bottle with a white plastic lid. Nibbling her lower lip, she carefully poked at it until she could see the label. Pantoloc. Probably what he said it was. That sounded familiar, and she was pretty sure it wasn't a narcotic or something. But there was another bottle beneath it. Hating herself, she slipped the Pantoloc out of the way to read the other label. Effexor. Both bottles were nearly full, but the date on the Effexor was from almost a year ago whereas the Pantoloc was brand new. She'd need to do a Google search.

Guiltily, she pushed the bag back the way she'd found it. She showered as quickly as she could then cursed herself for not bringing her clothes into the bathroom with her. Now she had to either get dressed in her sweaty workout gear or go out there in a towel. Shit! She opted for the towel rather than struggle back into spandex while still damp.

Dylan was seated in a chair he'd pulled up to the window, staring outside at the storm, water still pouring down from the sky, wind still pummeling everything out there. He glanced up when she came out then did a double take at seeing her with only a towel wrapped around her, and his smile was wicked.

She held up a hand. "Don't even start. I just need my clothes."

He wasn't shy about watching, unlike her, and she felt his gaze like a touch on her body as she found the dress she'd had on earlier. Despite the storm, it was still warm and humid. Her nipples tingled and tightened under his scrutiny and her pussy squeezed. God. Once more she carried her clothing back into the bathroom to dress.

They went down to the lobby, where Dylan managed to get some information on the storm, but did not, she noticed, even try to get himself a room. And even though she noticed, she said nothing. And she wasn't sure why that was.

"It should be blown over by tomorrow. But it's causing a lot of damage. Nobody knows when the airport will reopen. And there's no Internet access."

"Great." She couldn't even email the office to let them know what was going on. She sighed.

"I know you're frustrated." He took her hand. His big warm

fingers curled around hers and…it felt good. "But there's nothing we can do about it but ride it out."

"I know."

"Just be thankful we're in a safe place."

"I am."

"We'll get some dinner. After, maybe I can start reading some of the stuff you brought for me."

Why was he being so nice? She studied him. Probably because he was getting his way and they weren't leaving for San Amaro right away. "So that means you're coming with me? That you'll participate in all the things we have planned?"

"Do I have any choice?" His smile was crooked, giving him a vulnerable air that tugged at something inside her.

"Well, of course you do. But there are consequences to the choices you make."

"Yeah. There are always consequences."

After dinner, this time beers and hamburgers eaten in a corner of the lounge, they returned to her room and spent the evening sprawled out on her bed, reading. They both had magazines to flip through and Brooke gave him the information packages she'd put together on the various charitable groups they'd considered for Dylan. She kept glancing at him as he looked at them, wondering what he was thinking, what his reaction was. He didn't say much but did seem quite intent in his study of them.

"Did you know there's really only one ocean?" he said suddenly.

"Um. No. I thought there were like, five oceans."

"I know. That's what they teach you in school. But according to this, all the oceans are actually connected. There really is only one global ocean. So what happens to one ocean affects all the oceans, potentially."

"Huh. I did not know that." She hid a smile at his interest.

Her eyes started drooping at only about nine o'clock. "I must be jet-lagged," she said tiredly, rolling off the bed. Then she paused. "Where are you planning to sleep?"

He looked up from a brochure. He smiled and patted the bed. "Right here, babe."

She sighed. "Fine. But you sleep on top of the sheets."

He laughed. "If I decide to molest you, a sheet's not going to stop me."

Heat sliding through her, she turned to go into the bathroom. Just as she neared the door, a long, loud cracking noise split the silence in the room. She jumped a foot off the floor and whirled to face the doors to the balcony, where the noise had come from. "Jesus Christ!" she gasped, her hand flying to her throat.

Dylan surged to his feet and strode to the doors to peer outside. "It's hard to see anything. But it looks like a tree came down."

"Oh God."

"It's okay. There are probably a lot of trees down from this storm."

"But what if it fell on this hotel? Or the balcony?" It could have smashed the glass doors.

"It didn't. It's okay, Brooke."

Still trembling a little, she washed her face and changed into her pajamas. For a moment she actually considered sleeping with her clothes on, since Dylan would be sleeping in the same bed. Hell, that wouldn't be comfortable. She abandoned that thought.

Dylan had resumed his prone position on the bed and had turned out all the lights except the one lamp beside the bed, which shone on his reading materials. She crossed to the windows and tugged the curtain aside, once more staring out into the stormy night.

Weariness dragged her down and yet there was a jumpy excitement inside her, a fluttery sensation that she knew was because of the storm, but more so because of Dylan. She turned back to the bed and pulled down the puffy white duvet cover. The sheets slid cool and smooth over her skin as she climbed in.

"Will the light bother you if I read for a while longer?" he asked.

"No." She turned onto her side, facing away from the light. She closed her eyes.

Her body buzzed and hummed. She willed herself to relax. The workout had fatigued her body, the jet lag was clouding her mind, and yet still she couldn't go to sleep. She adjusted the pillow beneath her head. She fixed her tank top where it bunched under her ribs. She rolled onto her stomach and buried her face in the pillow, flipped onto her back, and then rolled to her side again.

She jumped when a hand landed on her back.

"Hey," Dylan said softly. "What's wrong? Can't get to sleep?"

"No."

His hand rubbed over her cotton top in small, slow circles. "Are you worried about the storm?"

"A little."

"Worried about me?"

"What do you mean?" She kept her face averted and nibbled her bottom lip.

"I'm not really going to molest you."

"I know that." Some of the tension released from her muscles at his gentle touch on her back.

"It'll all be fine."

She nodded. A slow lethargy began stealing over her and she sank into the bed. She rolled to her stomach again and he broadened his strokes, rubbing her back from her nape to the small of her back. Her buttocks tingled and then suddenly she was tense again. Geez! She wanted him to touch her butt! What was wrong with her? He was nice enough to give her a sweet, gentle, completely non-sexual back rub and she was getting turned on.

When his stroke pushed her shirt up a little and his fingers touched bare skin, she tingled and tensed. When his hand slid under her shirt to stroke up and down again, only now on bare flesh, she bit her lip. God, that felt good. She swallowed a moan.

"How's that?" he murmured.

"Good." The word was muffled by the pillow.

She felt the bed shift as he rose off it. The rustle of clothing reached her ears. The light clicked off, plunging the room into darkness, and then the bed again gave as his weight returned to it. He resumed his back rub, now lying beside her.

"You take things so seriously," he murmured. "You need to relax."

"I'm relaxed," she lied.

He laughed softly. "Yeah. Sure." He curled his fingers over her shoulder, briefly kneading the muscles there. "That's why your shoulders feel like rocks."

Just what her massage therapist always told her. She let out a long slow breath, trying to release tension along with it, and burrowed deeper into the bed. Dylan's hand spread warmth and languor as it moved it up and down her spine. Her jaw relaxed, her eyelids closed gently instead of being squeezed shut, and she actually drifted off to sleep.

Until she was awoken by a shout. Her heart lurched as she came awake, staring into the dark. What…?

A guttural, strangled noise came from the bed beside her and she flipped over to look at Dylan. She couldn't really see much in the dark. "Dylan." She set a hand on his chest. "What is it?"

He made another noise, threw her hand off with a jerky, reflexive movement and thrashed a little.

"Dylan! Are you okay?" She sat up and gave him a hard shake. "Dylan. Wake up."

His eyes fluttered open and stared at her unseeingly. "What the fuck?" he muttered. "What…"

"Ssh. It's me. Brooke. What's wrong?"

After a short pause, he groaned and rolled away from her. She touched his back, which was damp with sweat. Her heart pounded and her insides knotted. "What is it, Dylan?"

6

"Oh shit."

She shifted closer, stretching out on her side behind him, and slid her arm around his middle. He was shivering and sweating as if he had a fever, shaking a little even. "Are you sick?" Maybe he'd contracted some kind of tropical disease in all his travels. Malaria, or something. Was that contagious? Probably not.

It struck her then that he had not kept his promise and slept on top of the covers, because she was now pressed against his naked body. Mostly naked body. He'd kept on his boxer briefs.

His body was so big against her, all hot skin and muscle, and yet shivering, so she snuggled closer. She pressed a hand to his chest and was surprised when he covered it with his own and held it there.

"Brooke."

"Right here."

"Shit," he said again.

"You're scaring me. What's wrong?"

"Just a bad dream. Again." He groaned.

"Oh."

"I'm okay." But he didn't release the tight grip he had on her hand. She stayed like that, absorbing the warmth of his body, until she felt some of the tightness ease from his muscles.

After a long time, he shifted onto his back. She went to move away, but he reached for her and held her in place.

"You were supposed to sleep on top of the sheets," she said as he pulled her up against him.

"Oh yeah."

She couldn't help it, but her body fitted itself to him. He wrapped his arms around her and pressed her head to his chest.

"You feel good," he murmured. "You finally got to sleep and then I woke you up again. Sorry, babe."

"It's okay. You can't help it if you have a bad dream." But wow, that was some dream.

"Fuck."

"You swear a lot."

"I know."

They lay there, the only noise the sound of the wind howling and gusting outside and rain pelting the glass doors. Darkness cocooned them along with the soft sheets and fluffy duvet.

"Want to talk about it?"

"Not really."

"It might help."

He made a snorting noise. "Yeah, I've heard that. Look, I haven't had one of those dreams for a long time. I don't know why it suddenly happened again."

"What's it about?"

He was silent and she listened to his heart thudding beneath her cheek. "My accident last year."

"Oh." She'd read the newspaper and Internet articles about it. When it had happened, Barrett had been all pissed off because they'd just signed Dylan and he'd been all worried that their star athlete had been injured, and they weren't going to get their return on investment from him. She'd been horrified, because apparently Dylan had almost died in the accident and all Barrett had been worried about was their contract and the money. She'd also ached with empathy for Dylan, a rising star, unable to do the sport he loved. Luckily his broken foot hadn't been too serious. He'd healed, rehabbed it and gotten back in the water, and it had ended up being only a minor blip in his career.

But now she had to wonder if some of the other stuff that had been happening was somehow related to that. If he was still having nightmares about it over a year later…that had to have had some kind of powerful effect on him.

Without thinking, acting on instinct, she lifted a hand to his shoulder and rubbed him there. His skin was smooth, his bones big and hard beneath. She wasn't sure what to say.

"I got slammed," he continued without her prompting. "That's when a wave comes down hard, knocks you off your board and drills you deep. My leash got caught on a rock and I couldn't get free. I had a lot of nightmares at first. They were pretty bad. Then…they got better."

He'd skipped over something in the middle there, but she wasn't going to ask, just happy that he was talking about it.

"I don't know why I had one tonight. It's weird."

"Maybe it's the storm."

"Maybe."

His hand moved on her back again, stroking up and down like he had before, slipping beneath her tank top. An ache developed low down inside her and she had to resist tipping her pelvis against his body to seek relief.

"Your skin's so soft, Brooke." This time on the down stroke his fingers brushed under the elastic waistband of her shorts, which was folded over low on her hips. She tingled and the ache intensified. She squeezed her eyes shut against the rush of sensation, sucked in a long, slow breath, trying not to let on how she was feeling.

When his hand slid inside her shorts, she knew she should stop him. She couldn't explain why she didn't, except that it felt so good. His hand cupped her butt cheek and pulled her in closer and this time she couldn't stop herself from rolling her hips into him, trying to assuage that pulsing ache in her pussy. There in the dark, with a storm raging outside, she wanted this, even though she knew it was such a bad idea. She wanted more.

"Mmmm." He made a little noise of pleasure and turned into her a little more. His cock, hard inside the soft cotton of his underwear, twitched against her. She felt like she was in a dream, floating a little, in the dark, unable to see much, her other senses hyper alert. Heat. Strength. His warm male scent surrounding her. Her mouth longed to taste him and her lips parted involuntarily as he palmed her ass again and adjusted her body against his so that his erection was between them.

Her hips rolled in needy pulses against him, and he hardened even more and groaned. "Brooke. Oh God, Brooke, you feel so good."

"We shouldn't be doing this." She felt she should at least say it.

"I know."

But that wasn't stopping him either.

Lust burned inside her, hot and demanding, a hungry need whipping through her. And then he tipped her chin up with his knuckles and found her mouth in the dark with his.

Oooohhh God. His mouth closed over hers, opened and urged hers open too, and she kissed him back with hot need. His tongue licked inside, rubbed against hers, and she slid slowly, inexorably into desire, heat pooling inside her, sensations rocking through her. Flames built low in her womb, intense and burning.

God, he was a good kisser! His lips were smooth and warm, his tongue hot and silky, sliding in and out of her mouth with erotic intent, turning her on unbelievably. His hands cuddled her butt and pulled her in closer, and their hips rolled together in an instinctive rhythm of need.

When he rolled her to her back and moved over her, a thrill ran through her to her very core. He was strong and powerful, but she wasn't afraid, because God, she wanted this, so much, so very much. There in the dark, in their haven from the storm, she felt safe with him.

He kissed her mouth, her jaw, scraped his teeth over her flesh there and made her shiver. Then he dragged his tongue down the side of her neck and pressed hot, open-mouthed kisses to her collarbone. He tugged aside the neckline of her tank top to go lower then growled with frustration.

She wanted his mouth on her there and she tunneled her fingers into his hair and held his head, her hips still lifting against him. He covered one breast through her tank top with his hand and gently squeezed, her nipple puckering with instant excitement. A soft whimper escaped her lips and she closed her mouth and tipped her chin up as heat flashed from her breast to her pussy.

"Sweet." He gave her another gentle squeeze. "So soft. Oh man, Brooke."

She made some kind of inarticulate sound of agreement with whatever it was he was expressing with that comment, arching her back to push her breast further into his palm.

"Hot," he muttered. "You're so hot, aren't you?"

"Ungh." That too was agreement. His thumb rubbed over her nipple through the ribbed cotton of her tank top, then his hand drifted down and came to rest on her stomach as they kissed; more long, wet tongue kisses that sent her drifting dizzyingly among dark and sparkles.

She floated, her mouth open for him, her tongue tasting him. She nipped at his lips, so gently, and made him chuckle, let his hands roam her body, over her belly and hip, back to her breast, then down, down, fingertips once more sliding beneath the band of her shorts, this time in front.

His fingertips brushed her pubic hair and made her sizzle and shiver. She moaned into his mouth, sucked on his tongue and made him moan in return. Once more her hips lifted involuntarily, seeking his fingers. Oh God, what was she doing? This was crazy.

But he didn't satisfy that hot need inside her, just rested his fingertips there. He pressed in a little, right on her pubic bone which was ultrasensitive and made her jump, then toyed with the curls there, all the while kissing her with erotic heat. She parted her legs for him and her hands slid down to his shoulders, holding on while he kissed and teased her. Then she reached for him, slipping a hand between them to find his erection, hard beneath the soft cotton of his underwear stretched over it. He groaned.

Dylan wanted to say something, to ask her if she knew what they were doing, to ask her if this was what she really wanted, but her hand on his throbbing cock had his mind emptying, his body buzzing and aching. He gulped for air and with frantic, urgent motions he pushed her tank top up, over her breasts, sweet Christ, then off over her head. He grasped her shorts and tugged them down her legs, leaving her naked on the sheets. And then he shoved down his own underwear and kicked them aside, moving back over her.

She reached for him and they both gasped when their bodies connected again, this time no clothing between them, hot skin to skin, so hot he was amazed there was no sizzle as they pressed together. She parted her legs so he could fit himself into the cradle of her pelvis, and he took her mouth again in a hot, hungry kiss. She responded to him that way, opening for him, her tongue rubbing on his, her hands sliding up and down his sides urgently. She made needy little sounds in her throat that turned him on even more.

Crazy, crazy, this was crazy. He knew it and yet he couldn't stop, couldn't drag his mouth away from hers as he took the kiss deeper and it went on and on. Then he shifted to explore those beautiful breasts he'd barely got a glimpse of when he'd taken her top off. He kissed his way down over her chest again, this time in quick little kisses. He cupped one breast in a hand, so soft and full and perfect, and plumped it up so he could taste her nipple. He closed his lips over the budded tip and pulled it into his mouth.

Her gasp of pleasure, her fingernails raking over his scalp, had his blood rushing through his veins.

He suckled at one tip, then the other, until she writhed beneath him, hips lifting against him, and he knew she needed it as much as he did. He went up on his knees, spread them wide and fisted his cock to push inside her.

The room was dark, her body a shadow on the white sheets. He wished he could see better, but he wasn't about to stop and turn the light on, and somehow in the dark with the storm blustering outside, this seemed right. It felt sheltered, safe and secure. Private.

He let out a low moan as he pushed inside her, as her wet heat surrounded him, so hot, so good. Her body wrapped around his dick and squeezed and he fell over her. His elbows beside her head, one hand beneath her hair, he kissed her again, her mouth, her cheek, her eyebrows. She lifted to him, meeting his strokes with her own, and they rocked together in urgent need.

Her hands clutched his back, slid down to his ass and held on tight. His balls ground to her pussy as their bodies met, heat surging through him in waves of pleasure, his body rushing toward something. He fisted her hair, so silky.

This was crazy, incredible, sublime. It was fast and hard and fierce, both of them on fire, biting at each other's lips, hands groping, making delirious sounds of pleasure and need. Sensation poured over him, electric, tightening every nerve ending. Pressure built inside him, fast and dark, growing.

He didn't want to think about it, about what they were doing and the consequences of it. That seemed trivial and unimportant at that moment as a freight train of sensation roared over him, and he pressed his face into the side of her neck. She cried out and clutched him harder, fingers digging into his ass, her legs wrapped around him, going still beneath him. He let go, let it wash over him like the biggest wave, taking him down and submerging him in darkness and muffled sound, this time without the fear, without the panic, just exquisite pleasure slamming him, exploding through every nerve ending.

They lay together panting, hearts thundering, their skin damp as the world slowly came back into focus. Her pussy twitched around him in small aftershocks. Fuck, that was good. So damn good. Holy fucking shit good. He dragged air into his lungs and blew it out, keeping his weight on his elbows as much as he could so as not to crush her.

She slowly lowered and straightened her legs, but he didn't withdraw, not yet, feeling still so safe and peaceful there cradled against her. He pressed an open-mouthed kiss to the side of her neck and breathed in the scent of her, something sweet and fruity and tropical, like Tahiti. He murmured with appreciation, a relaxing languor stealing over him, weakening his muscles and fogging his brain.

Her hands rested limply on his back, then lifted to his shoulders and pushed at him a little. "Squishing you?" he muttered, moving. He didn't want to pull out of the clinging warmth of her body yet, but… "Shit."

He looked down at her face, shadowy in the dark. "Dylan. You didn't…use anything."

"I know. Shit, I just realized that. Fuck." He buried his face in the pillow beside her head for a few seconds, took a deep breath. "I'm sorry, Brooke."

He rolled off her and onto his back beside her. He gazed up at the pale ceiling. "Are you protected?"

She didn't immediately answer. "If you mean, am I on birth control—no."

He closed his eyes. "Oh Christ."

"Yeah, my thoughts exactly. What were we *thinking*?" He heard the anguish in her voice and felt it too.

"We weren't thinking. Jesus." It was kind of delicate and he wasn't even sure how to ask. He never had unprotected sex, for fuck's sake. "Uh…timing…?"

She sighed. "It should be okay. I hope."

Oh yeah. He hoped so too. "I'm sorry," he said again.

"It's not just your fault. I'm responsible too. I didn't even think until…"

"I know." They lay in silence for a few moments. "If it's any consolation, that felt fucking unbelievable." He turned his head on the pillow and she did too. Their eyes met, hers gleaming faintly. "I should have realized why it felt so good." He lifted a hand and laid it on her cheek. "It was amazing."

She gave a shaky little smile. "Oh yeah. It was."

"I never have unprotected sex," he told her seriously.

She held his gaze for a long moment. "Never?"

"Never. I swear. And I was tested not long ago, but I'll go again if you want."

She nodded. "I'll think about it. And same goes for me, except I'd venture to say you've been having a lot more sex than I have lately."

He closed his eyes, suddenly hating the fact that she'd walked in on him with two girls yesterday, girls he barely knew and didn't really care about. He reached for her and pulled her into his arms, and she settled against him, her curves fitting into his body. They heard another bang and a distant crash outside, followed by howling wind, and she flinched. He rubbed her back. She seemed to like that. "It's okay, I've got you."

"Mmm." He stroked her hair, now all tangled but still silky beneath his fingers.

"Are the nightmares the reason you don't want to go back to San Amaro?"

He went still. "What? No." He frowned into the darkness.

"Then why don't you want to go back?"

He sighed. "I'll go back with you, Brooke. I know I have to. Even though it pisses me off."

"I know, but I want to understand what the problem is. Maybe then I can help. That's what I'm here for."

"I thought you were here to chase me onto the plane with a big stick."

He felt her smile against his shoulder. "That too. But seriously, Dylan. I'm here to get you to cooperate so we can save this deal for you. For us. If there's something I can do that will help with that, just tell me."

"Well." With a flash of inspiration, he said, "There is something you can do for me."

"Okay. What is it?"

"I want you to come to a wedding with me."

7

Her head snapped up. "A wedding?"

He smiled, satisfaction rolling through him at this genius idea. "Yeah. A wedding. We were talking about my friend Matt Ferber earlier, remember?"

"Yeah…"

"He's getting married in a few weeks. Just before the competition. I need a date for the wedding."

She sat bolt upright in bed. "We are not dating! Just because we had sex doesn't mean—"

"Whoa, whoa. That's not what I meant."

"We shouldn't have done this! We barely even know each other. We're business colleagues, that's all. Oh my God, how are we going to work together now—"

"Relax, babe. It's okay. I get it." Hell, she didn't have to be quite so horrified by the idea of dating him. "I just need a date for the wedding to keep my friends off my back."

She shoved her tangled hair back and shook her head. "Oh."

"I know we have to work together. Look, this is one night. We're here in a tropical paradise—"

"Paradise? There's a cyclone going on out there!"

"Yeah, yeah. That's part of it too. It just happened, okay? Let's not beat ourselves up over it. We both know it was pretty good. Okay, stupendous, actually. But when we leave here, it'll be back to business. Except for the wedding you're going to accompany me to."

"Why should I do that?"

"Because it will help me. Remember? You said you'd do whatever you could to help. I've been trying to get out of going to this wedding, but if you come with me it'll all be good."

"I don't get it."

"What's to get?" He pulled her back down on top of him, enjoying the feel of her soft curves and silky skin. Thankfully, she didn't resist. He tugged the duvet back up over both of them and tucked it around her. "You know how when people are getting married they think *everyone* should fall in love and get married?"

Okay, he was stretching things now. He hadn't even seen Corey and Matt since he'd left and they were hardly pushing him to settle down.

"Oh yeah," she said with heartfelt agreement.

"Yeah. So that's why I need a date. Then they won't bug me."

"Oh." She was silent. "And that would make you feel better about coming back to San Amaro?"

"Yeah."

"So it wouldn't be a real date. Just a…pretend date."

"Yeah. Exactly."

"Well. I suppose I could handle that."

"Awesome." He tugged her hair so her head tipped back and once more he found her mouth and kissed her in the dark. And once more, heat built between them, climbing inside him, fast and hard. Thank God he had condoms in his bag.

In the morning, the storm continued to rage with ferociously gusting winds and torrential rain. The skies remained dark, palm trees whipped around by the wind. Hotel staff was keeping everyone inside, which seriously limited their options for entertainment. There seemed to be no shortage of food, but the restaurants were crazy busy, the atmosphere in the resort becoming almost party-like with the shared experience.

Others didn't seem worried, but Brooke couldn't help but be nervous at the fierce power of the storm. When Dylan spoke to someone at the resort, the front desk manager assured them that the brunt of the storm had missed them, with more damage happening at Uturoa.

They ordered breakfast but since there were no empty tables, they opted to carry the tray back up to the room and eat there. Even with the curtains open, it was so dark outside they needed lights on. Rain spattered against the windows in sharp gusts.

"Might as well go back to bed," Dylan said with a wicked gleam in his eye as they contemplated an entire day stuck inside the hotel. He lounged on the bed with his cup of coffee while she sat at the small round table.

Oh yeah, that sounded good. Brooke poured herself another cup of coffee from the thermos they'd brought up and added a splash of cream. It wouldn't take much to tempt her, even though she knew it was crazy. Last night had been incredible, and sitting there in the hotel room with him lazily eating breakfast while the storm rampaged outside created a feeling of cozy intimacy and a low-down ache of lust inside her.

"Is that all you think about?" She lifted her cup of coffee to her mouth.

"No. But I can't surf right now." He grinned. "It's called making the best of a bad situation. Right?"

She eyed him over the rim of the cup she held in both hands, trying to hide her smile. He was pretty irresistible, dammit. Last night he'd turned her inside out with pleasure, and her girl parts gave a squeeze as she had to admit she wanted more of that.

But she wasn't going to make it that easy for him.

"Well, I can think of other things to do."

"Really? Like what?"

"I have a deck of cards. We could play Crazy Eights or Rummy or something."

"Strip poker."

Now she had to laugh. "You do have a one-track mind."

His silvery eyes gleamed. "I don't deny it. Hey, come on. I'm not very good at poker. You could probably get me naked in no time."

"Why don't I believe you?" For some reason, she firmly believed that any kind of game in which there was competition was something he was going to excel at. Including poker.

The idea of getting him naked was pretty appealing though. Even if all she did was sit and look at his beautiful body with all those tanned muscles. Lord, she was melting all over again, slow liquid heat seeping down through her body to between her legs.

"You don't believe you could get me naked in no time?"

A smile tugged her lips as their eyes met across the room. "No. I mean I don't believe you're not very good at poker."

"Get the cards," he said softly.

"I don't want to play cards."

"Perfect. Neither do I." And his hands went to the buttons of his shirt.

"What are you doing?"

"It's called stripping without the poker."

She tightened her thighs and watched him. Her mouth went dry and her eyes fastened on him. He shrugged out of the shirt and let it drop to the floor. Her eyes feasted on the ripped abs, the slabs of his pecs with dark nipples, the thick muscles of his shoulders and upper arms.

She sighed.

"Your turn."

She swallowed and looked down at herself. She wore shorts and a swingy tank top. Biting her lip, her hands went to the hem of her top. Dylan's hot eyes fixed on her had her pulse racing as she lifted the top. Heat rushed over her body as she pulled it over her head then sat there in her bra and shorts.

He nodded approvingly and began to loosen the ties of the board shorts he wore.

"Stand up and turn around," she directed him.

He lifted an eyebrow and his hands paused. "I beg your pardon?"

She motioned with a circle of her index finger. "Stand up and turn around," she repeated, her voice husky. "I want to see your ass."

A slow smile spread across his face. "Oh you do, do you?" But he rose to his feet, turned his back on her and continued unfastening his shorts. "Who put you in charge?"

She knew the exhibitionist in him had no problem stripping like this for her. And why would he? His body was a work of art, male perfection. She watched the muscles in his back ripple as he pulled open the shorts with a rip of the Velcro fastener. He held them up and gave his ass a shake. She smiled. "I did. Drop the shorts."

"Bossy." He slowly began to lower the shorts, moving his hips. "I like it."

Inch by inch, he revealed more skin, paler skin, and her breath caught in anticipation as the curves of his butt were revealed. He had an amazing ass, so muscular and round, the skin so smooth. Her palms tingled to feel it.

"I want to bite you," she told him, shocking herself.

He gave her a sexy, amused glance over his shoulder. "Oh yeah?"

She nodded, wiping damp palms on her thighs.

"Bossy and kinky. Who knew? But I approve." He lowered the shorts another inch or two. She licked her lips, now picturing the front of him. Her pussy heated and squeezed. "You can bite me, but you have to be naked too."

"Okay," she whispered.

The shorts slid lower still on his muscular thighs. She drank in the sight of him with avid, hungry eyes. When he bent forward at the waist, tugging the shorts the rest of the way down his legs, pushing his butt out toward her, her pussy clenched hard. Oh God.

He stepped out of the shorts, still with his back to her, and bent to pick them up, giving her a clear view of that perfect beautiful ass. And when he parted his legs, giving her a glimpse of what was between his legs, a small whimper escaped her. He slowly straightened. Once more, she licked her lips.

"Can I turn around?" he asked, humor coloring his deep voice.

"Yes."

He turned. His cock thrust out and up from the thick patch of dark hair at the juncture of his thighs. Holy floating jellyfish, he was beautiful.

Her dry mouth began to water. She wanted to taste him. She made a move toward him but he held up a hand. "Naked," he reminded her, the corners of his mouth kicking up.

She wanted to rip her clothes off and dive on him, but he'd given her a wonderful show and now watched her with a warm appreciation that gave her the confidence to slow things down. She reached behind her and unfastened her bra then let it slide slowly down her arms and chest. For a few seconds it caught on her hard nipples and she paused, peeking at him up through her eyelashes. His cock jerked and his eyes darkened.

She rose on slightly unsteady legs and unfastened her shorts. Unlike him, she let them drop to the floor and kicked them aside. She hooked her thumbs into the sides of her thong panties.

"Turn around," he requested hoarsely. "You have a nice ass too."

Smiling, she pivoted slowly and did as he'd done, lowering her panties inch by inch. And then, bravely, she too bent over to pick them up. The sound of his sharply indrawn breath reached her ears and she smiled. She glanced at him over her shoulder as she rose and took in his parted lips and rapt expression.

"Beautiful."

She almost wanted to sigh. She'd seen the girls he'd been in bed with the day she arrived, and he'd probably been with so many women way more beautiful than she was. She was average —brown hair, brown eyes, average height, average size. Nothing really beautiful about that.

"What? Look at me, Brooke."

She turned to face him, some of that confidence dissolving.

"You *are* beautiful," he said, as if sensing that. "Look at you. You have the prettiest breasts."

She blinked. "They're not perfect."

"Yeah. They are. They're the perfect size, perfect shape…just the way I like, round and firm. I like how they fill my hand. Your nipples are pretty. I like how they get dark and hard…makes me want to suck them. And I like how they taste. Sweet."

Her legs wobbled as her knees turned to sand, and she reached a hand behind her to the table to steady herself. God. The man was sex and charm on a stick.

"Thank you."

"Should I talk about your perfect ass now?" His lips quirked.

She shook her head. "Let's talk about *your* perfect ass."

He laughed. "Still want to bite it?"

"Oh yeah."

They stood across the room from each other, naked, looking at each other with hot, hungry eyes, neither making a move. It was the sexiest thing she'd ever experienced. Maybe. Last night with Dylan had been pretty hot too.

She drew in a long slow breath. "Lay down on the bed," she directed him. "Face down."

He didn't move, lips still curved into that half-smile, and then he inclined his head and turned back to the bed. Once again she watched the play of muscle under smooth bronzed skin as he knelt on the bed, then stretched out long and lean. Her breath caught on another inhale.

She moved toward him, her legs trembling a little, and climbed onto the unmade bed as well. She pushed the covers aside to make room and then, biting her bottom lip, she laid her palms on his butt.

She could understand what he meant when he said he loved how her breasts filled his hands, because she loved how his ass filled her hands, firm and resilient, the skin smooth, the muscles beneath taut and compact. She gave a gentle squeeze and he flexed, and the muscles beneath her palms turned to rock. She sighed. He huffed out a laugh, his arms folded beneath his head.

He relaxed and she stroked and petted and caressed, up his back, down over the cheeks, brushing over the backs of his thighs, which made him twitch.

"Amazing," she murmured. "It's because you're a surfer, isn't it?"

"Surfing requires good gluts," he mumbled.

She sensed the tension in his body increasing, a faint vibration. He liked this. She dragged her tongue over her bottom lip, contemplating the crease between his cheeks, then boldly drew her fingers up through that tight channel. He made a noise in his throat, those impressive muscles flexing again. But his thighs moved just slightly apart.

That was all the encouragement she needed to keep going. She played more, dipping lower between his thighs, deeper between his cheeks, then teasing by drifting her hands over his back and lower spine, sliding her palms down the sides of his hips.

"I wish I had some massage oil."

"I have some."

"Of course you do." She smiled. "Where is it?"

He directed her to his bag and she found the small bottle and returned to the bed. She squeezed a trail of thick liquid down the center of his back, right to his butt cheeks, then tossed the bottle aside and set her hands back on his body.

He let out a long groan.

She studied him as her hands moved over him, now sliding easily in the oil, absorbing both the sight of him and the feel of him with carnal pleasure. Slowly, she eased his thighs farther apart and slipped her fingers down to brush against his balls.

He lifted his hips and reached beneath to adjust himself, and when he rested back on the bed she could see his cock now, between his thighs, stiff and flushed. Also so beautiful. Feasting her eyes on his well-formed shape, she again daringly dipped her fingers lower, cupping his balls, brushing the head of his cock.

And then, her mouth literally watering, she bent forward and pressed an open-mouthed kiss at the base of his spine. She drew the kiss out, long and slow, brushing her tongue over his flesh. Licking him.

She savored the salty male taste of him mingled with the oil, breathed in the scent of his skin. She kissed and licked her way lower, over the swell of his buttock, down to the crease where it met his thigh and drew her tongue over the soft skin there. His body trembled. She laid another trail of soft, pursed-lip kisses back up, and then right at the fleshiest part of him, she opened her mouth and sank her teeth into him, so gently.

"Christ!"

His muffled curse made her smile against his skin, and she did it again on the other side then licked over the spot. She nuzzled his flesh, nudged his thighs farther apart so she could touch her tongue to his balls. The skin there was so soft, his testicles drawn up tight against his body. He quivered.

"Fuck," he muttered, face buried in his arms. "I can't stand this much longer. You're making me insane."

"Should I stop?" She gave another nip with her teeth.

He groaned.

"I'll take that as a no. God, Dylan." Once more she drew back for the view, smoothing her palms over him. "You're so beautiful."

"Nobody's ever done this," he said hoarsely.

"Really? I can't believe that. I could worship your fine ass for hours."

"Yeah, that's not gonna happen. Because my fine dick is about to explode."

She gave a soft laugh and he rolled over. She was torturing herself as much as him, her insides all warm and achy. He reached for her and pulled her down on top of him, and they fit themselves together.

"Oh babe." He groaned, palming the back of her head to bring her down for a kiss. "You make me so fucking hot."

Their mouths met in a long, clinging bond. Their tongues slid against each other's in an erotic caress.

"Can't wait," he gasped a moment later. "You ready?"

"Oh yeah. I am so ready."

He rolled her to her back and now moved over her, kneeing her thighs apart. He reached for a condom from the bedside table and quickly sheathed his enormous cock, the veins so distended she bit her lip. Then before he did anything else, he slipped his hand between them, into her folds, gently exploring. "Ah," he said on a long exhalation. "So wet, baby. So good."

She gazed up at him, her heart warmed by his consideration, by how he'd made sure she was ready before he pushed inside her. She lifted her thighs wider and reached for him as he entered her, stretching her with a burning pressure. A small wail escaped her lips and he paused. "Okay?" His eyes met hers. His jaw was tight, his mouth firm, but his eyes held a warm question.

She nodded. "Just a little sore…"

"I'm sorry."

"No. Don't be sorry." Her fingers gripped his shoulders, pulling him to her. "Do it. I want you. God, I want you."

"Fuck, me too." He eased into her, inch by inch, filling her with a delicious pressure and her eyes drifted closed, her head falling to one side. "All day, Brooke. I want to do this all day. You and me in this bed."

"Works…for…me." She wrapped her legs around him as he moved inside her, now fully seated, their bodies pressed as close as they could be. "Got nothing…else…to…do."

He gave another huff of laughter, falling down over her to kiss her as he rocked his pelvis against her, his body bearing her down into the mattress, pressing on her clit, giving her the most exquisite abrasion that started tingles low down inside her. The tingles spread and intensified and swirled into an ever-bigger spiral of delight, rushing through her body, and she lifted into him, seeking more, more of that heaven until it became almost unbearable.

Their bodies both damp and slick, she dug her heels into that incredible ass and cried out as she came, tightening around him, her body contracting in hard pulses. And when he pressed his face into the side of her neck with low, feral growls of pleasure, she held on tight to his big body as he found his release too.

8

Two days later, the winds died down to gusty breezes, patches of blue appeared in the overcast sky, and Brooke and Dylan finally made it out of bed.

Okay they hadn't spent *every* minute of those two days in bed. But almost.

They explored the area, checking out what damage the storm had caused. The locals took it all cheerfully in stride, getting to work to clear downed trees and repair power lines. As the day went on, the sky cleared more and more and the sun evaporated all the rain that had fallen and turned it into sticky humidity.

Although the weather improved, the airport remained closed and there was no telephone or Internet access. Many places were still without power, although their hotel had luckily been spared and continued to operate semi-normally. The winds continued to whip the ocean into massive waves that Dylan eyed longingly. She shouldn't have cared, but the idea of him heading out into an ocean still so stormy and rough scared her. Thankfully he didn't seem inclined to actually try it.

They were finally able to leave Tahiti Faa'a Airport the next night. She tried to hide her nervousness from Dylan, but as the wheels of the plane left the ground, he unwrapped her fingers from around the armrest and held her hand between both of his.

"You okay?" He bent to speak in her ear.

She gave a tight nod and flashed what she hoped was a casual smile.

"Don't like flying?"

She tried to breathe, her heart thumping in her chest. He was going to feel how sweaty her palms were. "Not really," she said in an amazing understatement.

"It'll be fine." He rubbed her hand. "Want me to distract you?" He nuzzled her ear and she shivered.

She turned her head and their mouths met and clung in a long, warm kiss. Heat slid through her and she curled her fingers around his hand. Mmm. Yeah. That was probably the only thing that could distract her. She drew back and gave him another smile, this one more relaxed.

Once they were in the air and she'd begun to breathe normally again, when the lights had been turned off to allow people to sleep and they were passing high above the Pacific Ocean, a strange feeling of sadness fell over Brooke. After spending the last few days with Dylan, and that meant every *minute* of the last few days since he'd stayed with her, now that they were finally on their way back to San Amaro she found herself reluctant to leave. Tahiti was beautiful even though she hadn't had the best experience there, but it wasn't just that. Somehow she and Dylan had fallen into something, some kind of unspoken relationship where they'd become friends and lovers, and yet they both knew it was only a temporary thing.

Sleeping with him had been incredible, and even though she wondered how this was going to impact their working relationship once back in California, she'd done it anyway because... because...well she couldn't exactly explain it, other than—he was there. They were there, together, forced into close proximity by the storm and kept there by some kind of powerful physical attraction.

"Here." Dylan shook out a small airline blanket. He covered her with it and tucked it around her. He lifted the armrest between them and she slid toward him. Somehow they managed to snuggle together like they had the last three nights in her hotel room bed, even there in the airplane seats. She rested her head against his shoulder, his arms around her, and tried not to let that sadness take over. She needed to be thinking about work and what needed to be done as soon as she was home.

She'd fretted about her inability to contact the office or her family, to let them know she was all right. They'd probably seen coverage of the storm on the news and she worried they'd be freaking out especially since she couldn't reach them. Finally she'd managed a couple of brief emails to the office, astonished that the reaction from Barrett was, "What the hell is taking you so long? Get Dylan Schell back here RFN." She'd also managed a short phone call home to tell her parents she was fine. At least *they'd* been concerned about her. It sounded like her mother was almost ready to get on the next plane to come find her.

Dylan's breathing slowed as he fell asleep, and she tried to match her own breath to his to try to make herself fall asleep too. But it was hard not to think about him and the time they'd just spent together. It was hard not to get all warm and squirmy thinking about the things they'd done, in bed, even on the beach the last night in the shadows of the palm trees. She pressed her thighs together against the ache there. Giving up all that hot sex wasn't going to be easy.

She would be going to her apartment. She'd thought Dylan might stay with his friend Matt, since he said he'd stayed there with him last year, but he'd shaken his head at that and said he'd stay at a hotel. In fact he already had a room booked at the San Amaro Hilton but not until later in the month, so in one of her emails she'd asked Tim to change his reservation for him, and also to book a rental car for him at the airport. Once they landed in San Diego, they'd be going their separate ways.

Which made her heart contract and her throat tighten.

But it wasn't as if she wasn't going to see him again. They had work to do. It would just be…different. Back to reality.

She finally drifted into sleep too, a light sleep, still aware of the noise of the plane, the footsteps of the flight attendants moving up and down the aisle, still aware of Dylan's strong body against hers, his arms around her, that fresh air and water scent of his skin filling her head. She wanted to breathe that in and hold it inside her.

Hours later they both woke up, stretched, used the bathrooms and ate the breakfast the cheery flight attendants served them. Dylan read more of the materials she'd gathered about the charitable organizations and, surprisingly to her, used his laptop do some things—looked like he was reading some news stories, checking emails and responding to them. She'd forgotten that this was a business to him too. Or rather, no, she hadn't forgotten. Dylan liked to give the impression he didn't treat it like a business, but she was getting glimpses of a different side of him.

They claimed their luggage, including a special trip to the oversized baggage area for Dylan's carefully packed boards, then paused before she headed to the lot where she'd left her car and Dylan got on a shuttle bus to the rental car office. People passing by glanced at Dylan then took another look. He was surrounded by a magnetic field of coolness that people seemed to recognize, whether or not they knew who he was, with his athletic grace, tanned skin and shaggy hair, wearing sunglasses and a loose shirt over shorts.

They looked at each other and more emotion swelled inside her. Oh God, this should not be happening. It felt like she was saying goodbye to him forever, and the wrench of loss she felt inside at that was all kinds of wrong. He smiled at her. "Okay, babe. Here you go. You got what you came for. I'm back on U.S. soil. I guess I'll see you at your office Monday morning."

It was a little past noon on Friday. "Wait." She frowned. "What will you do all weekend?"

He shrugged. "Not sure yet. Why?"

She struggled for words, for what to say. "You need to stay out of trouble. And out of the media."

A shadow darkened his silvery eyes, but he grinned and gave her a look. "Oh yeah. Right. I'll see if I can manage to behave myself for the next few days."

"It's not just the next few days." She had to get back into business mode here and quick. "It's for good, Dylan. This isn't just a temporary stunt to make you look good. You seriously need to clean up your image if you want long-term sponsorship."

"Right." His mouth firmed and his eyes narrowed fractionally. "What do you do? Do you put your money where your mouth is and do some kind of charity work?"

She lifted an eyebrow. "Yes. I do."

"Oh."

"I'm a Big Sister. I have a Little Sister, she's twelve. She has no mom so I spend time with her doing girl stuff."

He pursed his lips and nodded. "Good for you."

She narrowed her eyes at him. "Yes. It is good for me, actually. I get as much out of it as she does."

He sighed. "I'm sorry, Brooke."

She hesitated. "Okay. My mom will be freaking out about where I was. I'm going over to their place for dinner tomorrow night. Come with me."

"To your parents'?" He lifted an eyebrow.

"Sure. Why not? We have a big family, they don't mind another person. My mom's a good cook. You can have a home cooked meal and it will be nice and safe."

He rolled his eyes and shook his head. "Whatever. Fine."

"I gave you my cell phone number. Call me if you need anything."

"I don't need a babysitter," he muttered.

"Fine." Back to cool and businesslike, she added, "Prove it by staying out of trouble all weekend. Want me to pick you up tomorrow night?"

He shrugged. "Sure. Drive carefully back to San Amaro."

She blinked. "I will. You too."

She watched him turn and push the cart loaded down with his gear out the door of the terminal. And swallowed hard through her suddenly tight, dry throat.

Yeah, he was real stoked to be here.

Driving the freeway reminded him of the last time he'd been here, headed back to San Amaro in a rental car just like this. Last time, his left foot had been in a cast and he'd been bummed about not being able to surf, but looking forward to seeing his buddy Matt.

He got that tight feeling in his chest, that feeling of not being able to breathe. Dammit. And even as he worked to control his breathing and get air into his constricted lungs, his heart started racing.

Fuck off, he was not having a panic attack now!

Maybe it was that fucking heartburn again. Sometimes it was hard to tell that from a panic attack. But he'd been taking the medication. For the heartburn. Not for the panic attacks. Because he hadn't had one in ages.

With sweat popping out on his forehead, he changed lanes and exited the freeway, pulling into a convenience store parking lot. Jesus.

He sat there for a while, trying to use some of the relaxation techniques he'd learned in therapy. This was whacked. Just because he was back in San Amaro? This wasn't even where his accident had happened, but last time he'd been here he'd still been recovering from his injury and then there had been all that shit with Matt and Corey that had gone down.

Memories of sitting in Matt's living room, drinking beer when Corey had walked in played through his mind. She'd been so damn sweet and sexy, yawning, with tousled hair, right out of Matt's bed, and she'd been hot as hell. Remembering how hot she'd been and how much fun they'd had, then remembering his last day there, how he'd wanted her to leave with him. How she'd refused.

He let out a long sigh. His heart still thumped, but in a more normal rhythm. The breeze wafting in the open window of the car cooled his face and he sucked in a big gulp of air. Okay. He was okay.

Remembering that time wasn't as painful as it used to be. He'd had a lot of time to think about things, to process everything that had happened, to sort out his feelings. He'd finally gotten back in the water and he'd won some competitions. He couldn't say he felt the same as he had before the accident, or before he'd spent those weeks in San Amaro, but he felt pretty good. He had goals.

Of course this sponsorship issue put a tiny wrinkle in his plans. Now he had a sexy little marketing and PR manager riding him about being on his best behavior. A smile tugged at his lips, remembering how earnest she was about cleaning up his image and doing all that charity work.

Him? Yeah right.

He'd go along with her and do what he had to do, but he wasn't doing any *more* than he had to do, because he had one goal—to win this competition. Okay, he had two goals. Win the competition, and get through Corey and Matt's wedding without making a fool of himself. That one would probably be the tougher one.

He started the car again and headed back to the freeway.

But no, the wedding didn't have to be the harder goal, because now he had Brooke. He grinned. He could do this. He could play along with Brooke, make nice with his sponsor so the money kept coming, show Corey and Matt he was A-okay with them getting married because he'd totally moved on, and he'd spend as much time as he possibly could working out, surfing and preparing for the competition. Yeah. It was all good. He flicked on his blinker and shoulder checked, then he made a series of daring lane changes as he approached his exit into San Amaro.

But once he'd checked into the hotel and hauled his stuff into his room, he sat on the bed staring out the window that overlooked Deep Sea Drive. A bleak, black feeling crept over him, that feeling that made him go out and smoke and drink and party and bring girls back to his room for sex so he didn't have to be alone. He closed his eyes briefly and sucked in a long breath. Maybe he'd call Matt and see what they were doing later. Get that over with before he did exactly what Brooke had warned him not to do.

He grabbed his cell phone and thumbed through his contacts till he found Matt's cell number and pressed the button to connect them. It was Friday afternoon; Matt was likely at the brew pub he owned. After a couple of rings, Matt picked up.

"Hey, dude," Dylan said. "How's it going?"

"Dylan? Hey! What the hell, man? You get caught in that hurricane?"

"Yeah. Sorry I didn't call but there was no cell or Internet service."

"You're okay though?"

"Yeah, yeah. It wasn't that bad. Holed up in the hotel for a couple of days."

"Probably not alone." Dylan heard the smile in his voice.

"As a matter of fact, no, I wasn't," Dylan drawled, speaking the truth. "And guess what? I'm back in the States and you'll get to meet her."

"Shut the fuck up! You're back? Already?"

"I am. I'm checked in at the San Amaro Hilton."

"Hey, that's great! So does that mean you'll be here for the wedding?"

"Yep."

"And you'll stand up with me?"

"If you still want me to."

"You know I do. That's fanfuckingtastic!"

"You're at work?"

"Yeah. Wanna come over?"

"I have some business shit to do." He rubbed the back of his neck. "Maybe we can get together later?"

"Come for dinner. Don't worry, we'll order pizza or something. But why a hotel, man? You could've stayed with us."

Yeah, right. Like that was going to happen. No way in fucking hell would he stay in Matt's little cottage with him and Corey. "I need space. Thanks anyway. I have a lot to do in the next few weeks."

"I guess. Okay, so I'll be home by seven. Come over whenever. I'll let Corey know you're here."

"Yeah."

A few seconds of silence told him Matt was wondering too how this was going to go."You bringing this new girl?"

"Oh. No. Not tonight. We just flew in this afternoon, she had work to do and family to see. They were kind of freaked out about the storm."

"Oh, okay. But she can come if you want."

"Sure, but I doubt it. Okay, see you later."

He clicked off. Okay. He was going to do this. He'd go over there and have pizza and maybe a beer and talk just like old times and…he'd leave and come back here to this hotel room all by himself.

Holy shit, he was really having a pity party. He had nothing to be so down about, for God's sake. That was all in the past and he was on a winning streak and this time he had a damn good shot at beating Heath Marlow. The Australian had been crowned ASP World Champion seven times, including five consecutive titles in the last five years. Dylan had come so close in Tahiti and he was frothing to come out ahead of the world famous surfer. He was determined it was going to happen this time.

Now he had calls to make to the rest of his team, finding out where they all were and when they could get their asses here. He needed Elroy, who shaped his boards, Brett, who coached him, his trainer Austin, and he'd have to call Holden and find out more about this whole deal with Jackson Cole. And oh yeah, find out how Holden's new baby was doing.

Shiz, a baby. That was pretty freaky. Holden was a former pro surfer with a good head for business who'd become manager and agent to a number of pro athletes—skateboarders, snowboarders and surfers. Dylan had a lot of respect for the guy, valued his opinions and advice and trusted him to do what was best for his career, but in the year since Holden had gotten married his life had changed. And now he had a baby.

Dylan located the rest of his team, assured them he was fine after the storm in Tahiti and was now back in San Amaro and ready to prepare for the next competition. He made plans with Elroy to have a look at his boards, and with Austin to meet on Monday to work out. But Holden reamed his ass out over this shit with Jackson Cole.

"Do you think I liked having them contact me like that?" he demanded. "Do you think I liked them telling me to go find you and get you under control?"

"They wanted you to come to Tahiti?"

"Yeah. But I couldn't leave, obviously."

So that was how Brooke had ended up there.

"We need to sit down in my office and have a serious discussion about your career," Holden said. "First thing Monday morning."

Well, shit. Dylan rubbed his eyes. More lecturing. Had he really screwed up that bad? "Sure. I'll be there."

He took a shower and changed before heading over to Matt and Corey's place. Because now it wasn't just Matt's place, Corey lived there too. Which made it all different. Christ, why did he find himself wishing Brooke was there with him?

9

Dylan stood outside the front door of his friend Matt's cottage near the beach, his insides in knots. Then the door opened and Matt appeared with a big smile on his face. "Hey, man! Come on in!"

Dylan stepped into the house, a house that now had a scent he would forever associate with Corey—a sweet mingling of chocolate and vanilla. His heart bumped against his ribs and he looked at Matt, who he hadn't seen in over a year, his best buddy from way, way back. Matt hadn't changed—same square jaw, same sparkling golden-brown eyes, same easy smile, but although the smile seemed genuinely happy, his eyes held a hint of apprehension.

They looked at each other and the few seconds seemed to stretch on interminably as thoughts and memories rushed through Dylan's head. He swallowed. Fuck it, this guy was one of the most important people in his life, even if he had ended up with the girl. He smiled. "Dude." He stepped toward Matt with arms outstretched, and Matt did the same. They threw their arms around each other and hugged, both of them holding on tight. Then they slapped each other's backs as they stepped away.

Matt's smile went crooked. "Good to see you, man. Thanks for coming." He paused. "Really."

Dylan knew they were both thinking the same things, both remembering the same things, and they both knew why this moment was so loaded. "Yeah." He'd make this easy for Matt if it killed him. "Of course I'd come. I wasn't sure how I was going to swing it, but as it turned out, the decision was made for me."

"How's that? Come on, let's get beer."

Matt led the way down a short hall to the kitchen at the back of the house.

"One of my sponsors wanted me to come back early and do some promotion work." Dylan cleaned up the story somewhat. "So here I am." He followed Matt, his eyes darting into the living room as they passed the arched doorway, looking for Corey. Not there. Maybe in the kitchen? His skin itched with the anticipation of seeing her again.

"Which sponsor?"

"Jackson Cole."

"Cool. So you're back well before the competition and in lots of time for the wedding."

"Yeah." No Corey in the kitchen either. Dylan's stomach jumped with nerves. "Speaking of wedding—where's the blushing bride?"

Matt grinned, looking over his shoulder from the refrigerator. "Blushing bride. Ha. She went to pick up some wine. She should be back any minute. Here." He handed Dylan a cold bottle. "Check it out."

Dylan looked at the beer in his hand, turning it to read the label. "I Do Brew."His eyes moved over the black and white cartoon picture of a bride and groom. He laughed and the real amusement relaxed him a little. "You gotta be kidding me, man."

"Made in honor of the wedding." Matt laughed too. "Try it. It's a pale ale."

Dylan tipped the bottle to his lips and drank. He nodded. "It's killer, dude."

Matt reached forward with his bottle and they clinked them together in a toast.

"Congrats. Can't believe you're tying the knot."

"Yeah." Matt shrugged. "It actually feels pretty good."

"You've been living together for what…a year?"

"Yeah. Just over."

"Obviously it's working."

Matt's eyes searched his and he nodded. "Yeah. It is."

"I'm happy for you, man. Seriously." And with a feeling of warmth unfurling inside him, he realized…he meant it.

The back door opened and Corey walked in. Her gaze fell immediately on Dylan. He smiled at her. "Hi, Cor."

She paused, holding a brown paper bag in her arms, her wavy hair in shades of honey and caramel flowing over her shoulders, her little nose dusted with gold freckles, as pretty as ever. She studied him for a few seconds, her expressive face not hiding her emotions at all—a hint of nerves, affection, relief. She turned to Matt, handed him the bag and moved toward Dylan for a hug.

His heart hammering, he set down his beer on the counter and enfolded her in his arms. She smelled like the candy she made, sweet and chocolaty, her wavy hair tickling his arms, and he held her and breathed her in. She felt good, slender yet soft, and he gave one last squeeze before releasing her to look down into her face.

"I'm so glad you came," she said softly.

He nodded, smiling. "Of course I came."

"There's no of course about it." Her gaze moved over his face. Trust her to say what they were all thinking. "I was afraid you wouldn't."

And once again, determination that he was not going to turn this reunion into something all full of drama and tension filled him. He was not going to ruin something as important as their wedding with his own issues. It had to be him who set the tone for this meeting, and yet he had to be honest. "Hey. It's been a while. I'm good, Cor." He touched a finger to the tip of her nose.

"I'm so glad."

Dylan glanced at Matt, looking for any signs of jealousy. He saw none, just Matt standing there watching, smiling faintly. Which was pretty damn amazing. After all, Dylan had slept with the guy's fiancée.

This could have been, *should* have been awkward, the three of them meeting up again like this. But dammit, he did not want them feeling sorry for him. And he really did want them to be happy. So he fought down that tension inside him and kept his smile firmly in place. He reached for the beer.

"I'll open the wine,." Matt set the bag on the counter with a clink of bottle. "Which one do you want, Candy Girl?"

Corey smiled and moved toward him. "The cold one. I'll put the other in the fridge."

She slid her arms around Matt's waist and hugged him, and Matt bent his head to kiss her mouth. Dylan watched and smiled, his insides tightening a little at their display of affection. He leaned against the counter and drank his beer.

They were good together. No, they were perfect together. They always had been.

He'd thought a lot about it at first when he'd left, his head all fucked up because of Corey and Matt and his busted foot and crazy fears. Mostly because of his crazy fears, if he was honest. He'd known he had no choice but to leave, alone. Leaving them together. At first he wasn't sure if they were going to figure things out. It had been clear to him that they were both crazy in love with each other. It hadn't been so clear to them. But the very next time he'd heard from Matt, via email, was to learn that they'd moved in together. So yeah, they'd figured things out.

Dylan had both wanted that and feared it.

He had to admit that hearing that news had thrown him a little, but deep inside he knew it was the right way for things to go. And now, back here again, watching them together without even a little bit of that pain that had eaten away at him for months after he left, he knew…he was over it.

He really was.

Why was it that suddenly it all didn't seem so dramatic? Almost as though he'd been all worked up over nothing.

"So tell us about this girl." Matt poured wine into a glass for Corey.

Dylan let the warm feeling inside him expand, let it loosen his tense muscles, and he laughed. "Brooke," he said, taking pleasure in saying her name, remembering their time together.

"You said she lives here? How the hell did you meet up with someone from San Amaro in Tahiti?"

"Let's go sit in the living room." Corey slid her arm through Matt's and tugged him with her.

"She works for Jackson Cole." In the living room, he sank into a chair and looked around. Subtle differences in the décor made him smile. The place looked less bachelor pad, with some nicely framed photographs on the wall, a soft beige throw draped over the arm of the leather couch and a big potted palm in the corner. It looked good. "She came down there to meet with me. I got booted out of my bungalow because of the storm and we ended up sharing a room." The story came easy when it was true.

"Dog." Matt grinned. "That would only happen to you."

Dylan laughed. "Yeah. We flew back together. She works in their Marketing and PR department and like I said, they have some things planned for me for the next few weeks leading up to the competition."

"I want to meet her!" Corey said. "Why didn't you bring her?"

"She had stuff to do." He wanted them to think there was really something between them because he did *not* want them feeling sorry for him or worrying about him. "She was out of contact with her office for a while because of the storm, so she had to get caught up. Don't worry, you'll meet her."

At the wedding. That was what she'd agreed to. Hopefully he could put Matt and Corey off meeting her until then. He *was* going to be busy. He planned to be doing a lot of surfing, a lot of working out and a lot of mental preparation for this competition. On top of whatever stuff he had to do for Brooke.

"How's the chocolate business?" he asked Corey.

She smiled and snuggled in beside Matt beneath the arm he had around her. "So good. I opened my store. I guess Matt emailed you about that."

"Yup."

"The place you found for me," she reminded him, and more warmth expanded in him. Hey, he'd done something good last time he'd been there.

"That's right. So it's working out well?"

"Awesome! I've got five people working for me now. It's great having a storefront and now being able to have some time off. And business is fabulous. I'm getting orders from all over the country. I may even have to hire more people to make chocolates to keep up with the orders."

"That's so great, Cor. You deserve it."

She grimaced, but then smiled. "Thanks."

"She still busts her butt," Matt said.

"So do you." She gave Matt a pointed look.

"I do not." He grinned.

"You totally do. You just make it all look so easy. And fun."

"I make beer. It *is* fun."

"Business is good for you too?" Dylan leaned back in the chair. While he admired the success Matt had made of his brewery, turning it into a popular brew pub, it had always puzzled him that Matt didn't have higher ambitions.

"Good enough," Matt said, unassuming as always.

"We've been doing some cool fundraising things with some other local businesses," Corey said. "Chocolate tasting, beer tasting, wine and cheese tasting, coffee cuppings...people really enjoy those."

"Fundraising. Huh."

He remembered the doubts he'd had about his surfing career when he'd been there last year. On top of being out of it for a couple of months because of his injury, he'd questioned what the hell he was doing. Surfing was basically a one-man sport. Yeah, he had Elroy and Brett and Austin, and they did work as a team, but when he was out there on the ocean, it was all him. No one else to rely on. Just him against the ocean, a force so much greater and more powerful than him. But also, no one else benefited from what he did. When he won, the glory was all his. Which was freakin' awesome and he loved it, but still…he'd seen Corey working her butt off to make her chocolates and he'd seen how many people loved them. She also worked with a group that helped families of people with mental illness. Matt had his business, which also made a lot of people happy, drinking his beer, hanging out in his pub, and he too participated in events like the one they'd dragged him to last year to raise money for a homeless shelter.

So the sport Dylan had dedicated his whole life to had felt… selfish. Pointless. He'd even had the crazy idea of giving it up.

Of course part of that had been the PTSD symptoms he'd experienced from his accident. The shrink he'd seen after that had told him as much. But surfing was all he had. Getting back into it had been the hardest thing he'd ever done and he was proud he'd accomplished that, even though his head was still kind of screwed up. He had a goal and he was working hard to get there.

"Tell me about the wedding," he said.

"We're having it at Laguna Dorada." Matt named his brew pub. "We're closing down the place that Sunday night. The ceremony will be out on the patio and then we'll eat and drink and party inside. Just fun and casual, with our friends and family."

"Sounds great. What can I do to help?"

Corey and Matt looked at each other, then back at him. "Nothing right now." Corey tapped her chin. "But I'm sure the weekend of the wedding we'll need help with some of the decorations and getting the chocolates to the restaurant. We're trying to keep it simple."

"The Saturday night before the wedding, Corey's girlfriends

are taking her out," Matt said. "So you and I and some of the guys should go out too."

"I'll take care of planning that," Dylan said. "A stag. We need strippers."

Corey choked on her wine. "Strippers. Oh God."

Matt and Dylan shared a grin. "What's wrong with strippers, hon?" Matt squeezed her shoulders.

She shook her head, smiling. Some girls might freak out at the idea, but not Corey. She probably knew Matt wouldn't go for strippers. Or…would he? Thinking about the things they'd done last summer, nice guy Matt did have a kinkier side…

"Tell us about your surfing." Corey changed the subject. "You've done great over the last year."

"Pretty good, yeah. I'm ranked third in the world now."

"That's awesome."

He grinned. "This time I'm gonna do it. This time I'm gonna beat Marlow."

"They're saying you can do it," Matt said.

"Of course I can." Some things were beyond his control. He knew only too well that the ocean was a force much greater than him. But all things being equal, he knew he could do it.

They ordered pizza, talked and laughed, and over the course of the evening the tension inside Dylan dissipated. In a way, it was weird. He could almost pretend everything that had happened between the three of them last year had been three other people. Not them. And yet, the easy fun they'd shared was still there, and he slid back into it, back into the jokes and teasing insults, becoming more comfortable.

It had always been like that between him and Matt. They'd been best friends since high school. They'd had each other's backs through thick and thin, Dylan teaching Matt how to surf, Matt coaching him through high school math and physics. They'd dated together and partied together, and Matt's home had been a refuge for Dylan when his own parents were too busy fighting to pay any attention to him.

Last year had made things strained and uncomfortable for them, and Dylan had left things like that. Which was at least part of the reason he hadn't wanted to come back. He had to smile at himself. When it came to surfing, he was aggressive and fearless. Well, mostly fearless. When it came to relationships, he was a big wuss.

Damn, he'd missed Matt's friendship though.

"I should get going," Dylan eventually said. Surprisingly it was nearly midnight, and holy crap, he was tired. He got to his feet and helped carry pizza boxes and beer bottles out to the kitchen. He hugged Corey and kissed her forehead with genuine affection. "Good night, Cor."

"See you soon."

Matt walked him to the door. "You could've stayed here," he said again.

Dylan was comfortable enough now for honesty. "No. I couldn't."

Pausing at the door, they shared a look of understanding. "We okay, man?"

Emotion rose up inside Dylan, including relief that he'd made it through this and things were…okay. Not great, but okay. And once again, there was no way in hell he was going to ruin this for Matt by being a jerk. "Yeah." He laid a hand on Matt's shoulder and squeezed. "We're good, dude."

Outside he breathed in the cool night air, the briny scent of the nearby ocean. Man, he was tired. He'd slept on the flight, but apparently not enough and probably all the tension he'd felt about seeing Matt and Corey again had sucked the energy out of him. For once, he was going to be happy to head back to the hotel and crash alone.

But as he drove back to the Hilton, he kept thinking about Brooke. What was she doing? Probably sleeping. He smiled, thinking about the way she curled her hand into a fist and tucked it under her chin when she slept. Weird that he knew that about her. Weird that he was going to miss having her in his bed tonight.

10

Brooke spent the rest of Friday and a good part of Saturday catching up with the work that had accumulated during her absence, including a meeting with Tim to get her up to speed on the things he'd been working on while she'd been gone. Saturday afternoon she took Amber, her Little Sister, shopping for new bras.

She picked up Dylan at the San Amaro Hilton later that afternoon. She texted him to let him know she was there, and he was waiting in the lobby when she walked in. He leaned against the back of a leather chair, flipping through some tourist brochure, dressed in his usual knee-length cargo shorts and a loose yellow and pink Hawaiian print shirt. She lifted an eyebrow over the pink shirt, but on him it just looked right. She caught the glances of others in the lobby, both men and women, some who probably recognized him and some who just wanted to look at him because he was so goddamn gorgeous. She sighed.

"Hey." She stopped in front of him.

He looked up and gave her that smile, white teeth and eyes gleaming in his tanned face, and her insides quivered. "Hey yourself." He dropped the brochure onto the table and slung his arm around her shoulders, pulling her in for a hug.

She went stiff, just briefly, surprised at his familiar contact. But why was she surprised? They'd spent days in bed together doing all kinds of wicked, naked things. A hug wasn't out of line.

Maybe because she'd been telling herself ever since they parted at the airport the day before that this was going back to strictly business. But he hadn't gotten that memo.

She slipped out of his embrace. "I parked out front. Come on." She led the way through the lobby and into the late afternoon sunshine, past big pots with waving palms and bright flowers, over the shiny brick sidewalk toward the parking lot.

In the car, she said, "So? What have you been up to?"

"Had dinner with my friends Matt and Corey last night."

"The ones who're getting married, right?"

"Right."

She bit her lip and cast him a sideways glance as she drove. "How was that?"

"It was…" His voice trailed off and he looked out the side window. "It was fine." He gave a nod. "Yeah. It was fine."

"Maybe you don't need me to go the wedding after all."

His head whipped around. "Oh hell yeah, I do. I already told them you're coming."

"Oh. Okay then." She had agreed, after all.

"Today I hooked up with Elroy and Brett, and we did some shaping on my boards."

"Oh."

"This is the place I can experiment a little. Normally I wouldn't try something new in a big competition, but here I can."

"Why?"

He shrugged. "Waves aren't as big here. Plus this is where I learned to surf."

"It sounds like you're pretty hands-on when it comes to your boards."

"Yeah. I took some CAD courses to learn more about

designing them. I'm making my board about an inch smaller, a little wider, and about a sixteenth of an inch thicker. Thinner through the tail and nose. I get better flotation, and the lightness lets me throw it around and look all whippy."

She laughed. "I have no idea what you're talking about. But it sounds impressive."

"I like doing that. It's fun working on the boards. Elroy's taught me a lot. And then I went to the gym and worked out with Austin."

"Sounds good."

"Where do your folks live?"

"Up on Seal Point. Not far."

"You're sure they don't mind me showing up like this?"

"Of course not. My family's exited to meet you. I have to warn you though, the whole family will be there. Or most of them anyway. My sister Fraya and her husband Kevin and their two boys, James and Jonathan. They're eight and ten. My brother Anthony and his wife and their new baby, Mimi. I'm not sure if my other brother Errick will be there. He broke up with his girlfriend a while back and is now leading a wild single life again."

Brooke loved her family, which was a big part of why she'd wanted to return to San Amaro to live after college. She loved San Amaro too, the nearly constant sunshine, the casual seaside feel of the small city, the beautiful beaches, the big pier and how pretty the streets were with their brick sidewalks and ubiquitous baskets and pots of flowers.

"Are your siblings older than you? Younger?"

"They're all older. Fraya's next, she's thirty-one. Errick's thirty-three, and Anthony's almost thirty-five."

"Wow. That's quite a family."

She smiled. "Yeah, I know."

"You're the baby, huh?"

Her smile vanished. "Yes. And they don't let me forget it." She pulled into the driveway.

"Nice place," he said as they walked from the driveway

through a big gate and into a large fenced backyard. They rounded a corner and climbed steps up to the deck overlooking the pool where her nephews were playing.

"Hey, Auntie Brooke!"

She stopped beside the pool and waved at them with a big smile. "Hi guys. Having fun?"

"We love Grandma and Grandpa's pool!"

Brooke looked over at her brother-in-law Kevin sitting in a chair beside the pool on lifeguard duty. "Hi Kev." She introduced Dylan to him and the boys.

"Get out of the pool and shake hands, guys," Kevin ordered them.

"That's okay," Dylan protested, holding his hands out as if to push them back. "You're having fun. Stay in."

"Are you gonna come in?" James demanded. "You too, Auntie Brooke! Come in and swim with us."

"I didn't bring a swimsuit," Dylan said. "Sorry. Looks like fun."

"Where are Mom and Fraya?" Brooke asked. "In the kitchen?"

"Yeah. Getting dinner ready."

"Come on." Brooke led Dylan into the house through sliding French doors.

"Oh there you are." Mom dropped the big spoon she was holding. She rushed across the kitchen and grabbed Brooke in a tight hold. "Thank God you're home safe and sound."

"I'm fine, Mom!" Brooke hugged her mother back then extricated herself. Her mom refused to let go though, still holding her arms and studying her.

"I was so worried about you! I kept thinking of that tsunami and how awful that was."

"It wasn't a tsunami."

"Too bad you weren't stuck there longer," Fraya said from where she sat at the big center island. At a look from their mother she added, "I just mean Tahiti's a good place to be stuck. How many of us get sent there on business? Not me, that's for sure." Fraya slid off her stool, her gaze fixed on Dylan.

"It was supposed to be a short trip." Brooke made more introductions.

Fraya grinned and extended a hand to shake Dylan's. "We're all big fans of yours. Welcome home to San Amaro for the Pro." She gave him an up-and-down female look that Brooke knew meant nothing. She'd been happily married to Kevin for nearly twelve years.

"Thanks," he said with that sexy grin. "It's good to be back." And he shot Brooke a fast, amused glance.

"You're going to win for sure," Fraya said.

Brooke caught the flicker in Dylan's eyes that belied his confident smile. "I sure hope so," he drawled. He turned to Brooke's mom. "Thanks so much for having me tonight, Mrs. Lowry."

"Call me Debbie." She too shook his hand. "And it's no trouble at all!" She studied him. "You are such a handsome boy."

Brooke rolled her eyes and suppressed a groan.

"Thanks." His grin spread across his tanned face again. He met Brooke's eyes and a shiver worked down her spine. "Sounds like you were worried about Brooke, but she was fine. We weren't in any danger where we were at the hotel."

"That's good to hear." Mom returned to the stove where she'd been stirring something in a big pot. "But we couldn't get hold of her, of course, so we had no idea. I tend to worry a bit."

"A bit!" Fraya and Brooke said at the same time, punctuated with a snort from Fraya. They laughed.

"Fraya, you're a mother, you know what it's like to worry about your children. And Brooke, you will too some day."

Brooke met her sister's eyes and they shared a small smile. Fraya and Kevin did often argue about how overprotective Fraya was of the boys, but everyone knew where she'd gotten it from, and even she recognized it and tried to loosen up a little.

"Tahiti is so far away," Mom continued. "How long was the plane ride?"

"Fifteen hours."

"And that's all over water. My God."

Brooke laughed. "True, Mom. To get to an island you have to get across the water somehow." It was obvious where she got her fear of flying from.

"Surfing's a dangerous sport." Mom picked up the steaming pot and poured it into the colander sitting in the sink. "You must be very brave, Dylan."

"He knows what he's doing," Brooke said.

"Well, I should hope so. Have a seat, kids. Help yourselves to drinks."

"Beer?" Brooke asked Dylan, heading to the refrigerator.

"Um. Okay."

She gestured at the stools at the island where Fraya had situated herself again, cutting up tomatoes for something, salad maybe.

Anthony and Jinny arrived, Jinny carrying Mimi in her car seat. Brooke hugged and kissed and made more introductions.

"Cool to meet you." Anthony shook Dylan's hand. "I remember watching you surf back when you were probably a teenager. You were great, even then."

"Thanks." Dylan cast Brooke a glinty-eyed look. "This visit is good for my ego."

"Like your ego needs it," she muttered.

Two dripping wet boys ran into the kitchen, towels wrapped around their shoulders, followed by Kevin. "You're dripping all over Grandma's kitchen, guys," Kevin said.

"That's okay." Mom smiled. "It's tile, it'll mop up. We're almost ready to eat, boys, so go get changed."

Anthony opened the fridge. "Mom! No beer?"

"I just gave Dylan the last one," Brooke said.

"There's more in the other fridge," Mom told him. "You can go get it."

Anthony heaved a long-suffering sigh and left the room. Jinny grinned and lifted Mimi out of her car seat.

"Oh let me have her!" Brooke rushed to Jinny's side. "Look how much she's grown!"

"You saw her a week ago," Jinny said.

"I know, but they grow fast! Don't you? Don't you grow fast, you beautiful girl, you?" Brooke took Mimi from her mom. Mimi gazed back at her with big blue eyes and a smile broke out on her round little face. She was so beautiful it made Brooke's heart squeeze, and she hugged her, breathing in the baby clean scent of her. She turned to Dylan. "This is my niece, Mimi. Isn't she gorgeous?"

Dylan was staring at her with an odd expression on his face. "Yeah." He shifted his gaze to the baby. "She really is." He smiled.

"So can you really earn a living as a surfer?" Mom asked.

"Shnippits." Brooke sighed. She was beginning to regret inviting Dylan for dinner. She should have known her family would say anything that popped into their heads. "Yes, Mom, they can make a lot of money if they're good."

"And if we win," Dylan added.

"Plus all the sponsorship money they get and whatever endorsements they do." Brooke bounced Mimi in her arms and once again her eyes met Dylan's with a heated jolt. She lifted her brows and he raised his chin.

Anthony returned with his hands full of beer bottles. "Dylan? How's your beer? Need another one?"

"No, I'm good. Great beer too, from Laguna Dorada. My friend Matt owns that brewery."

"Yeah. I know Matt. Good guy."

"Okay, call your father," Mom said. "Dinner's ready." She carried a big bowl of pasta primavera to the big round kitchen table.

"Dad!" Anthony shouted.

"Anthony," Mom said, "I could have done that."

"You said to call him."

Brooke grinned and took her seat. Her father wandered in from the den, the only one who hadn't yet met Dylan. One more introduction. Dylan rose to his feet and respectfully shook her father's hand.

"Pleased to meet you, Mr. Lowry. You have quite a family here."

"They get on my nerves," Dad said, and everyone laughed. "I'm serious."

While Brooke envied some of Dylan's travels, she knew she would always want to come home to San Amaro. And to her family, who she loved so much, and who, despite their teasing insults, were always there for each other no matter what.

Dad lifted his eyebrows as he took his usual seat, the only chair at the table with arms. He looked around. "Why isn't Errick here?"

"Hot date," Anthony said.

"Amazing." Fraya lifted salad onto her plate.

"Why is that amazing?" Mom asked. "He's a nice boy. Girls like him."

They all laughed again. "Yes, Mom, he is." Fraya passed the salad bowl to Brooke. "So Brooke, tell us more about Tahiti."

Tell them about Tahiti. Yeah, right. Dylan's eyes met Brooke's and heat slid over him. They were both remembering Tahiti, all right.

"Well, um. It's really beautiful," Brooke began. "I mean, I didn't get to see much because we were stuck in the hotel for a few days." Her glance collided with his again, and he felt like the air fairly sizzled around them at the heated memories of being stuck together—literally—in that hotel. Their eyes held for a long, smoldering moment. "But what I did see was gorgeous."

Dylan rescued her by talking about Tahiti, since he'd been there so many times, and then conversation turned to some of the other places he'd traveled to.

"Are you really a surfer?" James asked, staring at Dylan wide-eyed.

"Yes."

"Like, that's your job?"

He grinned. "Yeah. Cool job, huh?"

"I heard about a surfer who got attacked by a shark. Has that ever happened to you?"

Christ. "No," Dylan said. "Thankfully."

"I think the shark bit off her arm," Jonathan added. "Or maybe it was her leg."

"Or both!" James put in with gruesome delight. "I bet there was a lot of blood—"

"Okay, that's enough of that conversation," Fraya said. "Dad, what's new at work? How are those retirement plans coming along?"

"I'm not retiring."

Dylan watched Brooke and her sibling exchange exasperated glances.

"My parents are both doctors," Brooke told him. "Mom's been cutting back for a while now, but Dad refuses to."

Both doctors. Whoa. "If you love what you do, why quit?" He smiled at Brooke's dad.

"That's what I say! What would I do if I retired?" He paused. "Heh. Maybe I should take up surfing."

Dylan laughed with the others. Although Mr., er, Dr. Lowry looked pretty fit. He probably could surf.

The conversation then turned to other topics: Fraya's law practice, Mrs. Lowry, er, Dr. Lowry...*Debbie's* passion for gardening, and Mimi's teething and diaper rash.

"How come you can talk about poopy diapers at the table and we can't talk about sharks?" Jonathan demanded.

For a moment there was silence and Dylan waited with amusement for someone to respond. At his home, his parents would have told him to shut his mouth, but Fraya tipped her head to one side and said, "That's a very good point, Jonathan. We should not be talking about diapers at the dinner table."

Anthony pulled out his cell phone and read a text message. He frowned.

"Anthony, put that away," his mom said.

Anthony looked up. "Well, shit."

"What's wrong?" Brooke asked.

"Just got a text message from Brandy. She and Chelsea are at Slice of Heaven. Errick's there and guess who he's with?"

"Oh no." Brooke sat back in her chair.

"Tell us it's not Melissa," Fraya begged.

"Yup, it is," Anthony said. He shook his head.

Brooke caught Dylan's questioning look. "His ex-girlfriend. They broke up a while ago and we were all happy about it."

"Because she's a bitch," Fraya put in. Then she covered her mouth and gave a guilty glance toward her kids.

"Mom! You have to put a quarter in the cuss jar now!"

"I will."

"They're not good for each other," Brooke rephrased. "She really hurt him. I can't believe he's with her."

"I hope they're not getting back together." Debbie's forehead creased.

"He never said anything." Anthony frowned. "Just that he had a date tonight. He knows we all hate her."

"Kind of tough to have a relationship with someone when your whole family hates her," Dylan commented slowly.

Brooke sighed. "If they get back together, we have to put up with her. For his sake."

"I can't," Fraya said.

"Yes, you can. But maybe someone should talk to him and see what the…what he's thinking."

Debbie's mouth turned down at the corners. "Oh, now I'm worried about him. I don't want to see him hurt again."

"He's a grown man," Dr. Lowry put in. "He can handle himself."

"Not sure about that," Anthony muttered. "Not when it comes to her. He was an idiot about her."

"It's his life," Brooke said. "All we can do is be there for him, whatever happens."

They all nodded and made noises of agreement.

Dylan hadn't wanted to meet Brooke's family. He wasn't sure why, exactly. He didn't really do relationships, so it wasn't usual for him to meet the family of a girl he'd slept with. But this wasn't a relationship either. So he'd done hot nasty things to Mr. and Mrs. Lowry's—or should that be Dr. and Dr. Lowry's?—daughter for days on end in that hotel room in Tahiti. They didn't need to know about that.

Maybe it was because he didn't like the idea that she was babysitting him. Or keeping him on a leash. Or whatever. He wasn't going to go out and have some kind of public drunken orgy. Although, there'd been a time when he might have…

He also wasn't used to being around family. His own family hadn't exactly been a model of togetherness. The time he'd spent with Matt's family had been the closest he'd ever experienced to normal family life. He liked Matt's mom and sisters, and now that he thought about it, he kind of missed that. Spending time with a family of strangers wasn't going to be the same.

But from the moment he'd walked in the door, he'd felt at ease. They were all so open and friendly. Her sister was a little intimidating, but her brother seemed like a cool dude. Her dad didn't say much and had given him a long, penetrating look that had made his nuts shrivel a little, but after that he'd been cool too.

Seeing Brooke cuddling that baby, and kidding around with her nephews and seeing how much they loved her made his heart sort of ache. Or maybe he'd missed his Pantoloc. Nah. That wasn't it.

When they all started dissing the other brother's ex-girlfriend, he had a moment where he felt sorry for the chick, but then the way they were all on the same page about her and worried about their son-slash-sibling made him a little…envious.

In the past he'd probably been on the other side of that page, the guy everyone was hating on for hurting their poor baby sister or whatever. He kind of liked being on the inside.

After dinner they went out onto the big deck beside the pool, and the two boys insisted on changing back into their swimsuits and returning to the pool. Kevin too donned a pair of board shorts and went in with them, and they started tossing a big ball around.

"They're really good in the water," Dylan commented to Fraya, sitting beside him.

"They are! They love it. They're like little fish."

"They take swimming lessons?"

"Yes, they do."

"Hey Dylan!" Jonathan's head appeared at the side of the pool. "Could you teach me to surf?"

"There are no waves in that pool," Dylan pointed out, straight-faced.

Jonathan giggled. "Noooooo! Not here! I meant in the ocean!"

"Oh! Well, then, yeah, I could." He glanced at Fraya.

She bit her lip as if trying to stop herself from saying something.

"If your parents agree," Dylan added.

"You're kind of busy right now," Brooke put in from the chair on the other side. "Dylan's in the middle of an important competition," she told Jonathan.

He pouted. "After it's done, then?"

"Dylan won't be around that long."

Dylan hated the disappointment on the kid's face.

"I bet you're a good swimmer." James appeared at the side of the pool next to his brother. "Too bad you don't have a swimsuit."

"Yeah, it is," Dylan agreed. "That pool looks really nice. I like swimming." He set his beer down on the table and rose to approach the pool. He reached down and swished his hand into the water. "Man, I'd sure like to swim in there."

"Come in!" Jonathan said. "We want you to swim too."

Dylan pursed his lips. Then he reached into his pocket for his cell phone and wallet, tossed them to Brooke…and stepped off the side of the pool into the water.

Water closed over his head, cool and blue and quiet, and he let himself surface, emerging to shrieks of shock and laughter.

"What are you doing?" Brooke cried, while the two boys howled with laughter.

"Oh my God!" Fraya exclaimed, and Dylan caught Kevin and Anthony's guffaws.

He shook his wet hair back and grinned at the boys. "There. I'm in."

"Your clothes are all wet!"

"Hey, you're right. Oh well." He unbuttoned his shirt and tossed it to the pool deck, then dove and reached for a small ankle.

He played in the water for a good half hour then hauled himself out, his shorts dripping water all over the deck. "I'm sorry," he apologized to Debbie Lowry with his most charming smile. "I wonder if I could borrow a towel?"

She laughed and handed him one that someone had gone to get while he was in the pool. "Here. There's a bathroom right inside the sliding doors for pool users. Toss your wet clothes out and I'll put them in the dryer."

"Thanks."

He caught Brooke's eye as he walked past her into the house, shaking her head, a smile tugging her lips.

When he came back, the towel snugly fastened around his hips, he sat back down and picked up his beer. "That was fun."

"You're crazy," Brooke said to him.

He shrugged. "Probably. But it was fun." He turned to Debbie again. "Sorry to be a bother. It was just too tempting to resist."

"Those boys will worship you forever," she replied with a big smile.

He sat there while his clothes dried, drinking his beer, listening to teasing insults and banter interspersed with genuine concern. Brooke's mom was apparently still fretting over Brooke being in the path of the cyclone, even though she was home safe and sound. Did that overprotectiveness have anything to do with Brooke's fear of flying?

And yet he had to give her credit—it hadn't stopped her from flying all the way to Tahiti. Because she had to. Huh. He studied her, calmly reassuring her mother that she'd been fine, when he knew damn well she'd been freaking out herself. His heart gave a kind of squeeze in his chest thinking about that.

"How do you stay on the surfboard?" James asked him. "You must have good balance."

"Balance is one of the most important things to learn as a surfer," Dylan agreed. "Basically, if the downward force from gravity and the upward force of buoyancy are in line they add to zero and things are stable. When two opposing forces get out of line then the board will torque. When you move backward, the torque twists the board so the nose goes up and the tail goes down. The board rotates until gravity and buoyancy come into line again. So by shifting your weight relative to the center of mass of the board, you can tip your board nose down, nose up, right side down or left side down."

"That's physics," Kevin told his sons. "Listen and learn."

They talked more about the science behind surfing until Dylan looked up and saw Brooke watching him and listening, all silky brown hair and big eyes and soft smile.

"Pretty smart, aren't you?" she commented in a low voice.

He grinned. "You betcha." He reached out a hand to touch her soft hair, smiling. Then he caught her dad watching them with raised eyebrows. He drew back his hand.

"What'd you tell your parents about us?" he whispered, leaning toward Brooke.

She leaned closer still to whisper back, "I told them you fucked my brains out for three days straight."

His heart lurched in his chest, heat flashing through his veins. Jesus Christ! But nobody else had heard and a burst of laughter escaped him, earning another look from Brooke's dad.

But shiz, he wasn't sure when he'd ever felt like this—relaxed, mellow and…happy.

Brooke drove him back to the hotel later, and when she pulled up out front but didn't park, he turned to her with disappointment. "Not coming in?"

She gave him a level look. "No."

He pursed his lips. "Hell."

"This is business, Dylan," she reminded him.

It hadn't felt like business. He'd met her family. "I like your folks."

Her forehead wrinkled. "Thanks. I like them too. Most of the time. They boss me around a lot and treat me like a little kid, but I know it's because they love me."

"Thanks for inviting me over. What's up tomorrow?"

"You have the whole day to yourself. We'll get started Monday morning, when you and Holden come in for our first meeting."

He nodded. A whole day to himself should have sounded great. But it kind of didn't.

11

Monday morning, sitting in her cubicle, Brooke tapped her fingers on her desk and stared at her computer, waiting for Dylan to arrive. She'd already had another lecture from Barrett about taking too long to get back there. There'd been a cyclone, for God's sake! But she didn't bother to point that out to him and merely told him that Dylan had been perfectly cooperative and had easily agreed to come back to San Amaro and do whatever he had to do. Now she just had to hope he came through for her and did just that. Or she was screwed.

She was lucky to have this job and do work she loved. And she was going to do the best she could to make sure this contract with Dylan Schell turned out to be beneficial to the company, if it killed her.

She licked her bottom lip and stared at her computer monitor. She'd been having a hard time focusing for the last half hour as it drew closer to the time for their meeting. Dylan had wanted it later in the morning so he could meet with his agent first, and then his agent was going to attend the meeting with him. She didn't think it was necessary, but understood that Holden would want to be there to watch out for his client's best interests. They'd pretty much filled him in on what the plans were though.

Her phone rang and the call display told her it was the receptionist at the front desk. She grabbed the receiver. "Brooke speaking."

"Hi Brooke," Tammy said cheerily. "Dylan Schell is here for your meeting."

"Thanks. Be right out."

She hung up and resisted the urge to look in her compact mirror one more time. She picked up the folders she needed and poked her head into Tim's cubicle. "He's here. I'll go get him and Holden, and we'll meet you in the meeting room."

"Okay." Tim began gathering up the materials he needed.

Jackson Cole's home office was a large, new building on the outskirts of San Amaro, constructed with new green technology that allowed in a lot of natural light and used natural materials, solar energy and natural ventilation. Brooke took the stairs from her second floor office to the main floor, emerging into the lobby area furnished with sleek chairs and tables and potted trees.

Holden sat on one of the black leather chairs and Dylan stood in front of one wall, studying framed photographs of models wearing Jackson Cole apparel. Some of the images were quite sexy, shirtless men wearing jeans dangerously low on their hips, showing off impressive abs, or women in tiny bikini tops and equally low-slung jeans.

She studied Dylan as she walked toward him. He could pose for photographs like that, with his body. In fact, he *would* pose for photographs like that, wearing Jackson Cole clothing. That had originally been part of their plan, to use him modeling some of their clothing in their advertising, but they'd had a hard time pinning him down for a photo shoot. Last summer when he'd been there he'd had a cast on his leg. Now was their opportunity.

He turned at the sound of her footsteps on the wood floor. His dark hair hung over his eyes in that sexy way, his scruff of beard darkening his tanned face, his eyes gleaming that unique light silver as he smiled at her. "Hi."

Her heart leaped when they made eye contact and she became strangely short of breath. "Hello." She paused, clutching her folders to her chest. "How are you?"

"Good. Made it here on time." He held out a hand to the other man who'd risen. "You've met Holden?"

"No." She reached to shake the agent's hand. "We've emailed and talked on the phone a number of times though." She smiled. "Nice to meet in person finally."

"Likewise." Holden still had a fit athletic body, tanned face and wore his dark hair pulled back into a ponytail. He was dressed in casual pants and a golf shirt, but carried an expensive looking brief case.

"Come this way." She led him across the lobby, through a security door and down a short hall into a meeting room. One wall of the room was windows, overlooking the grove of Torrey pine trees. Tim and Dell and Luis sat at the long table, Tim with a notebook computer set up in front of him. "Can I get you coffee or something else to drink?" she asked Dylan and Holden.

Dylan gave her a look, clearly noting her businesslike demeanor. Meanwhile, inside she was all hot and achy thinking about Dylan's mouth on hers, his mouth on other parts of her body, his body inside hers…her breathing became shallow and she worked for self-control.

"Water?" He lifted an eyebrow.

"Sure. Of course."

"Nothing for me, thanks," Holden said.

She moved to a credenza where Tammy had provided a selection of cold drinks and a carafe of coffee. Tim and the others already had coffees, so she poured a cup for herself and picked up a bottle of water for Dylan. "I think you know Tim…but I don't think you've met the others." She made introductions all around, and Dylan and Holden shook hands and smiled.

She set the water on the long table in front of him and took her seat next to him. "So you and Holden have already met and discussed the situation?"

"Yes." He pursed his lips briefly and his eyes flickered toward Holden. She was going to guess that meeting hadn't been fun for Dylan. Hopefully Holden had made him realize the seriousness of it all.

"Good. Well, let's get started. You and I talked in Tahiti about some of the things we have planned, and in the meantime Tim and the team have been working to get things set up." She began by handing them each a folder containing information they'd put together on the two charitable organizations they'd decided on, as well as some additional background information Dylan would need to be aware of and an outline of their plan for him for the next few weeks. They reviewed some of the information and then started into specifics of event planning.

But it wasn't long before Dylan started giving them a hard time. "Dinner tonight?" He referred to the dinner that had been arranged with some of the Jackson Cole executives. "I don't know if I can do that. And tomorrow's out. I'm meeting with Elroy again about my boards."

"All day?"

"All day."

She looked down at the pen she held in her hands and the notes she'd made on a pad of paper. "Wednesday?"

"I'm meeting Austin at the gym in the morning. Then I need to get in the water in the afternoon with Brett."

She couldn't argue with the fact that he needed to stay in shape and to practice. She eyed him. "Thursday?"

"Same thing. Yoga class, working out, surfing."

"Yoga class?"

He grinned. "Yoga's very good for flexibility and balance."

She pressed her lips together. "All right. Well, Dylan, you're going to have to clear some space in your busy schedule for these things. We want you to meet with the folks at Oceans Alive and Daytrippers before the first events."

"It's going to be tough. I have a lot of work to do to get ready for this competition."

"Of course you do." Her back teeth ground together. "And of course training has to come first. But you have to fit these things in."

She caught Tim and Dell exchanging worried glances. *Damn you,* she cursed Dylan in her head. As if reading her thoughts, he smiled and leaned lazily back in the chair.

She took a deep breath. Was he doing this just to piss her off? Sure, he'd been all agreeable in Tahiti when he'd been sharing her bed, but now he was here, back in the real world, the business world, he was being a jerk. Words rose to the tip of her tongue and she wanted to let them loose, but this wasn't going to be pretty in front of everyone else.

"Dylan. Can you and I speak privately for a moment? Let's step outside."

She caught the open-mouthed stares of the rest of her team as she rose from her chair. She paused at the door, waiting for Dylan, who stood with lazy athletic grace and followed her.

"Excuse us," he said to the others with a smile.

She gritted her teeth as she stepped into the hall. She closed the door behind them and led him into another room, this one empty, then turned to face him. He was right there, right behind her, and she nearly bumped against him. Her heart slammed against her ribs as he reached for her, a sexy smile tipping up the corners of his lips. He crowded her up against the edge of a big table.

"What the hell are you doing?" she demanded, trying to escape his grasp.

He bent his head and nuzzled her cheek. "What do you think? Isn't this why you wanted to be alone?"

She slapped at his shoulder. "No! Stop that." But her skin tingled everywhere and her stomach did a little flip. He smelled good, and he was warm and…she smacked him again half-heartedly.

He kissed her cheek then drew back, smiling down at her, his dark hair falling across his forehead, so gorgeous and sexy she felt her knees wobble.

"Seriously," she choked out. "That's not what I wanted. I wanted to talk to you alone." She gave him a firmer shove and he took a step back. "Have you forgotten everything we talked about in Tahiti?"

"Of course not." He shoved his hands into the pockets of his jeans. Thankfully, Jackson Cole jeans. And dammit, they looked good on him. "But I did tell you that I would have a lot to do while I was here."

"You weren't even planning on coming until a few days before the competition! How can you be that busy?"

He eyed her coolly. "I made some phone calls over the weekend. I do have things to do. I'm not making this up."

"But you *are* making it difficult." She sat against the edge of the table, hands beside her hips. When Dylan's gaze moved up and down over her, heat flashed from her hairline to her pointy-toed pumps, and her skin tingled everywhere. She fought to ignore the fiery sensations. "Look, Dylan. We talked about the importance of doing these things. If you don't participate, Jackson Cole will pull the plug. What did Holden have to say about this?"

"Same thing you're saying." His gaze lingered on her mouth.

She resisted the urge to lick her lips under the warm weight of his gaze. Her nipples tightened inside her bra and she cursed her body for responding like that. How was she supposed to be all business when she was getting warm and wet just from the way he looked at her?

"I wasn't getting a cooperative vibe from you back in there. I thought we had a deal, Dylan."

He lifted his chin. "Yeah. I'm here, aren't I?"

She sighed. "Listen. Here's the thing. Surfing is a pretty individual sport. You need to learn to be more of a team player if you want to be successful."

He frowned.

"You're not just marketing yourself. You're marketing Jackson Cole. And you're marketing the entire sport of surfing. Surfing has grown a lot—it wasn't that long ago surfers didn't get big sponsorship contracts like other athletes. Now they do, and you need to be grateful for that."

Oh man, she sounded like a mother lecturing a little kid. She hated sounding like that. Dylan's scowl was deepening, a pissed-off glint in his eyes.

"You may think it's amusing to proposition flight attendants or make inappropriate comments to TV reporters, but this is a business and you are *that* far from losing this deal." She held out thumb and forefinger barely touching. "The surfing counterculture image can work for you, but only if you do it right. You need to be humble, honest and generous. You need to take responsibility for your actions."

"Jesus," he muttered. "You're sounding just like Holden. He was giving me all this shit about crisis recovery."

She sighed again. "This isn't a crisis. Yet. You're no Michael Vick or Tiger Woods."

"Gee thanks."

"I meant that in a good way." Shit. She didn't want to be a bitch. She softened her tone. "You have the potential to be huge, Dylan. You have the charisma, the easy surfer dude charm. You're well spoken in front of the camera as long as you say the right things. You've established a good social media presence on Twitter and Facebook. We can build on that by getting you out there doing some good things. But you need to cooperate and participate fully."

"Brooke." His clipped tone made her go still and blink at him. "I'm telling you I will cooperate. I'm here. I'm doing this. I get that I have responsibilities to other people than just myself. But make no mistake—this is about winning. I'm here to win this competition. That is my top priority. I'll do everything I can to cooperate, but we're going to have to work around my training schedule. Do you get that?"

She stared at him, then whispered, "Yes."

"Good. Let's get this done." And he turned and left the room.

She bit her lip. Frack. She'd really pissed him off. And she knew he was right. Maybe she needed to dial things back a little.

She hurried after him, back into the meeting room where the others were.

"Give me times and dates." He threw himself back into the chair and slapped his hand on the table. "I'll try to work my training around whatever you've got set up."

That was more like it. But he wasn't happy. And she found she wasn't too happy either, seeing the tightness of his mouth, the narrowed eyes and his refusal to look at her.

"No. We'll work around your training schedule. I'll set up the appearances at our stores. And an autograph session at Surf Sisters. They can be flexible. We want you to do a photo shoot modeling some Jackson Cole clothing, but I'll contact Jules and see if she can work around your schedule too. I want to set up a meeting with Daytrippers this week and Oceans Alive early next week. This weekend is a fundraising event at South Beach for Daytrippers. There'll be music, a traveling aquarium, activities for the kids, a silent auction, food and drinks. We'd really like you to be there. We've already sent out information to the media, and photographers will be there to get pictures of you interacting with the kids."

He nodded.

"Before then, hopefully you'll have time to study up on the group and what they do so that if reporters ask you questions, you'll sound informed." She leaned forward. "And this isn't an act, Dylan. You need to be genuinely interested in these groups. People will sense it if this all comes across as a PR stunt." She paused and glanced at Holden, then back at Dylan. "And like I said, since we've already announced it, it's important that you're there."

"I'll be there," he said shortly. "The only days that are absolutely out, other than the week of the competition obviously, are the Saturday and Sunday before the competition. I'm best man at my buddy's wedding," he explained to the others there. They all smiled and nodded.

Oh yeah, the wedding she'd agreed to attend with him. She studied him. Probably that was off the table now he was so annoyed with her.

They talked more, reviewing more details of what had been planned, until finally Brooke leaned back in her chair. "I think that about covers it."

Dylan nodded, looking down at the open folder on the table in front of him. "Guess I have more homework to do."

She bit her lip, doubts swirling inside her. Were they asking too much of him? It was true that the competition had to be his first priority. If he didn't surf well, there wasn't much point in doing all this other stuff.

"I've cleared my schedule for the next three weeks. Or mostly. There are a few meetings I can't change, but for the most part I'm here to help you with this."

He looked up and their eyes met. And held. Electricity arced between them. "Yeah?"

She nodded, nerves jumping. "I can pick you up and drive you to meetings. I'll help you with your schedule so you still have time to train."

"I said before, I don't need a babysitter."

"I know. I'm not babysitting you, Dylan. I'm helping. I told you in Tahiti, whatever I can do to make this easier for you, I'll do it." His eyes flickered and she knew with a flash of heat *exactly* what he was thinking. "It's my job."

She knew if they weren't in a room full of other people he'd be saying a lot more, but now he just nodded.

"Will you be at the dinner tonight?"

"Yes. In fact, I'll pick you up at your hotel. Our dinner reservation is at seven, so I'll pick you up about six forty-five."

He didn't like having plans made for him, she could see it on his face. No doubt he was used to calling the shots and doing whatever he wanted, whenever he wanted. But he gave a short nod. "Okay." He pushed back his chair and looked at Holden. "I'll see you then. Are we done here?"

"Yes, I think so."

They all filed out of the meeting room, making small talk about the weather and the upcoming competition. That would be the week it would be hard to keep Dylan out of trouble, with nonstop parties and concerts, and all his surfing buddies and beach bunnies and about five hundred thousand other people there. But they'd deal with that when they got there. Meanwhile she'd take things one step at a time, and right now getting Dylan to that dinner with the executive team was the next thing on her to-do list.

12

He'd made it through dinner with a bunch of suits, an office meeting with the director of Daytrippers and an appearance at a Jackson Cole store at a local mall. And this was just week one. It was only going to get worse.

The mall appearance had been sick. Crowds of people. Brooke had introduced him and her words still made him squirm a little, but also feel kinda good. "Dylan's amazing surfing, his unique personal style and positive attitude will help drive our Jackson Cole brand forward. We're excited to expand our relationship with such a talented athlete who influences so many young people all over the world, and not just surfers. We look forward to working with Dylan and cheering him on during the ASP World Tour this year and especially at our Jackson Cole Pro, San Amaro's hometown boy!"

And the crowd had gone nuts.

He sighed.

Yeah, he'd managed to fit in the other things he needed to do. He'd worked out at the gym a few times, done a couple of yoga classes and worked with Elroy on his boards. He'd even managed to get in the water at Breaker Beach and catch some waves. Damn that felt good.

He loved surfing like nothing else.

Determination burned inside him. He'd come so close to winning at Teahupoo, so close to beating Heath Marlow. This one was his.

Now, Saturday afternoon, he was at South Beach Park schmoozing with people the organizers wanted to spend money on silent auction tickets or to donate money to the organization. It was a good cause, and some of the kids were pretty funny. The way they hung on every word he said and stared at him worshipfully made him want to laugh, but also humbled him. Weird.

He tipped a can of pop to his lips, watching Brooke from behind his shades as she talked to a couple of people from Daytrippers. She'd worked the crowd, subtly directed him where to go and what do to, all the while looking so goddamn hot he wanted to drag her around behind one of these tents and roll around on the grass with her. Her long brown hair shone in the sun, her face half hidden behind big sunglasses, her lips shiny and perpetually smiling. She wore knee length shorts that left slender calves bare, and a loose top with little straps.

And he thought *that* was sexy as hell? Christ, he was used to tanned, blonde beach bunnies with serious breast implants. He shook his head. Maybe he'd grown immune to those kinds of charms.

He spotted a couple making their way across the grass toward him. Shit. Matt and Corey. What the hell were they doing here? He straightened and shot a glance toward Brooke. Probably Matt and Corey hadn't realized he'd seen them, so he legged it over to Brooke. "Excuse me," he said, taking her arm to draw her away from the conversation she was having.

She gave him a brief frown that she quickly turned to a polite smile. "Dylan. What can I do for you?"

"Need to talk to you."

She shot the two men she'd been talking to a brighter smile

and said, "Excuse us," as he dragged her away. "What's going on?" she asked in a low, tight voice.

"My friends are here. The ones who're getting married."

"Oh."

He paused, wrapped his arms around her and planted a big kiss on her mouth.

Startled, she didn't respond. Then she slapped a hand on his chest. Before she could shove, he murmured in her ear, "Please. Play along. Remember? I want to keep them off my back about finding a girl."

"Oh for—" She sighed. "We could have done that without making a big scene in front of all these people. Now the whole world will think we're together, not just your friends. I'm not sure how that would go over with my boss."

"Oh. Yeah." Shit, he hadn't been thinking about that. He'd just panicked seeing them. And there they were.

"Hey, Dylan."

"Hi guys." He gave them a beaming smile. "What brings you down here?"

"We heard you were here. It's been in the news that you're working with Daytrippers. Great cause. Thought we'd stop by and show some support."

"Awesome. It is a good cause, and the kids are great."

Matt and Corey looked at Brooke, whom he still had his arm around, with expectant smiles. "Matt, Corey, this is Brooke Lowry. Brooke, my friends Matt Ferber and Corey Fenwick. Soon to be Corey Ferber."

"Hi." Brooke reached out to shake hands with them, smiling. "Nice to meet you. I hear you're getting married next weekend."

"That's right." Corey studied Brooke. "And Dylan's bringing you to the wedding."

"Yes. I'm looking forward to it."

Corey looked at him, back at Brooke, back at him and he knew she was assessing Brooke. She grinned.

Okay.

"Hey, I think we went to high school together," Matt said. Then he looked at Dylan. "You didn't mention that."

"Oh yeah. We figured that out as soon as we met." Dylan slid his arm from around Brooke's shoulders then ran his hand down her bare arm to take her hand. "Not that we knew each other that well in high school."

"Yeah." Matt grinned at Brooke. "Weren't you involved with all kinds of clubs and committees at school?"

She smiled at him. "A few."

"And we were out surfing and getting drunk."

"Hey," Dylan said. "*I* was surfing. *You* were getting drunk."

Corey laughed. "I love hearing you guys talk about stuff like that." She looked at Brooke. "They're such good friends."

Dylan caught Brooke's smile. Totally fake. What was up with that?

Dylan, Matt and Brooke reminisced a little more about high school, chatting about some of the people they all knew and where they were now. Corey listened and laughed, not appearing to feel left out at all. Being from San Diego, and since she and Matt hadn't met until they were in college, she didn't know the same people they did. But that was Corey—interested in other people, warm, funny…he sighed.

"What's wrong?" Brooke looked up at him.

Huh? "Wrong? Nothing." Shit.

"So what's going on here?" Matt turned to survey the event.

Dylan welcomed the change of subject. "It's pretty cool. Check out the silent auction. Some awesome prizes are up for grabs. Let's go look."

The four of them made their way over to the silent auction, and Matt bought a bunch of tickets, spending a fuckton of money.

"Thanks, man." Dylan shot a glance at Matt. "You didn't need to do that."

Matt shrugged. "Like you said, it's a good cause. Hey, is that one of your surfboards?"

"Yeah. Autographed. Want to win it?"

Matt laughed. "There must be better prizes."

Dylan rolled his eyes but smiled.

Matt and Corey checked out the prizes, choosing which ones they wanted to spend their tickets on.

"You should have asked me for a donation," Corey told him. "I would have put together a gift basket of chocolates."

"Um. Well, I wasn't that involved in organizing this," he said, uncomfortably aware he'd had nothing to do with it, even though people kept complimenting him. "But for sure, next time I will. Corey makes chocolates," he said for Brooke's benefit. "She owns Decadent Indulgence."

"Oh my God, I love those chocolates! They're amazing."

Corey gave her a pleased smile. "Thanks."

"And Matt owns the Laguna Dorada Brew Pub," Dylan added.

"I knew that." Brooke smiled. "It's a great place."

They wandered around and listened to the band that played. A ten-year-old boy came up to Dylan. "What's your favorite maneuver?"

Dylan grinned. "Hey dude. I like any kind of air—airs and barrels. Backside Finner."

"Cool."

"You surf, buddy?"

"Yeah. I'm coming to learn from you next week."

"Awesome. I can't wait. What's your name?"

"Cody."

"Mondo, Cody. I'll see you then." He fist-bumped the boy. Straightening, he caught Brooke's eye, surprised to see a look of soft warmth on her face.

"I have to go talk to the people from Daytrippers again for a few minutes," she said abruptly. "Excuse me."

"She's gorgeous," Corey said to him when she'd left.

He smiled. "Yeah. She is." And that wasn't him faking.

But Corey was looking at him searchingly. "So you two met in Tahiti, but she's from here."

"Yeah."

Her mouth kicked up at one corner. "But you're only here for a couple of weeks."

"True that. Why?"

"I was just thinking, that makes it kind of hard for anything long term to develop between you."

Oh hell. Long term. *Get those ideas out of your head, Corey*. "I don't do long term," he said lightly. "You should know that. I'll be off in a few weeks for the next event. But we can have fun while I'm here."

"Sure. Okay."

The way she looked at him made him want to squirm. He pasted on a big grin to assure her he was fine.

"We should all have dinner tonight." Corey glanced at Matt. "We could go to the brew pub."

"Sure," Matt said. "Great idea."

Hell. "I'd have to check with Brooke," Dylan said. "I'm not sure what's up for tonight."

"Okay. Where is she?"

He wasn't going to get out of this, apparently. He scanned the crowd and spotted her near the stage. She was laughing and then she looked right at him and said something, and the people she was talking to looked at him too. He lifted his eyebrows and started towards her. "Be right back," he told Corey and Matt.

"This is Leila Cruz from Channel Six news," Brooke introduced him when he arrived at her side. "They're interested in doing a little spotlight piece on you for the news next week, about you being home for the San Amaro Pro. Hometown boy has a chance to win it all."

Oh man. He'd had a million requests for that kind of thing.

"Oh. Well, sure." He smiled and shook hands. "Sounds great."

"We want to highlight your involvement in local organizations," Leila said. "Like this one today. We try to support those kinds of things."

"That's great. Appreciate that. This is an awesome cause."

God, how many times could he say that? "I'm happy to contribute and if you can shine more light on it, all the better."

He caught Brooke's open mouth and raised eyebrows.

"I hear you're working with Oceans Alive too," Leila said.

"Yes I am. I haven't yet had a chance to be very active but I'm very aware of the issues facing our oceans. Oceans are the largest ecosystems on Earth, our biggest life support systems. We need healthy oceans to survive and prosper."

Brooke's eyes widened even more. What? Wasn't this what he was supposed to be doing?

"I spend a lot of time in oceans," he continued. "Which makes it even more important to me."

"Definitely," Leila agreed.

"Dylan being here has really added some star power to this event," Brooke said, her eyes still fastened on his face. "The folks from Daytrippers are thrilled with the turnout today."

He met her eyes and held her gaze with a challenging look. She tipped her head to one side and pursed her lips.

They chatted for a few more minutes, Brooke talking him up and making him look like a freakin' saint.

He knew he wasn't a saint, he was nowhere damn close to being a saint, but her praise and smiles made something warm and soft expand in his chest. It made him smile too, and stand taller and regard the TV news reporter more benevolently.

"My agent looks after things like that." He handed the reporter Holden's card. "But I'll tell him we talked."

"Thanks so much. I appreciate it."

When Leila had left, he turned to Brooke. He found himself feeling very warm toward her now too. "Thanks for your support. I know you were just doing your job, but…thanks."

She gave a slow nod. "You did great, Dylan. I'm impressed."

Her comment made his chest swell even more. Maybe she really meant all those things. "So, this is going the way you wanted?"

"So far. As long as we get some positive attention, it's all good."

"Well, I'm not drunk or stoned or stripping my clothes off in public, so it should be positive."

She rolled her eyes, but he caught the twitch of her lips.

"Holden has all kinds of things lined up. ESPN, Extreme Sports."

She nodded. "Yes, I know. That's good too. These are just some things to emphasize the things about you that make you a positive representative for Jackson Cole."

"Business."

"Of course."

He nodded. "Matt and Corey want us to have dinner with them tonight. But you don't have to. If you have something else planned. Or even if you don't, we can make some excuse."

She blinked.

"Because I only asked you to come to the wedding with me. Just to keep them off my back. I don't expect you to do more than that."

"Oh no?" She smiled. "Just kiss you right in front of hundreds of people, that's all."

He grimaced. "Oh yeah."

She narrowed her eyes at him. "Maybe it would be a good way for me to keep an eye on you tonight."

"You want to keep an eye on me?" He moved closer, deliberately turning the comment into something more.

Her eyes flashed. "You know what I mean."

"You think I might get into trouble tonight?"

She studied him. "I don't know."

"Haven't I been a good boy all week?" he asked, a touch of bitterness edging into his voice.

"I'm sorry," she said, surprising him.

"Sorry for what?"

"For making it seem like I don't trust you."

He hesitated. "Do you trust me, Brooke?"

Brooke's heart thudded lightly in her chest, just fast enough that she could feel it. Did she trust him? That all depended on what they were talking about.

"You've never been unreliable," she said finally. "You always do what you say you will."

He nodded, his usually smiling, happy face looking unusually serious. "Yes."

"But you *do* like to have fun."

"Doesn't everyone?"

"Of course. Everyone likes to have fun. But—"

"Even you?"

She frowned. "What's that supposed to mean? Of course I like to have fun."

"I mean…" He leaned closer and stroked some of her hair off her face and down behind her shoulder. Her skin quivered. "You're so professional, so serious. So buttoned up."

"Buttoned up?"

He nodded. "The first time I saw you, that's exactly what I saw."

Her cheeks flamed as she remembered walking in on him and those two women. "That might have been because you were naked and in bed with two women," she said stiffly. "And I was dressed."

"Oh yeah." He grinned. "I was hoping you were going to join us."

"As if."

"No threesomes for you?" He shook his head, a sorrowful look on his face. "And you just said you like to have fun."

Her eyes went wide and then slitty. "A threesome is your idea of fun?"

"Hey, it's just one of many."

"Along with drinking, drugs, partying…"

"Dancing," he added helpfully. "I like to dance."

She gave him a look.

"And surfing. Don't forget surfing. The most fun there is."

"More than sex?" Oh holy guacamole, why had she said that?

"Hmm. I'd have to give that some thought…okay, no. Sex is the most fun there is. Surfing is the most fun I have with my shorts on."

She choked on a laugh. "How did we get talking about sex?"

"I don't know. But I like it. Oh wait. We were talking about how buttoned up you are—"

"I'm not 'buttoned up'!"

He leaned forward and nuzzled her ear. "It's okay, babe. We can work on that. Anyway. You should come out with us. You know…to keep me out of trouble."

She opened her mouth for the obvious reply and then the answer came to her, the way to put him in his place. "Okay, fine. I'll come with you to dinner."

He frowned.

Ha. She studied him, standing there all gorgeous in the late afternoon sun, all tanned muscles, athletic grace, his dark hair gleaming, his sunglasses hiding his beautiful silvery eyes. She wanted to see his eyes. "What's wrong? Don't you want to have dinner with them?"

"Huh?"

"I got the feeling you didn't want to."

He went very still. "What makes you say that?"

"You seemed kind of…tense around them. And the way you said, 'we can make some excuse' sounded like you *wanted* to make an excuse."

His mouth tightened. "I'm not tense around them. They're my friends."

"Yes. You *were* tense around them." Maybe it was intuition, she couldn't really put her finger on it, but when his friends had approached them earlier, she'd felt the subtle tightening of his muscles in the arm he had around her, sensed the tension in his words and his smile.

"I am not. Fine. Forget it. I'll tell them you're busy and I'll go out with them myself."

"Are they putting that much pressure on you to settle down? Is that what it is?"

He paused. "Um. Yeah."

"So let's go then. We'll show them."

But he didn't look happy about that, and she suspected she'd been right—he didn't want to have dinner with his friends. And he hadn't wanted to come back to San Amaro. And she was starting to wonder why.

13

They'd agreed to meet Matt and Corey at Matt's brew pub. When they'd done with their duties at the beach, Dylan and Brooke went their separate ways, but he had her address entered into his phone and an arrangement to pick her up at seven o'clock. Kind of like a date.

He returned to the hotel to change. He checked his emails, fooled around on Twitter a little, then showered and changed into jeans and a T-shirt. He looked down, making sure it wasn't a Jackson Cole competitor T-shirt. That wouldn't impress Brooke.

Why did he care about impressing her? Maybe it was more that he didn't want to annoy her. Staying on her good side was part of his strategy for this trip. Play along with what she and Jackson Cole wanted him to do. Maintain his sponsorship. Win this competition. And oh yeah, convince Corey and Matt that he was doing fine now.

Brooke lived in a small apartment building a few blocks off the beach. Looked like only about four apartments in the building. He buzzed and she let him in, and he found her apartment on the second floor on the right.

She opened the door before he had a chance to knock,

stepped out and closed the door behind her. For some reason he was disappointed. He'd wanted to see inside, to see where she lived. To see if her home was as buttoned up as she was. He smiled, remembering her reaction to him saying that earlier.

"You seem in a good mood."

"I'm always in a good mood." *That* was a big fat lie. But she didn't need to know that. Although she'd already seen him after one of his nightmares. Which reminded him that they'd been in bed together when that had happened. And reminded him of the things they'd done in bed, which made his groin tighten. Goddamn. He studied her as he followed her down the stairs. Maybe this date could end like a "real" date and they could have some of that again…

She too wore jeans, which surprised him. Sexy jeans, low on her slender hips, hugging her thighs and butt. On top she wore a sky-blue loose tank-style shirt with deep cut armholes that left her shoulders and some of her back very bare. He wanted to drag his tongue over those sexy bare shoulders. "You look hot."

She gave him a look, as if she was trying not to smile. "Thank you. You look nice too."

"Nice? I look *nice*? Jesus."

Her smile twitched again. "What do you want to hear?"

"You're supposed to tell me I look hot too."

She shook her head as he opened the passenger door of his rental car. "You know damn well you look hot."

"I do?"

"Oh my God."

He closed her door with a grin and bounded around to the driver's side.

When he was in, she said, "Your ego doesn't need any more stroking."

"I can always use more stroking. And not just my ego." He gave a meaningful glance at his lap.

He caught the flush that stole into her cheeks as he started the car and grinned. He shoulder checked and pulled away from the curb. "So. A threesome is out of the question, huh?"

She choked. "What?"

"We were talking about it earlier. You seemed opposed to the idea."

"Uh…" Her fingers curled tighter around the purse she held on her lap. "Well. If I was ever going to be involved with a threesome, it wouldn't be two girls. It would be two hot guys in my bed, all their attention on me."

Oh Jesus fucking Christ. Now it was his turn to make a little choked noise.

She shot him an evil grin. "What? Not seeing yourself in bed with another guy?"

Oh hell yeah, he was seeing himself in bed with Matt and Corey, he and Matt both focused on her and her pleasure. Brooke thought she was taunting him because the idea was so out there, but little did she know she was torturing him in a different way. And little did Miss Buttoned Up Assistant Marketing and PR Manager know he'd actually done that.

"Yeah, let's drop that subject. Tell me what's up next week."

Back to business. That was nice and safe. They talked about the things she'd scheduled, working around his practices which he was intensifying in preparation for the competition now only two weeks away.

Matt and Corey were already there at a table for four with beers in front of them. Dylan focused on relaxing, because Brooke had been scarily perceptive earlier, noticing that he tensed up around them. Even though things had gotten easier that night when he'd had dinner with them at their place, obviously some uneasiness remained.

So he pulled out his best jokes and stories, teasing Corey, entertaining them all while they ordered beer and then burgers. He asked Matt about new beers he was making, and Brooke got Corey talking about her chocolates, who in turn asked Brooke about her job, and a few hours later he was stoked to realize he'd had a lot of fun with these three people. Like he and Brooke were actually a couple. Which they weren't. Although he couldn't seem to stop touching Brooke throughout the meal, leaning closer, brushing her hair back, stroking her arm…

"I have to plan some kind of bachelor party for Matt," he told Brooke on the way home. "Not sure what to do about that. Any suggestions?"

"Geez. I don't know much about bachelor parties. When my friend AJ got married, the guys flew to Vegas for a weekend."

"Yeah, that's not going to work so much. Seeing as you've got me all handcuffed here."

"Handcuffed. Very funny."

"Vegas'd be fun, though. Damn. What else?"

"I hope you don't expect me to tell you where to find strippers."

"Well, we have to do something raunchy. We can't just go out for steaks somewhere."

"I don't see why not. *You* have stay out of trouble, remember?"

"Shit. Matt's getting married. We have to do something."

"Well, either you have it at someone's home where nobody will know what happens, or you go out for a nice dinner. Or maybe miniature golfing."

His horrified laugh nearly choked him. "Miniature golfing! I don't even do real golfing. Golfing is for people who don't know how to surf."

"Remember, my brother Errick's the golf pro at the country club here."

"Oops. Sorry. Didn't mean to insult your brother."

"Don't worry. He does know how to surf. He's a pretty good athlete all around. But back to your bachelor party…maybe bowling? Oh wait! I have the perfect idea."

"What? I'm all ears."

"There's an adventure company just outside of town. They take people kayaking, hiking, rock climbing, and they do this high ropes thing. They do it for groups, like corporate team building and stuff. You guys could all go there, and then maybe go for beers somewhere after. As long as you behave."

"You had to add that in there." He thought about that. "You know, that's a pretty cool idea. You have the name of this place?"

"It's Intrepid Adventures. I know the two guys who own it. Their girlfriend does photography for us. I'll find the number when we get to my place."

"That'd be great. Thanks, Brooke." He paused. "Uh...*their* girlfriend?"

"Yeah." She smiled. "The three of them live together. Ménage à trois relationship."

"Seriously?" He gaped at her. "Like, a permanent relationship?"

"Apparently. I don't know them well enough to talk to them about it, but they don't hide it."

"Huh. How about that?" And he thought he'd been shocking her when he'd talked about having a threesome. Not so much.

When they pulled up in front of her building, she said, "Come on in and I'll find that brochure about Intrepid Adventures."

"Okay." *And* he got into her apartment. *Yes!* He followed her inside, breathing in a warm, almost tropical scent. She flicked on a light and dropped her purse on the coffee table in the small living room. He looked around. The lamp created a warm glow that illuminated the beige sofa and two matching chairs piled with red and orange cushions. The coffee table looked like an old farm table with a rough wooden top, the legs cut down to make it the right height. A stack of magazines sat there along with a trio of thick candles and a remote control. He studied the framed black and white photographs on the wall then took a few steps closer. Yep, as he'd thought, some of them were nudes, with low key lighting. Stunning.

Brooke crossed to a desk in the corner, an old oak desk with a modern laptop sitting on it and some papers. She slid over a wicker filing tray and dug through it, pulling out a small glossy brochure. "Here it is."

She turned and he admired her as she moved back toward him across the small room, the light shining on her hair.

"What?"

"Nothing. Just thinking how pretty you are."

"Um. Okay." She handed him the brochure, and he took it and studied it. He flipped it open and checked out the photographs inside, people climbing rugged rock faces, kayaking on the ocean, and then an image of the high ropes course. "The rock climbing looks cool. Matt might like to do that." He looked up at her. "Thanks."

"No problem. I just hope they're not too booked up to do something in the next week."

"Yeah. I hope so too." He moved closer to her. She stepped back. He smiled and followed her, reaching out to slide a hand around the back of her neck. He wanted to kiss her. Her lips parted and she gave him a nervous look. "What's wrong?"

"Um…"

He bent his head and brushed his lips over hers, once, twice, then opened his mouth over hers and captured hers in a long, clinging kiss. Heat sizzled over his skin and arousal stirred inside him. Nice.

She broke away and slipped out of his grasp. "We can't do that, Dylan."

He gazed at her with disappointment. "Why not? We've already done it."

"We have a business relationship."

One corner of his mouth turned down. "I had fun tonight though."

"It wasn't a real date. I'm just helping you out, remember?"

"Yeah. But…" He shifted closer again and this time she put the couch between them. He ached to touch her, to feel her soft skin beneath him again, her body clasping him, rippling as she came with him inside her… His dick swelled and his skin tingled.

But she shook her head.

"Seriously?" he asked softly, sorrowfully. "You don't want that? Man, it was so good…"

He caught the flash in her eyes, the way her lips softened. A pulse fluttered at the base of her throat where the skin was thin and sensitive, and when she pushed her hair back, her hand trembled a little. She did want it.

"We can't. I-I'll see you Monday. For the meeting with Oceans Alive."

He stood there for a minute, his heart thudding, wondering how far he should push it. Nah. He gave a short nod. "Okay. See you then." He turned to leave and she followed at a safe distance as he let himself out. "G'night, Brooke."

"Thanks for dinner," she said. "Dylan…"

He paused, a tiny flicker of hope flaring to life, and turned to look at her.

"It *was* fun."

He gave a crooked smile and nodded, then left.

Damn.

Brooke leaned her forehead against the closed door after Dylan left and focused on breathing. Sweet Jesus, she'd wanted him to stay. Wanted him to take her into her bedroom and…well, take her. His kiss had brought to life all kinds of tingles and flutters and aches, his mouth on hers so warm and delicious. She'd been aroused all evening, sitting there in the restaurant talking and laughing with his friends, eating and drinking beer. They hadn't had to do much to pretend they were a couple. After being together like they had in Tahiti, it felt comfortable to sit beside him, to touch his hand, to let him lean into her, to meet his eyes and smile and let the heat between them build. He was so damn sexy, the way he looked, the way he smiled, the way his eyes crinkled at the corners. And seeing him with his friends, the easy way they interacted, the history he had with Matt, made her heart tumble a little.

He *had* seemed a little…manic. No, that was an exaggeration, but he'd definitely been a bit hyper. He was always energetic and dynamic, but he seemed to be putting on an extra bit of a show. Was that for her? Or for Matt and Corey? She remembered the tension she'd sensed in him earlier that day when they'd appeared. She'd attributed it to them bugging him about finding someone and settling down now that they were doing that, and he'd agreed, but she'd had no hint of that pressure from them during the evening. Of course, that made sense given that Dylan had found someone. Supposedly.

She straightened and laid her hands on her hot cheeks. She didn't know Dylan all that well, so his demeanor during dinner could be just the way he was. She locked her door then turned to go down the hall to her bedroom. Only another couple of weeks of this and he'd be off to the next event. Where was the next event?

She found herself detouring back into her living room and sitting in front of her computer, looking up the ASP World Tour schedule. Huh. The next event was in Brazil, and wow, it started not long after this one. Then Portugal, then oh wow, back to California, Santa Cruz.

That was his life, traveling the world to exotic locations. And her life was here. And there wasn't any point in even thinking about anything more than that. Dylan's friends wanted him to find a woman and settle down, but how the hell was he supposed to do that when he barely even had a real home?

She looked again at the schedule, at the intervals between some of the events. What the hell did he do during those times? Besides party wildly and get himself into the news. She shook her head as she put her computer to sleep then closed the lid.

Alone in her bed, she found herself reliving those nights with Dylan in Tahiti. They'd been back a while now, and sometimes it seemed like a dream, distant and nebulous. Other times it seemed like he should be there with her, in her bed, wrapping his body around her and making her feel so good.

She missed him.

That was stupid.

Okay, he was starting to feel some serious pressure and he did not like it.

His agent was booking him for interviews like crazy, with magazine and newspaper reporters, bloggers and television people. He was ramping up his time in the water, working out at the gym, doing yoga. He was spending time with Elroy, working on his boards. Brooke had set up stuff for him to do with these damn charities and store appearances and a fucking photo shoot. And now he had to organize a bachelor party. Christ.

She didn't need to worry about him getting into trouble. He didn't have *time* to get into trouble. He barely had time to take a leak.

It started Monday morning when they met with the people from Oceans Alive.

"Our current big undertaking is a five million dollar project designed to divert urban runoff to an onsite treatment facility that will clean the water before discharging it into the ocean at Silverado Beach," Director Brian Humbert said. "This beach has had a lot of complaints about water quality and has consistently been rated F. There's a large residential community upstream that has resulted in bacteria loading. But it's a popular family beach, so we want to improve the quality for visitors."

"How does the water get treated?" Dylan asked.

"With ultraviolet technology. The plant will be able to treat over a million gallons of polluted runoff water a day."

"That sounds amazing. I've been reading about the problem. I see the problems first hand obviously, but I've only recently come to realize the magnitude of it. The impact on the climate. Survival of our oceans is vital. Everything really requires healthy oceans."

"Absolutely. Urban runoff is only one part of the problem of course, but it's something we can take positive steps to help."

"I'd never thought about it before," Dylan admitted. "I didn't realize that most sources of marine pollution are land-based."

"That's right. Direct discharge of waste into the oceans is one problem. Also runoff due to rain."

They talked about Dylan's role in helping to raise money for the project. "This ties in really nicely with work I'm doing with Daytrippers," he told them. "I can talk to the kids about ways to keep the oceans healthy. It's always good to make younger generations aware of the problems, right? And if they're into surfing and they like to have fun in the ocean, taking responsibility for it goes hand in hand with that."

He caught Brooke's eye and gave her a small smile.

After that meeting, he needed to get to the beach but found himself lingering outside the office of Oceans Alive, standing there on the sidewalk in the bright morning sun, so he could talk to her. Look at her. He wished he could touch her.

"You did great in there. You must have been studying all that info I gave you."

"Some. It's interesting. I really do love the ocean. I kind of feel guilty for not taking more responsibility for it sooner."

"You did come across as very sincere."

"I *was* sincere." He rubbed his face. "I'm just…this is a crazy week."

"Is it too much?" Her eyebrows slanted down.

He sighed. "No. I just need to manage my time. Holden's got a lot of stuff lined up for me too, but most of all I need to make sure I'm focused on the competition. First I have to get things set up for the bachelor party and then get through the damn wedding. Next week it has to be all about the competition."

She nodded, her eyes searching his. "Okay. I don't want this to interfere with your training, Dylan. I know how important that is to you. And obviously, as one of your sponsors, we want you to win. It benefits us too. It benefits everyone if you do."

Business. Oh yeah, she was all about business. He nodded. "Okay. I better get going."

He did get through the week, satisfied with the training he'd been able to do. The yoga was not only good for increasing his flexibility, but also for stress relief. Much as people thought he was laid back, he'd never been good at relaxing. At first yoga had driven him crazy, but he'd worked at the meditative part of it, worked at slowing himself down, centering himself. The mental part of competition was hugely important too, and it was good to use those times for some visualizing, imagining himself riding the hugest waves, latching onto those waves, painting the canvas of the wave with his moves, seeing himself do that. He incorporated that into his training in the water too, while sitting on his board on the ocean, letting the swells lift and lower him, only the water and the sky and the wind around him. The ocean had always amazed him, the incredible power and beauty of it. The ocean had nearly killed him but had also given him the most incredible joy of his life. Had given him his whole life, really, since surfing was everything to him. He loved and feared it. He respected it.

He spent time with his coach, Brett, who gave him some ideas of things to try, things to work on, both in the water and out.

The "bachelor party" took place on Saturday. He and Matt and a bunch of other guys spent the afternoon kayaking to a small beach that could only be accessed by boat, climbing the rock cliffs there, eating lunch that the adventure company brought while sitting in the sun on a small sandy beach dotted with rocks. They worked their muscles hard, but had a lot of laughs.

Dylan knew two of the guys from high school and it was cool catching up with them. They were all impressed with him and his surfing career, but shiz, Boone was a doctor for chrissakes, and Nick ran the San Amaro Golf and Country Club. The other guys were friends and neighbors of Matt's who he didn't know. Funnily enough, Carlos and Mike, the two guys who ran the adventure company, lived next door to Matt, and when Dylan had told him what he was doing and asked who he wanted to invite, they were both on the list. Carlos and Mike had put together a great day for them when Dylan had contacted them and explained about the bachelor party. At the end of the day, Dylan had arranged reservations at a local steakhouse and they all gathered for steaks, beers, more joking and talking about the day.

He'd pulled off a successful bachelor party that hadn't involved naked women or any police involvement whatsoever. A few months ago he would have sneered at something so tame, but now, he was kind of proud of himself.

And found himself wanting to tell Brooke all about it.

As the party broke up around eleven o'clock Saturday night, he debated driving over to her place. Would she let him in if he dropped by out of the blue like that?

Nah. Stupid idea. And he'd see her tomorrow at the wedding. That was one good thing.

The wedding was still something that filled him with dread. Not sure why. He'd already faced Corey and Matt a couple of times. He'd had Brooke with him to ensure they didn't feel sorry for him. She'd be there with him tomorrow at the wedding. It would be fine.

14

Brooke gave one last look in the mirror as the buzzer at her door sounded. She was ready.

It wasn't a real date. She had to keep reminding herself, even as she'd carefully shaved her legs, styled her hair, applied makeup and spread mango and pineapple scented body lotion over her skin. She'd become addicted to the tropical scent after leaving Tahiti, and every time she used it she thought of Dylan. That scent and him would be forever imprinted on her olfactory memory.

She'd talked herself out of buying a new dress for the occasion for that same reason—it wasn't a real date. Dylan had never seen the dress she'd chosen, nor had other guests, although it was possible there were people she knew among the invited guests.

Because Dylan was the best man, he was picking her up a little early. She opened the door to see him standing there in a suit and tie, and she lost her breath. "Hi."

Her gaze tracked down from his smoothly shaven face, over the pale gray collar of his dress shirt, the silky blue-and-silver tie that matched his eyes, over the way the dark suit fit his broad shoulders and tapered down his athletic body to his waist and hips. "You look nice."

"Nice," he snorted. "Again."

She grinned. "You do clean up pretty well for a surfer dude."

He smiled. "Thanks. You, on the other hand…" He moved inside her apartment and, holding one of her hands, twirled her around. "Look fucking amazing."

"Thanks."

"Great dress." His gaze left heat in its trail as he looked her up and down. "Holy crap, Brooke."

The heat spread to her cheeks as he studied her bare legs and high-heeled shoes. "It's okay for a wedding?"

"Oh hell yeah."

The pinky-peach dress was strapless and hugged her body from armpits to mid-thigh. It was saved from being too plain by a pin on the left side of her waist made up of a large flower centered with pearls and rhinestones. On her feet she wore nude-colored high-heeled pumps.

"Okay, good. Well, I'm ready." She picked up a pashmina in a darker peach shade and her little beaded clutch purse.

She caught Dylan eyeing her backside as she turned back and flushed again. Damn. She liked it that he liked how she looked. But *this wasn't a real date.*

"We're a little early." Dylan helped her into his car. The short skirt made that maneuver a little tricky, but she carefully kept her knees together and swung her legs in. "I was already at the restaurant helping with some last minute things."

"How did it go yesterday?"

"Great!" He told her about their expedition, kayaking and rock climbing, sounding so enthused she couldn't help but smile.

"Sounds like you enjoyed it."

"I did. It wasn't your typical bachelor party but I had a lot of fun. Of course I like stuff like that, but I think everyone else had fun too."

"And today? You've been helping Matt?"

"And Corey. We went and did some decorating at the restaurant. They're keeping it pretty simple, but we got things set up on the patio for the ceremony. They had some flowers delivered that had to be arranged, and we set up chairs. Then Corey went home to change and get ready with Matt's sister Neve, and Matt stayed a while longer to supervise the food prep and get the bar all ready. I offered him my hotel room for him to get dressed so Corey had the house to herself. We went back and got changed. Matt'll meet us at the restaurant. You'll just be one of the first guests to arrive."

"No problem."

The restaurant was empty when they walked into it, closed to the public for the day, but delicious smells wafted from the kitchen. Dylan led the way onto the patio where Matt stood talking to a couple of his staff. Matt too wore a suit, dark like Dylan's, his shirt snowy white. They hadn't gone as formal as tuxedoes for the wedding.

"Hi Brooke," Matt said with his easy smile. "Nice to see you again."

"You too."

"I'll get you a glass of wine," Dylan said. "Since there's a little time until the wedding starts."

She found a seat and let Matt and Dylan check out the sound system they'd rigged up for music for the ceremony and dancing later. Sipping her wine, she looked around the patio. Vines grew across a pergola above them, the evening sky midnight blue beyond that. Baskets of colorful flowers swayed gently in the soft breeze. Chairs had been arranged in rows with a center aisle, and at the front were two large arrangements of flowers, bright gerbera daisies and delicate cascading ivy, and more hanging baskets. Lamps on the walls and fence cast a soft glow, and large pillar candles flickered beneath glass shades at the front. She let out a sigh of pleasure. Lovely.

With the music playing softly, guests began to arrive and take their seats. She waved to a couple of people she knew. San Amaro wasn't that big. How much talk was this going to cause, that she was there with Dylan Schell?

She wasn't worried about her boss, despite her comment to Dylan about that last weekend. She'd just tell Barrett she was doing her job, keeping Dylan out of trouble. And really, there was no need to worry what anyone else said about it. He'd be gone in a couple of weeks and her only contact with him would be business as they continued their sponsorship arrangement. Hopefully they continued with it. Dylan had been on the bubble a few weeks ago, but he'd definitely made an effort to clean up his act.

She just hoped he kept it up.

She took another sip of wine, uncrossed her legs, and crossed them the other way. She watched Dylan up front laughing with Matt about something. He didn't seem to be having too hard a time behaving himself. He was dedicated and focused when it came to his sport. She knew his schedule, she'd been to the beach to watch him in the water, she knew how much time he spent with his coach, with his shaper, and working out. Despite the laid back attitude, he was dead serious about surfing. And about winning.

He'd done everything she'd asked of him, again with seeming ease. He'd talked to people at the charity organizations with knowledge of their business. He'd charmed the kids from Daytrippers. He'd signed autographs and smiled and talked to long lineups of people without complaint. He'd modeled Jackson Cole clothes for photographer Jules Stockwood as if he'd been trained to do it, laughing with her about the bachelor party he had planned with Mike and Carlos. And he hadn't seemed to miss going out and getting drunk or high every night.

She sipped her wine, thinking about all that and what that might mean.

She now watched Dylan seating guests. He led a man and a woman to seats adorned with big tulle bows at the very front, but before they sat, the woman embraced Matt in a tight hug. His mom, no doubt. Then Dylan seated a man and a woman who slightly resembled Corey. Possibly her parents. And then another man and a woman in the seats next to them.

The patio now full, murmurs of the crowd mingled with strains of music, until the music stopped and a hush fell over the crowd. Brooke saw Dylan and Matt looking toward the back of the patio at the entrance from the restaurant, and she turned along with the other guests to see a young woman in a pretty fuchsia dress holding a small bouquet of flowers. That must be Corey's maid of honor—Matt's sister? Corey and Matt had only one attendant each.

The music changed to soft piano chords, and the girl gave a beaming smile and started down the makeshift aisle. When she reached the front and stepped to one side, all eyes again turned to the back. Corey appeared in the doorway, wearing a white, knee length slip dress of a heavy silk that skimmed over her slender body, clutching a bouquet of pink gerbera daisies. Rather than a veil, she wore a spray of tiny pink and white orchids pinned in her hair with white ribbons trailing to her shoulder. With a hesitant smile at the guests, she lowered her eyes then started forward to Ingrid Michaelson singing the classic "I Can't Help Falling In Love With You."

Brooke hardly knew Corey, but even so, seeing a bride start down the aisle looking that beautiful, lifting her eyes to find her groom and flash him a luminous smile so full of love and happiness, made her heart squeeze. Smiling, she watched with all the other guests as Corey took her place beside her husband-to-be, then handed her bouquet to her bridesmaid. They waited for the song to end, the haunting voice and moving lyrics trailing off into silence.

The ceremony was completely untraditional, officiated by another sister of Matt's, very personal and meaningful to the couple. They each spoke vows they'd written themselves, bringing tears to Brooke's eyes when she listened to their heartfelt words about friendship and love and finding the courage to admit their feelings for each other.

She found herself watching Dylan as he too listened to their vows, trying to read the expression on his face as various emotions flickered there. Matt and Corey's words seemed to have personal meaning for him too, as he dropped his gaze to the stone floor of the patio at one point, lips pressed together, then raised his head again with a determined smile.

She was swiping one corner of her eye with a fingertip when Dylan looked right at her. She smiled and he gave her a small smile in return. Weddings always seemed to arouse a lot of emotions in people.

Following the ceremony, guests rose and mingled while Corey and Matt disappeared into the restaurant for a few minutes. They returned to applause and spoke to their guests, inviting them to move inside for drinks and food.

The meal was informal too, with all kinds of selections set out on the bar in a buffet-style meal. Dylan moved to her side and smiled down at her. "There we go. Duty is done. Let's eat."

She smiled back at him. Damn he looked good.

They loaded up plates and carried them to the table at the far end of the bar where Matt and Corey sat along with Corey's maid of honor, who was Matt's sister Neve, and her date. Dylan introduced Brooke to Neve and Jason.

"That was a lovely ceremony," Brooke said to Corey and Matt. "Very personal."

"Thanks." They exchanged a warm look. "We just want tonight to be fun."

Brooke watched Corey cast a glance at Dylan that held a hint of worry. Once again, that slight tension vibrated in Dylan's body where his shoulder pressed against hers and his smile seemed strained. She looked between him and Corey one more time, then caught Corey's glance at her new husband and the exchange between them.

Acting completely on instinct, she turned to Dylan, leaned into his body and whispered in his ear, "Did I tell you how hot you look in that suit?"

He shifted a little to slide his arm around her and squeeze her waist, lifting his other hand to touch her cheek, smiling into her eyes. "No. The word you used was nice," he murmured. "Not hot. I'd definitely remember if you said I looked hot."

"Well you do." She kissed his jaw and held his gaze for a moment. His rough fingertips on her cheek felt nice.

It was all an act. Well, sort of.

They settled back onto their chairs and resumed eating. "This is so good." She picked up a piece of flatbread topped with cherry tomatoes, arugula and goat cheese drizzled with a balsamic vinaigrette.

"I like the shrimp." Dylan lifted one. "Try it."

He fed her a bite of the crisply breaded shrimp. A burst of jalapeño heat warmed her tongue. "Mmm. Spicy."

"I like things hot."

She grinned. "Oh, me too."

His wink made her insides flutter.

She turned back to Matt and Corey, happy to see them watching. "So are you two going away on a honeymoon?"

"Not right away," Corey said. "This week with the Pro going on is one of our busiest times of the year. Matt will be super busy at the brew pub and I expect increased business at my shop too, with all the people in town. So we're going to go away for a week later."

"Yes, I guess this is a busy time."

"San Amaro's always busy in the summer, but this is a big event."

"True. Are those your parents, Corey?" She nodded to the couple she'd noticed on the patio, the woman who resembled her.

"That's my mom," Corey said with a smile. "And her boyfriend. And at the next table is my dad and his wife. My parents split up a long time ago."

Brooke nodded. "You look like her. Beautiful."

"Aw. Thanks. It's kind of special having my dad here, since I only recently reconnected with him."

The three couples chatted through their meal, interrupted frequently by guests stopping to say a few words with Corey and Matt and congratulate them. Almost as many people stopped to greet Dylan and ask about the upcoming competition. Dinner was also interrupted frequently by guests clinking their cutlery against glasses in a demand for the newlyweds to kiss. They laughingly complied.

As she finished eating, Brooke shifted her chair even closer to Dylan so she could lean into him, and he obligingly slid his arm around her shoulders again. His fingers played with her long hair, a sensation that she quite enjoyed.

Matt got up and spoke into a microphone attached to the sound system. "Hey everyone. Corey and I just want to say a few words before we all move out onto the patio for some dancing and more drinks, and some of Corey's special chocolates."

A murmur of appreciation rippled through the group. Matt smiled and Corey moved up to stand beside him. He slid his arm around her waist and pulled her closer, and they exchanged a brief, intimate smile.

"We want to keep this really informal, so no long speeches or toasts," Matt continued. "We wanted to thank all of you for coming and being a part of our day. We especially want to thank folks who came from far away." He named off a few relatives of his and Corey's that Brooke didn't know. "And last but definitely not least, we want to thank my best man, Dylan Schell."

Brooke felt Dylan's body tense next to her and she shot him a smile. He looked relaxed and happy, but there was no mistaking the tautness of his muscles and the way his fingers tightened on her waist.

"Many of you know Dylan or know of him, and know that he flew in all the way from Tahiti to come to our wedding. Now, I'd like to say he came just for us." Matt gave a wry grin. "But the truth is, Dylan's competing next week in the ASP World Tour event and has a good chance of winning. So he was coming anyway, but we managed to get him here a little early so he could be part of our wedding. Which was really important to both Corey and me, because it's Dylan we have to thank for Corey and me ending up together."

Once more Matt and Corey shared a look, and then they both looked toward Dylan. Dylan shifted in his chair beside Brooke.

"You heard us say in our vows that Corey and I were friends for a long time before we became a couple," Matt said, speaking to everyone, but his gaze fixed on Dylan. "That friendship is a really solid basis for our love. And our marriage. But when our feelings for each other started changing, we both needed a little kick in the butt to make us admit that. To ourselves, and to each other. And it was Dylan who gave that to us." Now he spoke directly to Dylan. "Your courage and willingness to take risks inspired both of us. And your unselfishness is something we'll never forget." Matt lifted his glass. "We both love you, and we owe all this to you, man."

As Corey and Matt touched their glasses together in a toast to Dylan, the wedding guests did the same, murmuring amongst themselves. Brooke turned a little toward Dylan, smiling, but instead of lifting her glass she leaned up and kissed his cheek. "Wow. That was so nice."

Dylan's cheek was hot and as she drew back, she saw the color that had washed up into his face. His body nearly vibrated with tension. Was he that embarrassed? He didn't seem like the type to embarrass easily, but maybe he wasn't used to such public displays of affection from his friends.

Dylan lifted his own glass toward Matt, still smiling, in acknowledgement of his friend's words. "Jesus Christ," he muttered.

"Okay," Corey now said to their guests. "Let's go eat chocolate and dance!"

Brooke leaned closer to Dylan again. "Are you embarrassed?"

Dylan cleared his throat. "Fuck yeah. I don't deserve their thanks."

She wanted to know what he'd done to get Corey and Matt together, but this didn't seem the time to ask. As the crowd gradually moved outside, people stopped at their table to greet Dylan and chat with him. Dylan kept his arm around Brooke, sitting there, playing with her hair, nuzzling her ear, whispering things to her about other guests as they passed by.

"We aren't having cake," Corey explained as she and Matt eventually made their way back to the table. "Just the chocolates."

"I saw them on the bar," Dylan said. "They look amazing."

"We meant every word of that." Corey bending down beside his chair. She settled a hand on his shoulder and squeezed. "You know we love you."

Dylan's mouth tightened and he gave a short nod. "Love you both too, babe." He pushed back his chair and stood, and enveloped Corey in a big hug then kissed her forehead. He turned to Brooke. "I need to find the restrooms. Be right back."

She watched him walk through the restaurant.

"I think you embarrassed him," Brooke said lightly to Corey.

Corey too had followed Dylan with her gaze and she looked at Brooke. "Yeah. We didn't mean to embarrass him. But we…" She stopped and Brooke sensed her discomfort, a thickening in the air around them. "Well, I'd better go serve those chocolates." With a bright smile, she turned and headed out toward the patio.

Brooke awaited Dylan's return. When he dropped into the seat beside her, he seemed more relaxed. He picked up his wine glass and finished what was left, then slid his arm around her again.

"Weddings make me horny," he whispered in her ear, nuzzling her hair and making her shiver.

She laughed. "Breathing makes you horny."

"True that." He turned her face toward him and this time kissed her full on the mouth. And Matt and Corey weren't even there. She let herself be seduced by his warm mouth, firm yet gentle, teasing her lips apart, his tongue sliding over her bottom lip. "Mmm. Actually it's you that makes me horny. You taste good."

"So do you." She sighed against his mouth. "And smell good. And feel good." She ran her fingers through his hair. "But we shouldn't be making out in the middle of a wedding."

"You're probably right. Dammit."

They followed the other guests out onto the patio. The music started again and Matt and Corey began dancing to Colbie Caillat singing "Lucky".

"The perfect song for them," Dylan murmured as they watched the couple move to the music, arms around each other.

"They seem really happy."

"Yeah. They do." He stood behind Brooke, his arms around her waist, and he kissed the top of her head. She longed to turn and ask him if he was really happy for them, but instead bit her lip.

When the music moved into the next song, she turned in his arms. "Dance?"

He smiled. "Sure."

They joined Corey and Matt, and she linked her arms around Dylan's neck as he settled his hands on her waist.

It was all an act. Except for the heat settling low in her core, the ache of her breasts, her hardened nipples brushing against his chest. Except for the curl of desire inside her that was oh so real.

They finished the sexy slow dance and the music changed to a faster tune, so he led her from the dance floor. "Another glass of wine?"

"Sure." A nice cold glass of wine was just what she needed.

They strolled to the bar and got drinks, then returned outside. Dylan led her around the corner. The patio was L-shaped with only a few tables on the short side. Nobody was there, and they sat on the padded wicker loveseat and set their drinks on the small table.

The music wasn't as loud here, the shadows deeper, and he tilted her face up to him one more time. "You're so beautiful," he murmured and he kissed her again, a deep, open-mouthed kiss that stole her breath and had her heart pounding. She held onto his shoulders as he pushed her back into the cushions.

She kissed him back, letting his tongue slide into her mouth so sweetly. His big body pressed against hers, one hand coming up to cup her breast through her dress. Her nipples tingled and her pussy squeezed with delight. "Mmm."

"Oh yeah," he groaned, scattering hot kisses over her cheek and her jaw. He held her head with both hands, thumbs tipping her chin up, and gazed down into her eyes, his blazing. "It's not the wedding that makes me horny. It's you."

She smiled as he dipped to kiss her throat. His tongue dragged over her skin and shivers cascaded down her body. She moaned.

"This dress is so sexy." He kissed her collarbone. "You have killer legs, Brooke. I noticed that in Tahiti."

"You did?"

He snorted. "How could I not? We were naked together for basically three days straight."

She shivered again, more heat melting between her legs. "Oh yes. We were." And she wanted to be again, with him. Naked.

He ran his hand from her breast down her body, outlining the curve of her waist and hip, squeezing her butt, all the while his mouth devouring hers. Her head spun as heat sizzled over every nerve ending and built hotter inside her. "Dylan!" She gasped when she realized he'd hiked her dress up and his hands found the bare skin of her thighs.

He smiled against her mouth. "Nice. Very tiny panties."

"Well." She tried to formulate words as his hands slid higher and played with her bare butt cheeks. "Can't have panty lines."

"No. That wouldn't do at all."

"This dress is pretty snug."

"Really? I hadn't noticed."

"You can't do that," she panted. "Someone will see."

"I don't care."

A vague rational thought flitted through her mind and she tried again to protest. "I'm supposed to be keeping you out of trouble. If someone sees us like this, oh my God..."

"It's dark." He kissed her ear, and then shockingly, he dragged her panties down over her hips.

"What are you doing?"

"What do you think I'm doing?"

"Not here!" She pressed a palm on his chest, but oh dear God, his hands and mouth felt so good on her. Somehow he'd managed to slip the panties all the way off. They snagged on her heel, just briefly, and then he crumpled them in his hand and tucked them in his jacket pocket.

Heat flashed through her veins and her tummy did a little flip. "Sweet Jesus."

"Mmm." He kissed her again, his mouth magic on hers, warm and sexy.

And then his fingers were between her legs, finding her slick folds, making her shudder with delight. "Dylan, God, Dylan, we can't..."

"Sssh." He opened his mouth on her jaw. "Relax. Wanna make you feel good."

Her head fell back against the back of the love seat. Done. She didn't care if the whole wedding watched at that point, she just wanted his fingers to continue stroking her, deeper, brushing over her sensitive clit. She was wet, and he spread her cream over her flesh, up to her clit where he gave a firm rub.

She parted her thighs as much as she dared, given their near public location. This was risky and scandalous and shamefully exciting. She was supposed to be the voice of reason, the one keeping him from any kind of outrageous misconduct, and here she was *participating* in it, for God's sake!

The buzzing started at his fingers, spread through her body, a coil of heat twisting inside her at his touch. She bit her lip and gave herself over to it, lifting her hips, pushing her pussy shamelessly into his hand, let the pleasure build higher and higher. Heat swept over her body and weakness slid down her legs as pleasure burst inside in a small shower of sparks. She turned her face into his neck and panted through the orgasm.

"Oh, there you are."

She and Dylan both froze at the voice.

15

Dylan looked up to see Matt standing across the patio. "Oh hey Matt." His voice came out oddly gruff.

"Oops, sorry. Didn't mean to interrupt."

"I'll catch you in a few," Dylan said.

Matt nodded, grinned and turned to leave.

"Oh. My. God," Brooke moaned against his neck.

"It's okay." He slid his hand out from under her dress and tipped her chin up. The feminine scent of her arousal rose to his nostrils. "Look at me."

She forced her eyes open. "How will I ever face him again?"

Dylan grinned. "Don't worry. I'm sure it just looked like we're sitting here making out. He couldn't see any of your pretty pussy."

Even in the dark, her cheeks practically glowed with heat. She slapped his chest weakly. "You are a bad, bad man. I can't believe I let you do that."

"You loved it." He brushed a kiss over her mouth. "Admit it."

"*So* bad."

He smiled. "You okay?"

"Yes, I'm okay." She wriggled and tugged her skirt down. "Give me my panties."

"No."

"Dylan!"

"I'll give them to you later. Let's go dance again." He kissed her once more then rose and took her hand to pull her to her feet. She stared at him in speechless astonishment. Then she blinked, tugged her short skirt down again on firm thighs and reached for her glass of wine.

"Fine." She moved past him. His dick so hard he wasn't sure if he could actually walk, he watched her ass. He swore she gave it an added little twitch, just to torment him, knowing she was naked under that dress.

Christ. He almost groaned aloud. This might have been a mistake. He grabbed a paper napkin off a nearby table, wiped his fingers and tossed it into waste basket as he followed her.

Around the corner, other guests sat at tables, stood at the narrow bar running along one wall, or danced on the area that had been cleared for that purpose. He spotted Corey and Matt in the corner, talking to their families.

"I am so embarrassed," Brooke moaned beside him.

He looked down at her. "I'm not."

"And it's all about you," she muttered.

His head jerked and he stared at her. Ah hell. She was really upset. And he was a dick. "I'm sorry, Brooke. You're right. I was being a selfish jerk. I'm sorry if I embarrassed you."

Her mouth flattened. "You're probably happy he saw us like that."

"Eh." Was he? He examined that. "No. I wasn't doing that on purpose so he'd see."

"No?"

"God no! I just wasn't thinking. I was…well, I told you, I was just…excited. I wanted you to feel good."

She licked her lips. Her gaze dropped briefly to his crotch, where he was still hard.

"So I'm not *happy* he saw us. I just don't care."

"Really?" She stared up at him wide-eyed.

"Damn, you're pretty."

Her eyelashes dropped. "Stop it."

"What? It's true."

"God, Dylan. We're not really together. This is an act to get your friends off your back about finding a girl and settling down. Right?"

"Oh, Brooke." He sighed, disappointment filling him up. "I'm not that good an actor."

She bit her lip and studied his face.

"Are you?" He moved closer, finding himself tensely awaiting her answer.

"Um…"

"You didn't fake that orgasm."

"Oh my God."

Her blush amused him. He bent and placed a soft kiss on her cheek. "Wanna dance again?"

"Oh. I don't know. I guess so."

"Don't sound so enthusiastic." He plucked her wine glass from her fingers and set it on an empty table. "Come on."

He pulled her onto the dance floor again, this time a faster number, enjoying watching her dance, lifting her arms, shaking her hips a little as she gradually got over her embarrassment and got into the music. He watched with aroused fascination as her skirt rode up a little higher on her legs. Because shiz, she was bare under there.

"You're a good dancer." She leaned into him.

"I like slow dancing better."

"Oh I know."

Their eyes met and held with a sizzle of sparks.

"I'm not done." And he knew she knew what he was talking about as her eyes darkened.

They danced, ate decadent chocolates made by Corey, talked to guests. He introduced her to Matt's other sister, Jenna. They talked to the Surf Sisters, Bella and Jaden, who owned a surf shop on the beach and gave surfing lessons. And they talked to Carlos and Mike and their girlfriend Jules, who'd taken all those half-naked pictures of him the other day. Their relationship still blew his mind a little, but hey, to each his own. It wasn't as if he'd never had a threesome, but his just usually lasted a few hours, not a lifetime.

And speaking of lifetime commitment…Corey and Matt were having a blast tonight, celebrating their marriage. Like the words of the song she'd walked down the aisle to, some things were meant to be. And they were meant to be together.

As if she knew he was thinking about them, Corey appeared at his side. "Hey Dylan."

He smiled at her. "Hey Mrs. Ferber." And for the first time, he felt truly relaxed around her, at ease teasing her by calling her that.

"I really like Brooke." She nodded toward Brooke where she was talking to Carlos and Mike, then beaming up at him. "I'm so happy for you."

"I like her too," he said honestly. But a mix of emotions tangled inside him. It didn't matter that this thing with Brooke wasn't real, the fact of the matter was he was leaving. Real or fake, they couldn't have any kind of future together. Which was kind of a downer actually. And confusing. But along with that was relief that Corey and Matt didn't feel sorry for him anymore. And all of that put together kept him from saying to Corey that he and Brooke had no future together.

"She's crazy about you."

He started. "Oh. Uh. You think?"

She smiled. "Oh yeah. And I can tell you're feeling the same about her. I was watching you, how you couldn't take your eyes off her."

He shifted his feet and resisted the urge to tug at his collar. He smiled though. "Huh. I do like looking at her." So he did, finding her across the patio now talking to Jaden and Bella. And remembering that she was naked underneath that sexy little dress made heat pulse through his body.

Guests were starting to leave. Could they escape now too? Actually it wasn't so much of an escape as he'd feared. The wedding had actually been enjoyable and seeing Corey and Matt together and so happy felt…pretty good. Meant to be.

"Dylan."

He looked down at Corey again. "Yeah?"

"When you left last time…we were really worried about you."

"I was fine."

"No. You weren't." She frowned at him. "Why can't you just admit it?"

He sighed and thrust a hand into his hair. "Okay, I wasn't fine. My head was fucked up from my accident. That made me do and say and think crazy things. But now…a year later…I can see that it was a lot of drama over nothing."

"Nothing? You call that accident nothing? Geez, Dylan, you wouldn't even tell us about it when you came, we had to find out on the Internet. Clearly it was affecting you, but you wouldn't even talk about it."

"No, no. The accident wasn't nothing," he said slowly. "I meant all that other stuff that happened."

"Oh." Her forehead crinkled. "Really? That was nothing?"

"No. It wasn't nothing." He blew out a breath. He really did not want to go there with Corey. "I mean, I was messed up and I didn't really understand what I was feeling. But you did."

They looked at each other.

And then Brooke was beside him, slipping her arm though his. "Am I interrupting?" she asked lightly. He looked down at her pretty smiling face and read the concern shadowing her eyes. She was rescuing him.

He didn't need rescuing. He could look after himself. Probably this conversation was one he and Corey needed to have, to acknowledge what had happened and move past it. But the fact that someone was looking out for him, someone had his back when he'd never had that before in his life, made his chest tighten. For a moment he couldn't even speak as emotion rose up in his throat. He drew Brooke closer to his side. "No," he said gently. "Not at all." He looked back at Corey. "You were right, Cor. And I really am fine."

She smiled and nodded, and then moved away to talk to someone else.

Dylan returned his focus to the woman wrapped around his arm. "Thanks." He eased a strand of hair off her face then ran his hand over her hair.

"Everything okay?"

"Everything is great." Really. "Wanna leave now?"

"Um. Sure. If you're done. You're the best man."

Only a few guests remained and they were saying their good-nights to Corey and Matt. Some of Matt's staff were discreetly cleaning up, picking up empty glasses and beginning to rearrange the patio furniture.

"Let me check with Matt. Come on." They crossed to where Matt stood as Corey hugged someone. "Hey dude. Anything you need me to do here?"

Matt shook his head and laid a hand on Dylan's shoulder. "Nah. We're good. The crew will clean up tonight." He paused. "Thanks for being here, man. It meant a lot to me. To both of us."

"I'm glad I was here too. It's been good to see you guys. Really good." Hard. At first. But good. "Brooke and I are heading out then."

"Great." Matt winked. "We'll be there next week to cheer you on."

"Mondo."

Corey hugged him and then Brooke, Matt hugged Brooke, and then they left.

Brooke wrapped the silky shawl thing she'd brought around her bare shoulders as they walked out of the restaurant. The ocean breeze blew her hair back off her face and she looked utterly gorgeous in the moonlight.

"Okay." He gave his tie a yank and loosened it, then undid the top two buttons of his shirt. "Your place or mine?"

She met his eyes. "Dylan. The wedding's over. The pretend date is over."

"Yeah. It is." Her eyes flickered as he agreed with her. "From now on, shit gets real, babe. Your place or mine? Let's not play games."

They stood there looking at each other for a moment. And she said, "My place."

He followed her into her apartment, so close behind her she could feel his body heat, and when he closed the door firmly behind him, he took hold of her and pushed her farther into the apartment, crowding her up against a wall. He pressed her there, his body hard against hers, the wall flat at her back, and kissed her, hot and urgent.

She kissed him back, her need for him just as urgent, her body aching for him. The orgasm he'd given her earlier had only been a tease, exciting her even more, amping up her hunger for more.

God, she'd never been so turned on in her life! But it wasn't just the orgasm. It was being with Dylan, watching him interact with people, all the people who admired and liked him, people who knew him as more than just pro surfer, second place, third ranked ASP Dylan Schell, people who cared about him. Yes, he could be a selfish bastard at times, but he could also be generous and caring and sweet.

He dragged his open mouth over her cheek, nipped her earlobe with his lips, making her tremble in his arms. "Brooke," he murmured. "God."

Just how she felt too. She wound her arms around his neck but he reached for her wrists and lifted them above her head. With one hand, he captured her wrists and pinned them to the wall above her, while his other hand slid up her thigh, pushing her short dress higher, and then his fingers delved into her wet pussy. She gasped, her head falling back against the wall as he played there, between her legs where she was so wet and sensitive.

"Sweet. Christ that was hot, knowing you were bare under that dress."

"I know. And I was so wet…I felt it every time I moved."

"Jesus." He crushed her mouth with his again. "And now…no panties…you're all ready for me. Right here. Right now."

"Yes. God, yes."

He kissed her again and again, sliding his tongue into her mouth, sucking on her tongue, biting softly at her lips. She gasped and kissed him back as he crushed her into the wall, and then his hand slid from her pussy and down her thigh. He lifted her leg to his hip, ran his hand up the back of her thigh and cupped her ass.

She might be bare and ready for him, but he was still wearing a suit, which was way too many clothes, and she managed to get one hand free and pushed at the suit jacket to get it off his shoulders.

"This isn't going to work." He groaned, releasing her other wrist and lowering her leg to the floor.

"I know. But that was hot."

He grinned as he yanked the suit jacket off and tossed it aside.

"Dylan! Not on the floor!" His beautiful suit jacket lay in a heap.

"Jesus. I don't care. I just want to be inside you." He was working the buttons at his wrists, so she started on the other buttons, leaning in to kiss his smooth hard chest as she bared it. She tugged the shirt out of his pants, ran her palms over his chest and abs, following them with her gaze, admiring his sleek muscles and bronzed skin, then down his sides to his waist while he undid his belt and zipper. The pants loosened around his hips and her breath hitched in anticipation of seeing more of him, of having his naked body right there with her again. It felt like forever ago that they'd spent those steamy few days in her hotel room, gorging themselves on hot sex while a tropical storm raged outside.

She melted even more inside, almost panting as he dropped his trousers to the floor. She grabbed for his boxer briefs. He captured her hand in his, but not before she'd brushed over his huge erection behind the soft cotton. "Easy, baby."

She pressed herself up closer against him, sliding her free hand back up his chest. "Do it," she urged him, kissing his jaw. She nibbled him with her lips and he sucked in a sharp breath.

"Fuck yeah." He tugged his underwear down, just far enough that it pushed up his cock and balls. Her blood rushed hot and fast through her veins at the sight, his cock so thick and hard, veins prominent, his balls propped up by the underwear. Her knees went soft, but right away he hoisted her up, slamming her back against the wall. Her dress was still up around her hips and once more she wrapped her arms and legs around him. With his hand pressed between their bodies, he managed to find his cock and push up into her.

The air whooshed out of her lungs and her head thunked back against the wall. "Holy shnippits!" He filled her, completely, deeply, and thank God he was holding her up because her bones melted and she went liquid around him.

He went still, then his body started shaking. She lifted her head to see him laughing. "What?"

"Holy shnippits? Christ, Brooke, you make me laugh. Even at a time like this."

She stared, then smiled back at him, warmth spreading inside her. He gave her a fast, hard kiss and then bracing herself on his shoulders, she lifted herself on him while he used his hands beneath her butt to help, sliding her up and down on his shaft. The friction sent pleasure zooming through her veins, spreading from her center all the way through her body until she was tingling everywhere. He found her mouth with his again, devouring her, and she kissed him back, as desperate and hungry as he was. Her hands moved over him, his shoulders, his neck, his face, holding him there as they kissed and fucked up against the wall.

"Fuck that feels good," he mumbled. "Brooke…ah, man."

She sucked his tongue, bit at his bottom lip, all the while

moving against him so he slid in and out. She tightened her thighs around him to tilt her pelvis just…there, oh *yeah*, and now the additional friction on her clit made her insides tighten.

"Christ…I love that."

They bounced together, finding a rhythm. She held on tighter, squeezed her body around him tighter. Her breathing quickened, her heart crashed against her ribs, every nerve ending sizzling.

"Yes," she said through gritted teeth. "Oh God, Dylan, yes, fuck me, just like that."

"Holy hell, Brooke…gonna come."

"Me too." She rubbed against him more, sensation building in a tight twist inside her, her body clenching hard around his thick column of flesh. "Oh God…oh God, me too…." And pure ecstasy peaked inside her, sharp and hard. She cried out again and again, buried her face in the side of his neck while his hands tightened on her ass and held her snug against him as he pulsed inside her.

"Oh fucking hell. Goddammit."

She moaned, still quivering around him, luscious sensation pulsing through her veins.

"We didn't use a condom." He let out a groan, his body still taut from his orgasm. "Again, dammit."

"Oh for…" They were cursed. Why were they so damn stupid with each other? This was ridiculous. She sighed. At that moment, she still felt too good to get worked up about it. "It'll be okay."

"Fuck," he muttered again. "I'm sorry, Brooke. You make me lose my damn mind."

He eased out of her body with a rush of fluid and she bit her lip.

"Hold your dress up." He stepped back. He tucked his half-hard penis back into his boxer briefs and kicked at the trousers around his ankles. "We need to clean you up. Fuck, I look like an idiot." His shirt hung open over his underwear and he wore dark socks and shoes. She couldn't help the giggle that escaped her.

Their eyes met and his lips quirked too. He toed off his shoes, bent and tugged off his socks and tossed them aside, then pulled off his shirt and shoved down his boxers.

"Your clothes are going to be so wrinkled."

"Whatever. That feels better." He stood there in her hall, completely naked and completely at ease.

"You like being naked, don't you?"

"Yeah." He grinned. "You need to be naked too."

"I wish I had your confidence."

His eyebrows sloped down. "You look gorgeous naked."

"Pfft."

His frown darkened and he grabbed for her hand. "Hey. Come on."

16

He dragged her down the hall. She only had one bedroom so it wasn't hard to find, and in the dark room he found the lamp beside her bed and switched it on. He turned and looked around. "There." He pulled her toward the dresser with the big mirror above it.

He situated her in front of him, in front of the mirror, and he found the zipper at the back of her dress and drew it down. The strapless dress slid down over her hips, and she stepped out of it as he unfastened her bra, leaving her naked.

She dropped her gaze to the dresser and he reached around her, his big, hot body pressing against her back and her ass. He lifted her chin and met her eyes in the mirror. "Look at yourself. You're beautiful."

"I'd rather look at you."

He smiled and cupped her breasts, thumbs rubbing over tight nipples. Ripples of exquisite pleasure ran over her body. "Your breasts are perfect. Round and soft. I love your nipples." His hands flattened on her ribcage just below her breasts. One hand slid down over her waist and hip. "Your hips are beautiful." The other hand glided over her abdomen and then covered the small patch of curls at the juncture of her thighs. "Your stomach is so smooth and pretty."

He turned her so she was sideways to the mirror, staying behind her but putting some distance between them so he could palm her ass. "Your ass is spectacular," he said, his voice a little hoarse. His erection nudged at her back. He was getting hard again. He cupped her butt with both hands and then, to her shock, he went to his knees behind her and pressed his mouth to the small of her back. In the mirror, she watched his eyes go heavy-lidded then close as he kissed her butt cheeks, opening his mouth slowly on her skin, then rubbing his lightly-stubbled face on her sensitive skin there. Sensation sizzled across her body, up and down her spine.

Her pussy clenched hard on a wave of intense arousal and she found herself cupping her own breasts, heavy and aching. He held her hips as he worshipped her ass with his lips and tongue, possibly the most erotic thing she'd ever experienced, especially the visual of it in the mirror, his dark hair hanging over his forehead, his beautiful face pressed to her ass. She began to tremble, and when he slipped his fingers between her thighs, her entire body jerked.

"Your thighs are all wet. From my come. I was going to clean you up."

"I like it."

He turned his head and met her eyes in the mirror, his gaze lifting briefly to where she held her breasts. "Hot," he growled. He rose gracefully to his feet and once again turned her to face the mirror. His body was big and darkly tanned behind her, his eyes glowing in the lamplight. Bravely she studied her own image, her tight breasts pink with a flush that spread all across her chest, her nipples puckered. She lifted her chin and shook her tangled hair back. Her cheeks were also blushed pink, her eyes sparkling, her lips full, and damn, she did look…sexy.

He took hold of her hands and moved them to the dresser in front of her then laid a palm on the middle of her back and pushed her down a little. She lifted her gaze to his, loving the erotic promise on his face.

"Gonna fuck you again. Like this. Right here. And you're gonna watch."

Heat zoomed low in her belly as he kneed her legs apart. In the mirror, her breasts looked bigger as she bent forward. He slid a hand around to fill his palm with one and gently squeeze, and she widened her arms to accommodate his touch. "So beautiful…see?"

She nodded mutely, taking it all in, excitement tightening inside her. Behind her, he ran his thick cock up through her wet pussy, up the crack of her ass, making her shiver, then back down. "Have you ever tried anal?"

Heat flashed beneath her skin, into her face and she shook her head, still holding his gaze in the mirror.

"Want to?"

"Um…maybe."

"Okay. Not now." He rubbed his cock over her butt, then between her thighs again. With some thrusts of his hips, his cock slid between her thighs, back and forth. He groaned. "We'll get you ready for it some time."

Some time. When would that be? She pushed away the memory that he wasn't going to be in San Amaro very long. His fingers at her nipple, pinching and rolling it, distracted her, and ribbons of pleasure tugged from her nipple all the way to her core. She moaned.

"So wet." He rubbed his cheek against her hair. "Your pussy is so sweet. Hot and wet, like liquid fire."

Sweet Jesus, his sexy words turned her on even more. She gripped the edge of the dresser and watched as he turned his face against hers, rubbing his stubble over her jaw then kissing the side of her neck. Erotic. Exotic. Hypnotic.

He slid one hand up to her throat and cupped her there, the sensation exquisitely dominant and protective. Their eyes met once more in the mirror and heat and light sparkled between them.

With his big thigh he pushed her legs even farther apart, opening her for him, pressed her lower so her butt was out. She bent her arms and rested her elbows on the dresser as he found his cock and pushed into her once more, her tissues there swollen and sensitive. "Oh God. Oh yeah."

"Feel good, baby?" He leaned over her and gathered her hair into his hand, twisting it tightly. Sensation cascaded from her scalp all the way down her spine to pool in thick liquid heat in her pussy. He pulled aside her hair and sank his teeth so gently into the back of her neck. She gave another soft mewl of ecstasy as he filled her again, stretching her, easing slowly into her body until his crisp curls were pressed against her ass. The strength and heat of his body pressed into her, and she bent her knees and her elbows to adjust the angle so she could push back against him and take him deeper still.

"Yeah." He licked her neck, then down her back. He kissed her between her shoulder blades. "Fuck me back, Brooke. You're so fucking hot."

He began to move, in and out, the pull and drag of his hard shaft on her flesh so sweet, so very deep, this angle hitting so deep inside her it edged on pain. He tugged her hair again, lifting her head, and tears in her eyes blurred the vision in the mirror. She blinked, not wanting to miss a minute of this, watching Dylan Schell fuck her from behind. It looked so amazing, so...beautiful.

"Oh my God." She gasped as he hit deep inside her again. And again. "God, Dylan."

She fucked him back, pushing her ass back at him, meeting every thrust, and she pressed a hand to her abdomen where he filled her with such delicious pain. Once more she lowered her face to rest on her folded arms, and his hands roamed over her body, her waist, her hips, her back, her hair. Every drive hit harder, deeper, and pushed a cry from her throat, soft sounds of pleasure/pain.

His hand slid around her hip, dipped to her pussy and his fingers settled over her clit, rubbing in small circles.

She cried out.

That was just what she needed, just where she needed it, sensations twisting up inside her once more, every plunge of his cock inside her sending sparks sliding through her veins, illuminating her from the inside out, setting every nerve ending on fire. Noises slid helplessly from between her lips, formless sounds of pleasure and delight. "Dylan! God, Dylan…"

"Look at me." He growled out the words as he tugged her hair again, lifting her head. The image in the mirror was surreal, erotic and beautiful, sexy and sensual, her face glowing, her eyes hazy and lost in sensation, her lips parted and gleaming wetly in the low light. Dylan's face behind her had tightened into taut lines of near agony as he held back his release until she had hers.

"Yes. Oh yes…" His fingers worked magic on her clit, and as he hit the exact right spot with his fingers and with his cock, she exploded, a storm of lightning blinding her vision, thunder in her ears, waves and waves of bliss pouring over her like the ocean, endless and immersive and powerful. She cried out once more, her forehead landing on her forearms as Dylan pumped into her again, again, and…

"Fucking hell," he yelled and pulled out.

Her head jerked up as she tried to rise, but he held her down with a hand on her upper back while liquid heat spread over her lower back.

"Shit," he muttered moments later, his taut body relaxing a little behind her. "I know it's too late, but we forgot the fucking condom *again*."

Dylan sucked big gulps of air into his straining lungs and gazed down at the semen on Brooke's back. Jesus Christ, what was the matter with him? He never fucking forgot protection, and now he had with Brooke how many times? And pulling out like that was so stupid, with his semen still on her thighs from the first time he'd nailed her up against the wall.

He closed his eyes. He was a risk taker, always had been, but never with sex. Getting a girl pregnant had always been one of his biggest fears. He valued his freedom more than anything, and if having a kid wasn't the fastest way to lose that and get tied down, he didn't know what was.

Looking down at her back, also rising and falling with her still labored breathing, with his seed splashed there was goddamn hot.

"Now we really need to clean you up." He reached for a box of tissues on the end of the dresser. He wiped her back mostly clean and dropped the tissues into a waste basket, then turned her into his arms and picked her up. With a gasp she grabbed his shoulders.

"Dylan!"

He headed toward a door that looked like it might be a bathroom and sure enough, it was. "We need to shower." He lowered her feet to the small rug on the tile floor. He started to reach for the light switch then paused. Instead of turning the light on, he left the door open and some illumination filtered in.

Once again they were both reflected in the big mirror above the vanity, the lines and curves of their bodies shadowy. He reached into the shower and cranked it on, barely taking his eyes off Brooke. "You okay?" He settled his hands on her shoulders.

"Yes." She met his eyes and gave him a rueful smile. "I know I should be pissed off and worried, but I'm not. I mean, it's both our faults. And…" One slender shoulder lifted beneath his hand. "It'll be okay."

He nodded. "Brooke…we should talk about it."

She shook her head. "You don't need to remind me that you're leaving. I know what your life is like."

"That's not what I was going to say." He searched her face with his eyes. "If anything happens…fuck it, if you get pregnant, I'll be there for you. Fuck the tour. Whatever you want or need from me, you'll have it."

He said that without even a hint of terror that should have accompanied such words. He meant it. And with a strange sense of Zen, he felt completely calm about it and completely protective of Brooke.

She nodded slowly. "Okay." She swallowed. Steam began to fill the small room and he turned her by the shoulder toward the bathtub. She stepped in and he followed, pulling the curtain behind him.

In the small space, nearly dark with the shower curtain blocking much of what little light came in the bathroom, he positioned them beneath the pouring water, facing each other. With both hands he tipped her head back a little to wet her hair, and she closed her eyes. He pushed his fingers into her hair, dragged them down through the soaked strands and reached for a bottle of shampoo sitting on a corner shelf.

He took his time soaping up her hair then rinsing it. She handed him the conditioner and he worked that into her hair, loving the way it slicked up the strands and made them slip through his fingers. Then he washed her body, using a big pink puff and lots of sudsy body wash that made her body gleam. He watched rivulets of water and bubbles trace their way over her chest, her breasts, down her stomach, collect in the small patch of dark hair. He turned her to face away from him and scrubbed her back, then down between her legs so gently. When he was done he gathered her up in his arms once more and pulled her back against him, pressing his face to her wet hair and breathing in the tropical scent that surrounded them.

His hands slid over wet skin, smooth and sleek, cupping her breasts, her throat. She gave a low moan and his dick twitched. Christ. He was fucking insatiable around her.

She picked up the puff where he'd hung it and used it on him, dragging it over his shoulders and chest, down his abs to his crotch, and then she abandoned the puff and used soapy hands to wash his cock and balls, sliding her hands between his thighs, up into the crease of his ass, and heat surged through his body.

"You're getting hard again already." She looked down where she held him and rubbed him.

"Fuck yeah. What do you expect when you touch me like that?" He slapped one palm on the shower wall and held her hip with the other.

"I can't do it standing up again. My legs are still weak. You have to wait until we're in bed."

He grinned. "If I must."

They toweled off, watching each other with heated, admiring gazes, and tumbled naked into her bed. It wasn't the biggest bed, queen-sized he guessed, but the sheets were silky soft and smelled like Brooke, and stretching out in it with her pressed against him, skin to skin, from knee to chest, felt so damn awesome it took his breath away.

He kissed her, holding her damp hair, and this time they took it slow, with lots of long, leisurely kisses, sliding tongues and nipping teeth. Their hands moved over each other, exploring, stroking, eliciting soft moans and sweet sighs. He loved touching her, tasting her, breathing in the scent of her. His cock thickened and lengthened yet again, and his body pulsed with arousal, but he ignored it and focused on kissing and tasting her everywhere.

"Mmm. Hold on." He hated to interrupt but this time he had to make sure she was protected, so he rolled out of bed. Jesus, his pants were still lying in a heap in the hall. He dug through them to find his wallet and the one condom he had in there, then returned to the bedroom, depositing the condom on the bedside table close at hand. Because they *were* going to need it.

He moved over her, kissed her breasts, sucked on her nipples, loving how they tightened and lengthened against his tongue. He rubbed his face on her curves then dragged his tongue down the center of her abdomen. He nuzzled her stomach, brushed his fingers over the dark curls, then parted her thighs and moved between them. Her body quivered beneath his hands, and he pushed her legs up and back. She was beautiful there, so damn pretty, glistening pouty folds, and he leaned in to kiss her there too. He pressed soft kisses to one side then the other and then licked a long, luscious line up one soft-as-a-cloud plump lip, and then down the other. He pressed a closed-mouth kiss over her clit and she moaned, her hands coming to his head.

"So sweet." He slipped his hands beneath her ass to lift her up to his hungry mouth. "God, I want to eat you up like candy." He licked again, letting his tongue go deeper, finding the arousal that melted out of her. Her fingers tangled in his hair and tugged. He opened his mouth and sucked soft flesh into a suckling kiss, feasting on her, tonguing her deeper and deeper.

"Dylan...please..." Her hips moved with need, and he knew what she wanted, where she wanted to be touched, licked, sucked, but he smiled against her soft skin as he tormented her longer by taking his time, filling himself with her taste and scent, pleasuring both of them with long licks and gentle nibbles. He used his teeth on her taut thighs, slid a finger inside her, letting her hungry body close around him and squeeze.

He licked her taste off his lips as he watched his finger slide in and out then added another finger, and another, pumping his hand in and out of her pussy while she groaned and twitched. He lifted her higher so he could see all of her, including the tiny star of her anus. Heat flashed beneath his skin at the thought of doing her there. He wanted that, fuck yeah, but not this time. Still...they could play there...and he lubed up his thumb with her cream and rubbed over the opening.

She gasped, hips lifting even higher off the bed. "Dylan..."

"It's okay, baby." He teased her there a little more, her body tightening as she gave soft little whimpers. "Just playing here. It's okay."

He slicked up a little more of her feminine liquid and this time pressed in, not too far...just a little...

"God!"

Now. He bent his head again and kissed her pretty pussy, found her clit with his mouth and kissed it again, licked around it and around it...and then over it. Her cry echoed in his ears, but he lost himself in the pleasure of pleasing her, licking her clit over and over as her body trembled and constricted, clamping down on his fingers in her pussy and his thumb in her ass. And when he felt she was getting close, he opened his mouth and sucked the tiny bud into his mouth. It hardened and swelled against his tongue and he sucked firmly as she came apart beneath him.

"Sweet Jesus," she gasped. "God, Dylan."

"Mmm. Good, baby?"

"So good…so good…" Her head tossed and turned on the pillow and satisfaction swelled inside him at giving that to her. He moved over her again, kissing his way back up her body all the way to her mouth while he extended a hand and groped around for the condom he'd set there.

"One sec, babe." He rose up onto his knees to roll the latex on, and then he came down over her again and pushed his throbbing cock inside her. Her body closed around him, so fucking hot, so tight, still pulsing from her orgasm. He grunted as sensation wrapped around his cock and sparks slid up his spine. He wanted this to last, this time, he really did, but pressure built inside him, fast and dark. The condom helped, a little, made him miss the erotic sensation of being bare inside her, but even so, the feeling of fucking her was sublime, and he moved in her clinging body.

Her hands held onto his shoulders, gripping him then sliding across them to his biceps, back to his chest, moving all over him and making his skin prickle everywhere. When she brushed over his nipples, he jolted at the flash of sensation, and when her hands slid into his hair and scraped across his scalp, pleasure poured over him in waves.

"Fuck, I need you," he gasped. "Brooke…need you."

"I know." He kissed her mouth again. "I know."

She moved beneath him, lifting her knees, hooking her ankles behind him as he drove into her, again and again, fucking her hard, and when she cried out and said, "Harder!" he *loved* that and hammered into her. His skin buzzed, his balls drew up tight, grinding against her body, the base of his spine burning. He growled as his body tightened, his consciousness narrowing to her, just her, there beneath him, not only taking what he was giving her but giving it back with fierce pleasure. She lifted her hips against him, meeting every stroke, and goddammit she came again with a long, soft wail, her fingers digging into his shoulders, nails giving him stinging bites of pleasure. His body lost it, roared toward the peak, crazed for that ultimate satisfaction, and then he came too with a blinding surge of ecstasy, fire rushing down his spine and out his cock.

His grunts and groans of pleasure were loud and unstoppable, and he was only vaguely aware of them above the pounding of his blood in his ears and the surge of pleasure that cascaded over his entire body.

17

An incredible languor and satisfaction seeped through Dylan's body, right to his bones, lying there with Brooke in his arms, wrapped up in her limbs and the soft sheets of her bed. Jesus, she was amazing.

She'd been there for him tonight at the wedding, and it hadn't been so bad with her at his side, even when Matt had got up there and started spouting shit about him being responsible for Matt and Corey being together, reminding him painfully of how that had happened. They were fucking grateful to him, for chrissakes, when what he'd done could have split them apart forever. Guilt had smacked him in the back of the head, remembering how back then, he'd almost wanted that to happen, guilt along with relief that he'd buggered off in time for them to work things out and end up in their happy ever after and the wedding they'd all celebrated today.

Brooke had been there for him all along, really, from the time she'd showed up in Tahiti and pissed him off with her demands that he come back to San Amaro with him, then pushing him to do all this charity stuff that turned out to be not so bad too. Kinda fun. Kinda made him feel like he was doing something worthwhile. And listening to her praise him to others for what he was doing made him feel so damn good, he just wanted to hug her and kiss her and smile like a fool.

Jesus. What kind of sappy shit was he thinking here?

He stroked a hand over her shoulder and upper arm, slowly up and down. Her soft breathing told him she had dozed off, and so she should after going how many rounds with him? She'd come more times than he had, including at the wedding—his dick twitched remembering how hot and wicked that had been—and if he was exhausted, she must be too.

She shifted against him and he felt her lips press to his chest in a kiss.

"You awake, baby?"

"Mmm." She let out a long, heartfelt sigh that made his dick twitch yet again. She rubbed her face against his chest and her fingers tapped over his shoulder and curled around it.

"We should get some sleep. You have to work tomorrow, right?"

"Yeah." She sighed. "My alarm is set for seven-thirty. You probably have a lot to do too."

"You should know." He smiled.

She gave him a lethargic swat on the shoulder. "I don't have every minute of your week planned out."

He laughed. "Yeah. But this is it. Things really ramp up tomorrow."

"Your first heat is Wednesday, right?"

"Right. Wednesday at eleven-thirty." He hesitated. "Are you going to be there?"

"Of course! I'll be working, but yeah, I'll be there."

That made him happy. "I probably won't see you much before then," he said slowly. "Tomorrow and Tuesday I'll be working with Coach and the rest of the team to get ready."

"It's funny that you have a coach who's not a surfer."

"I kind of like it. He has a whole different perspective. And he knows what it's like to compete at this level, since he was a world champion snowboarder. He even works with me on nutrition and what I should be eating, and how I should be working out. He's the one who encouraged me to try yoga. And another great thing is, he's tall, and he knows how to coach me to use my height to my advantage, project where I want to go a little earlier when I'm winding up into turns. And I need to do some fine tuning on my boards with Elroy."

"I don't think I realized how much of a team you have working with you."

"Yeah. I guess. But when it comes right down to it, it's just me out there, me and the waves."

"You're going to do great this week."

He smiled and kissed her head. "Yeah? What makes you say that?"

"I just know." Her voice grew drowsy. "You're talented and you've been working hard."

"Thanks." He cleared his throat a little. Coming from her, he found that really meant a lot. He stroked her arm and shoulder and then her breathing slowed. She'd fallen asleep.

He glanced at the digital alarm clock on the table beside the bed. It was after one in the morning—should he stay the night? Or head back to his hotel and sleep alone?

Yeah, like he really wanted to do that. He was starting to drift too, sleep rolling over him like gentle waves, and so he slid a little lower into the bed, settling Brooke's sleeping curves next to him and closing his own eyes.

Brooke rolled out of bed first after her alarm went off and shut herself in the bathroom to get ready for work. When she emerged, Dylan was sitting on the side of the bed, dressed in his dark suit pants and dress shirt, in the process of rolling the cuffs back on his arms.

"Are you hungry?" she asked as she put on earrings in front of her big mirror. The big mirror where they'd, uh…watched themselves the night before. Heat flashed low down inside her.

"Starving." He grinned and rose to his feet, all big and sexy in his rumpled dress clothes, hair tousled, beard darkening his jaw.

"I can give you some toast or cereal. Or a bagel."

"Got any eggs?"

"Mmm. Yeah, I think I do."

"I can scramble some up for myself."

He made himself at home in her small kitchen, cracking eggs into a bowl.. "Want some?"

"Okay. If you're making them anyway." Half the time she didn't even eat breakfast, which she knew was bad. He whipped eggs together and poured them into a skillet while she made coffee and popped bread into the toaster, then they sat at her small counter to eat.

"I had fun at the wedding."

"Did you? That's good. Thank you for coming with me. I liked having you there."

"Your friends are nice. Corey and Matt. They seem so happy together."

"Yeah."

"They care about you too."

"I guess."

She lifted her head. "Why do you say it like that?"

"Like what?"

"As if…as if they *shouldn't* care about you."

"Huh. Maybe they shouldn't. You know I'm not really worth caring about."

She blinked at him. "What are you talking about?"

"You weren't all that impressed with me when you showed up in Tahiti. I was messing up my career. You were pretty clear that I was in danger of losing my sponsorship and needed to clean up my act. I'm an asshole."

She was silent for a moment, processing that. What he said was true, but… "No, you aren't."

He smiled at her. "Thanks, babe."

"Seriously, Dylan. I've gotten to know you better since we've been back and you're not really an asshole. Corey and Matt clearly care a lot about you. Tell me…what was that about, when Matt said you were responsible for him and Corey being together? How did you get them together?"

He bent his head and looked at his eggs. "Uh…no idea."

"Oh come on." She smiled. "It must have been great, for him to mention it at the wedding like that. I want to hear."

He sighed. "Corey and Matt were friends for a long time. Then they started sleeping together, so they were friends with benefits. Last year when I came back for a visit, I was staying with Matt, and…well…we ended up *all* sleeping together."

She stiffened. Replayed those words in her head. What? Had he really just said that?

"I mean, not Matt and me," he hastened to add. "But you know…"

"You slept with Corey?"

He swallowed. "Yeah. But with Matt there. A threesome. You know."

"Um. Yeah." Yeah, she knew what a threesome meant, and she knew he'd done it. Many times apparently. She'd walked in on him in bed with two other girls in Tahiti. But with Matt and Corey? Holy floating jellyfish!

"They weren't 'together' then, as in, a couple. They were just friends. With benefits."

Her heart felt like a rock in her chest. "I see. But I, uh…still don't get it. How did that bring them together?"

He sighed and set down his fork. "I was leaving to go to France for the next part of the tour and I asked Corey to go with me. She turned me down." He shrugged. "Because she was in love with Matt. She just didn't realize it. He didn't either. I mean, he was in love with her too. So basically, it was because of me that they realized they weren't really just friends with benefits, and that was how they ended up together."

"You asked her to go with you to France?" Her lips felt stiff as she said the words.

"It was a stupid idea. Of course she couldn't do that. I wasn't thinking right at the time."

She cleared her throat, which was surprisingly painful.

"That was a long time ago," he added.

Did he still have feelings for Corey? Was that what this was all about? Having to come home and go to the wedding of the woman you loved to another man…yeah, that would be hard. "That's really why you wanted me to go to the wedding with you, isn't it?"

"Ah…"

"It wasn't because they were bugging you to find someone. Was it…were you trying to make Corey jealous?"

His mouth dropped open. "Good Christ, no!" He shook his head. "Why would she be jealous over me? She's in love with Matt."

"Okay. Not trying to make her jealous, exactly." She laid down her own fork and stared at the toast on her plate. "But it was because of that you wanted someone there with you. Right?"

"Well. Yeah."

"You should have told me that."

"Why? What difference did it make? I was honest about it just helping me out. Not being real."

"Yes." Her heart contracted. "You were. I just wish I'd known that you…" She stopped. She didn't look up at him. "I just wish I'd known."

"It doesn't make any difference to us."

She closed her eyes, her chest hurting so bad. Last night had been incredible—the wedding, afterward at her place, the amazing sex, even this morning…up until the moment he told her he'd slept with Corey Ferber and had wanted her to go to France with him on the tour.

She wasn't jealous. She was just pissed off that she hadn't known, that she'd been made to feel foolish all those times they'd been with Matt and Corey, and she'd had no fucking clue that Dylan had apparently had pretty strong feelings for Corey. That Dylan and Matt and Corey had all slept together in a fun threesome.

That thought made her stomach heave.

"Okay." She opened her eyes with a bright smile. "You're right, it doesn't make any difference. Now, I'd better get going or I'll be late for work and you need to meet with Brett."

He didn't move for a moment, just looked at her, a faint crease between his eyebrows. "Yeah. I guess so."

"Just put the dishes in the sink." She slid off her stool. She reached for her cell phone where it was charging and dropped it into her purse. She slid her feet into her pumps while he gathered up the rest of his clothes.

"So I'll see you Wednesday?" he reminded her as she locked her door behind them.

"I'll be there!" She paused, wanting only to get away from him in case her emotions broke free and she made a complete fool of herself. But if she wouldn't see him again until after his heat... Her heart squeezed. "Good luck, Dylan," she said seriously. She went on her toes and gave him a kiss on the mouth. "You'll do great."

He wrapped his arms around her and pulled her up against him in a tight hug and her throat ached as he pressed his face to her hair. Dammit.

"Thanks." Then he released her and she had to drag her eyes off him to climb into her car.

She held herself together until she was in her office and alone, sitting there at her desk staring blindly at her computer screen.

It shouldn't have surprised her. After all, the first time she'd seen Dylan since high school, she'd walked in on him with two other girls. She'd heard the rumors of his wild escapades, including sexual ones. The fact that he and Matt and Corey had done that should not be a surprise.

Okay, so it wasn't exactly surprise that she was feeling.

She wasn't even sure *what* it was she was feeling. Disturbed. Very disturbed. Foolish. Angry. The way her chest ached made her think she was hurt, but why would that be? Just because she and Dylan seemed to have something between them, the way he'd taken charge as they left the wedding…what had he said? *"From now on, shit gets real, babe. Let's not play games."*

That had made her think what was happening between them was real. Big mistake.

He was a player. He'd slept with his best friend's girlfriend.

She gave a sharp tap to her keyboard to bring the computer to life and opened her email program. She had work to do. She couldn't sit here all day pouting about Dylan Schell.

What had that all been about, them *thanking* him for God's sake? How did *that* work? She shook her head, then leaned back in the chair and looked at the ceiling. That was messed up.

Corey seemed so nice and normal, and so in love with her new husband. She certainly didn't seem like a trampy, sexy siren who guys were falling all over themselves to be with, a girl so sexy she ended up in bed with two guys. Imagined scenes flashed through Brooke's mind, of Corey and Matt and Dylan—gah! She sat up straight and fiercely rubbed her eyes, as if to erase the images. *Don't even go there!*

Why was this bothering her so much? She'd seen Dylan with two other girls, all of them naked, for God's sake, and that hadn't disturbed her nearly as much as hearing about this. Was it because he'd wanted Corey to go with him on the tour? Ouch. Yeah, that stung a bit.

"Hey Brooke. Have you got the consumer research and sales data for the launch of Jolt?"

She looked up to see Tim. She blinked. *Get it together, woman.*

"Yes. Right here. I was doing some analysis on the data for the launch plan." They were launching a new male fragrance, Jolt. She handed the file to him, and with a smile and thanks, he backed out of her office.

Once more she sank back into her chair. She began to put

things together into a more complete picture, although a lot of the puzzle pieces were missing. Dylan's reluctance to come back to San Amaro now made more sense. He'd been trying to avoid the wedding, not just because his friends thought he should settle down, but because he'd slept with the bride. Maybe because he didn't want to see them get married.

Obviously he'd had pretty deep feelings for Corey. Curiosity burned inside her about what all had happened between them. Clearly he'd only given her minimal information about the whole thing. It confused her. And goddammit, it made her ache and want to cry.

She leaned forward and dropped her forehead to her desk. Flerkinschmidt! She was falling in love with him.

That could not happen. It had to be back to business for them, business and nothing *but* business. She had a job to do and Dylan did too, his job being to win a competition. And in less than a week, that would be over and he'd be flying off to Brazil, and if she'd successfully kept him out of trouble, her boss would be happy and she'd be on track for moving into a management position. That was all she had to worry about.

18

The bleachers had been set up since last weekend, but only now when the senior men's qualifying rounds began were they filling up with people. The weather was cooperating, with cloudless blue skies that almost hurt to look at, the ocean an equally blinding blue, tossed into decent waves by the wind.

White tents had been set up along the beach, home to all kinds of vendors of food, clothing, jewelry, sunglasses and a hundred other things. At the end of the beach, the stage sat empty right now, but later on there'd be a fashion show and at four thirty the first of the headliner bands would take the stage to rock the beach.

Crowds meandered along the sand, girls in tiny bikinis, ripped guys in low-slung board shorts, everyone wearing sunglasses and a sheen of sunscreen on tanned skin, music pulsing in the background.

Dylan grinned. This was so familiar to him, it felt like home, and he loved it. He soaked up the atmosphere, the sound of the waves a backdrop to voices talking and laughing and the chords of "Party Rock Anthem" blasting from some giant speakers; the briny scent of the ocean mingled with coconut sunscreen and from somewhere, the smell of popcorn. The sun warmed the sand beneath his bare feet and his face as he turned it up to the sky. He held his board beneath his arm and shifted from one foot to the other as he waited for his scores. Adrenaline still surged in his veins from the run he'd just had.

It had been radical.

He didn't even need to know the score to know how he'd done.

He'd sat outside, waiting, everything still around him, watching the rolling water swell all the way to the horizon, and then he'd felt it move beneath him and he was ready. He'd latched onto that wave, sensing the movement of the water, anticipating where he was going, surefooted and steady. He'd felt like he was flying out there, like he was one with the waves, like he could do no wrong. Inside a wave, he'd experienced that strange effect of being perfectly still on the water even as he was tearing across it, an oxymoron of speeding stasis.

When his score was announced, easily qualifying him for the next round, another broad grin broke out across his face and he waved to the cheering crowd. Cheering for *him*.

More adrenaline rushed through him, his heart pumping, his muscles twitching, and he found himself searching through the sea of faces for Brooke. Where was she? He'd only caught a glimpse of her earlier, but he knew she was there somewhere.

There were Matt and Corey, and he gave a wave to them, watching them lift their arms above their head to applaud, smiles stretched across their faces too.

Dylan hugged Brett and Elroy, and began the trudge through the sand. He needed to find Brooke. But before he could get very far, a microphone was thrust in front of his face and he found himself being interviewed by half a dozen reporters.

He pushed back his impatience to see Brooke and flashed smiles, threw out some lines about his run. "Yeah, it was fun out there, today." He shoved his wet hair back off his face. "The waves are fun, it's pretty consistent. I saw some barrels before my heat so I wanted to find some, and find some air. The wind is perfect for the airs."

It seemed to take forever, even though he never minded talking to the media. Hey, what was more fun to talk about than surfing, especially when it was going well? But he found his attention drifting, his gaze sliding away to search for Brooke, and he had to give himself a mental slap on the back of the head and focus.

When he finally managed to break free of the reporters, he was surrounded by girls, gorgeous, half-naked, tanned girls in bikinis and sunglasses. Jesus.

He almost laughed at himself, at how uninterested he was in them when only a month ago he would have been in heaven surrounded by a bevy of sexy chicks. When he spied Matt and Corey making their way across the sand toward him, he excused himself to the girls. "I gotta go talk to my friends, ladies. Catch you later."

"Hey dude," Matt said. "Great run."

"Thanks. Hey, you guys seen Brooke?"

Corey grinned. "Looking for your girl already?"

Dylan grimaced. "Yeah. She's here somewhere. I'm gonna get out of this wet suit and then check out the VIP Lounge."

"Okay. When's your next heat?"

"Tomorrow afternoon. Five o'clock."

"We'll be back to cheer you on."

Dylan paused. Emotion tightened his chest. He slapped a hand onto Matt's shoulder and squeezed. "Thanks, man. That means a lot to me."

"I'm sure you have tons of people cheering for you everywhere you go," Corey said, glancing at the girls who'd ambushed him moments ago.

"Well, yeah." They laughed and he grinned too. "I'm not bragging, it's the truth. But seriously, it means a lot more when it's your friends here for you." Christ, he was getting all sappy.

"And Brooke," Corey added.

"Yeah," he admitted.

"Go find her," she said. "We'll talk to you later."

"Come up to the VIP Lounge," Dylan said. "I'll get you in."

"I have a pass," Matt said. "We're one of the sponsors. They're stocked up with our beer."

"Well shit, yeah, I should've known that. Okay, I'll see you up there."

He quickly changed into his usual baggy knee-length shorts and a loose Hawaiian print shirt and headed to the VIP lounge constructed on the second level of the massive tent on the beach. When he walked in, he scanned the room for Brooke. He did a double take at seeing the Beckhams there, schmoozing with Adam Levine and a blonde girl…hey, wasn't that Wayne Gretzky's daughter?

He spotted executives from the big sponsors and then Matt and Corey and—yes!—Brooke stood there talking to them too, along with the bigwigs from ICON, the big entertainment company that put on the event. He made his way through the crowd, but people kept stopping him to say hi and congratulate him. Hell, he hadn't won yet. This was early in the competition, but he accepted the good wishes with smiles and handshakes and paused to say a few words to the people he knew he should.

"Hey Dylan." Jancy Barnes stepped in front of him and laid a hand on his arm, her smile wide and friendly. "Haven't seen you since Fiji."

He smiled. Jancy was a good kid, a talented surfer with a promising future. They'd hung out a few times on the tour. He gave her a hug. "Hey yourself. How're you doing, babe?"

"Great." They chatted about their heats and Jancy introduced him to her friend Tiffany, another cute tanned blonde.

"It's so awesome to meet you!" Tiffany gushed, shaking his hand and beaming up at him.

Then he paused to talk to Heath Marlow, his main rival in this competition, the man he was determined to beat. But Heath was a good guy and they could shoot the shit and hang out with each other and still be competitors. Deuce and Jimmy, both from Australia, joined them as they talked.

Finally he made it to the group where Brooke stood, and he positioned himself beside her. The others greeted him immediately and included him in the conversation. Brooke glanced up at him with a professional smile and said, "Congratulations, Dylan."

"Thanks." He smiled into her eyes, but she immediately looked away. Hell. He'd been hoping for a bit more reaction from her than that. Maybe he needed to get her alone.

"I was just telling Matt and Corey how lovely their wedding was."

Why did her voice sound funny, kind of strained?

"Yeah, it was nice. Lots of fun."

"Thanks," Corey said. "That's what we wanted."

They continued to make small talk about the event, and when he had the opportunity Dylan looked back at Brooke. "I'm gonna get something to eat and drink. Would you like something?"

"I'm okay, thanks."

He tightened his jaw. "Oh come on. Come with me and see what there is." And he firmly drew her away from the crowd.

"I already ate," she said in a low voice, still smiling that tight smile.

"I just want to talk to you for a few minutes. Without everyone else there."

"Talk about what?"

He paused. "Um. I thought…well, never mind." He thought she might have more to say than just "congratulations" but, okay, whatever. "I wanted to see you. Did you watch the heat?"

"Yes, I watched from here. Great view."

"True that." He paused. "So what've they got to eat here?" He steered her toward the long table laden with food.

"All kinds of things."

"I'm starving." He always ate light before he competed. "And I'll grab myself a bottle of Gatorade."

"I'll get it for you." She moved away from him toward the bar where all kinds of drinks, both alcoholic and non-, were being served by sexy bartenders.

He watched her, something settling inside him like a stone in his gut. She was so pretty, her long brown hair loose and shiny down her back, wearing a yellow sundress with tiny straps that showed off a lot of her smooth gold skin. But she didn't seem very pleased to see him or very excited by how well he'd done.

He started loading a plate up with shrimp and chicken fingers and raw veggies, and she returned with his bottled drink. "Thanks. Sure you don't want something?"

"I'm sure." She flashed another smile that didn't reach her eyes.

"I thought you might sit with Corey and Matt to watch."

Her eyes flickered and the corners of her mouth tightened. "I had to come up here and act as hostess on behalf of Jackson Cole."

"Huh. Yeah. You look really nice." His gaze moved over her nearly bare shoulders.

"Thanks."

Matt and Corey approached them then, and at Corey's knowing smile, watching them, he remembered that they thought he and Brooke were really a couple.

He felt like they were really a couple. Weren't they? After Sunday night at her place, how could they not be?

So he slid a free arm around Brooke's waist and did what he'd wanted to do earlier—he kissed her. She blinked at him in surprise, then her eyes shuttered and her smile went crooked.

"I'm glad you're here," he said in a low voice, but loud enough for Corey and Matt to hear. And he meant it.

"Of course I'm here," she said through that brittle smile.

"What are you up to this afternoon?" Matt asked him.

Brooke answered. "This afternoon you've got an autograph session down on the beach, and a bunch of kids from Daytrippers are coming."

"Awesome."

"Sounds cool," Matt said.

"And then another TV interview," Brooke said. "For a film being put together for Extreme Sports."

"And then another dinner," Dylan remembered with a grimace. He released Brooke so he could eat. He picked up a shrimp. "There's a party at Aura tonight. Wanna come with me?"

Her eyes narrowed. "A party?"

"Yeah." He met her eyes and smiled, lifting one shoulder. "You know…a bunch of people get together and eat and drink and talk and dance and generally have fun." There were endless parties going on at these events, all night long if you wanted.

"Should be a good time," Matt said. "We're going to stop by there later."

Brooke's mouth tightened. Jesus, what was with her? Was she worried about his behavior again? He hadn't done anything wrong in…weeks. But these events were supposed to be fun.

"You have a heat tomorrow," she reminded him.

"I know." Now his own eyes narrowed. He might like to party and have fun, but when it came to competing, he took that very seriously. He knew what he had to do to be in prime shape and he'd do it. "But it's not until later in the day. What—you're telling me I can't go to the party?" His voice went low and hard.

Corey and Matt exchanged glances.

Shit.

Brooke gave a light laugh. "I can't tell you what to do!"

"Coulda fooled me," he muttered. He handed his plate to a passing waiter with a tray, half the food still on it. He opened the bottle of Gatorade and drank deeply.

Brooke bit her lip, glanced at Corey and Matt then said, "If you want to go to the party, we can go. Sure."

"Great," Corey said. "We'll see you there. We'll be there around nine, nine thirty."

"Awesome." Brooke glanced at her watch. "I have to go talk to a few people and then it'll be time for your autograph session. You know where it's being held?"

"Yeah."

"Good, I'll see you there." And she disappeared into the throng of people.

Dylan glanced at Matt and Corey, who seemed to have sensed the tension between him and Brooke.

"Everything okay, Dylan?" Corey asked.

"Um. Yeah. Great."

More people joined them then, once again shaking his hand, and he accepted more congratulations and good luck wishes, and entertained everyone with his surfing stories until it was time to get to that autograph session.

As he trudged through the soft sand back on the beach, irritation rubbed inside him, but he wasn't sure what that was about. Maybe because he wasn't used to having his time so structured, all these things planned out for him, when he usually liked to just hang out and cruise around town and have some fun.

And that reminded him of why Brooke had come to Tahiti to bring him back and why they were doing all these things. His sponsorship had been in jeopardy and he needed to clean up his act if he wanted to keep it.

And he'd been doing it. Truthfully, while he liked having more freedom, it hadn't been that hard. Yeah, he'd had to fit all these meetings and events in around everything else he had to do, but he'd actually enjoyed much of it. And before a competition, he was focused on the things he needed to be—eating right, getting enough sleep, working out, shaping his boards, going over things with Brett and most important of all, time in the water practicing. Despite what Brooke thought of him, it was only *after* a competition that he liked to let loose. And what the hell was wrong with that anyway?

His mood dipped when he arrived at the tent where the signing was being held and he had to force a smile and act all relaxed and happy, all the while casting glances at Brooke who appeared to be doing the same.

"We need to talk," he muttered to her at one point during a break in the action.

"Sure. But I'm really busy. How about later?"

He frowned. He didn't want to wait until then. "I'll come to your place when I'm done with dinner. Then we can go the party with Matt and Corey."

Her lips tightened and she cast her eyes down but nodded. "Okay."

19

Brooke focused on her work for the rest of the day, ending up back in the VIP tent networking with local business people, a couple of clients and members of the media. The party atmosphere and beautiful sunny weather put everyone in a good mood. The waves were great for the surfers and some terrific scores were being posted.

Matt and Corey had left earlier to get back to their businesses. No doubt Laguna Dorada was packed all day with all the tourists in town for the Pro, and Corey was probably busy too, as people explored all the little shops and restaurants along Shore Drive. It had been so awkward earlier, seeing them now that she knew about them and Dylan.

Thinking about that made her stomach pitch. But then Dylan had showed up and wanted to be all friendly and she remembered that Corey and Matt thought they were actually a couple, and even though she'd only agreed to attend the wedding to help him out, she couldn't just abandon him now. They were stuck with this act for the rest of the week until Dylan left town. So she'd agreed to go to that damn party.

"Brooke."

She turned at hearing her name and saw her boss standing in front of her.

"Hi Barrett. What's up?"

"I need to talk to you." He jerked his head and she followed him away from the group of people she'd been talking to. In a quiet corner he turned to her. "What's with you and Dylan Schell?"

She blinked. "Nothing."

He gave her a look, chin down, eyes narrowed. "Right. And I'm about to win the Jackson Cole Pro."

She pressed her lips together.

"You two looked very friendly, and I'm hearing talk that you've been looking pretty friendly all over town."

She rolled her eyes. "Oh for heaven's sake. Yes, we're friendly."

"You're supposed to be keeping him on a leash."

"I am. Have there been any problems? Any hints of bad behavior?"

"No." He eyed her then smiled. "Oh, so that's how you're doing it."

Her mouth dropped open. "What are you talking about?"

He smiled knowingly. "Attagirl, Brooke. You do whatever it takes to keep him in line and keep the higher-ups happy."

"I'm not…" She paused. "I mean, I'm not…" Oh Jesus. She didn't even know what to say. She'd been about to assure Barrett that she wasn't sleeping with Dylan, but…she was. But not like he thought. Except, telling him the truth wasn't an option.

She stared at him. Did she want him and the rest of Jackson Cole management thinking she was that ambitious and manipulative that she'd use sex to control Dylan? Good God.

"It's not what you think. It's just business."

"Well yeah, I should hope so." His smile faded and he gave her another calculating look. "Because we didn't give you this account so could you hook yourself a rich surfer."

Pressure built inside her, fast and hot. A red haze floated in front of her eyes and she took a deep breath. "That's really uncalled for, Barrett." She gave him the haughtiest look she could muster. "If you have problems with how I'm doing my job, let me know."

"Dylan Schell *is* your job. Just remember that."

And he turned and left.

She stood there for long moments, marshaling her thoughts and trying to control the emotions that churned inside her. She'd never really liked Barrett, but she'd never hated him more than she did at that moment.

Furious, she whirled around and left the VIP tent. She was done for the day anyway. Her face hurt from smiling and she was tired of schmoozing and networking. And dammit, she had to go that damn party with Dylan.

A mistake, yet she'd said she'd go and she'd also committed to helping him, which in turn made sure that he was staying on his best behavior. She felt squeezed, as if she couldn't win no matter what she did.

But this only reinforced her determination that from now on, things between her and Dylan had to stay just business.

At home, she made herself a grilled cheese sandwich for dinner. She'd grabbed a few bites of food earlier in the day, but hadn't really been hungry, her stomach in knots, first with nerves for Dylan as he surfed, then anxiety about seeing Corey and Matt, and Dylan wanting to talk.

She didn't want him to know she was all twisted up about him. This was supposed to be a casual thing, a wedding date to help him out and gain his cooperation in the business part of their relationship. She wasn't supposed to be feeling like this. Whatever "this" was—she couldn't even identify it. Jealous? Hurt?

She had no right to be jealous of him and relationships he'd had in the past, and she certainly had no reason to be hurt. Everything that had happened was no big deal. They'd get through the week with Dylan's reputation intact, hopefully a championship under his belt and his sponsorship and her job secure. She needed to keep Dylan happy so he'd behave, cooperate with the charity events and hopefully win this event.

She'd been so casual to Dylan about watching him surf earlier, but the truth was she'd been gnawing on her thumb, her stomach a mass of tight knots as she'd watched. God, she'd wanted him to do well.

And then, watching him, something weird had happened. She was no expert on surfing, but she knew a little, and she knew when she was watching something amazing. Something almost magical. The grace and power of his body as he'd ridden the wave, the way he moved with the board, the way he kept his balance with such ease, was mesmerizing. When he'd caught that air, he'd been flying.

And then she hadn't been nervous any more. She'd been calm and smiling, and when he'd finished, a feeling of awe and admiration swelled inside her, a feeling of…pride. She was proud of him. Not like a parent is proud of their kid. Not even like she'd had anything to do with it. It was hard to explain, but she was impressed and happy for him, wanting more than anything for him to do well so he'd be happy.

And he *had* been happy, and that had made her heart expand in her chest so much it had been hard to breath, a warm soft feeling growing inside her. Then it had been even harder to maintain her professional demeanor when he'd shown up all jubilant, flashing that sexy grin around and hugging half-naked girls.

She changed into a short purple dress that was tight around her hips, blousy on top, with narrow spaghetti straps, and redid her makeup in preparation for Dylan picking her up for the party. When he arrived at her door, she was ready, wearing a cheerful smile along with her stilettos.

"Wow." Dylan gave her a scorching up and down look. "You look hot."

"Thanks. You look good yourself." And he did, even though he was wearing his usual baggy shorts and loose, brightly-colored print shirt. "I'm ready to go."

"Hey, we have a few minutes. I wanted to talk to you."

Damn. "Oh right. Okay. Do you want something to drink?"

"Nah, I'm good, thanks. Did I tell you the other night I like your apartment?"

She made a face. "Uh, no. But thanks. It's nothing special."

"It's just like you." He strolled into the middle of her living room. "On the surface it's all neat and tidy and buttoned up, but underneath it's hot and sexy."

She stared at him. "How the hell do you get that from my apartment?"

He grinned. "It's the little things. The hot red and orange cushions on a beige couch. The pictures on the wall." Her framed black-and-white photographs were done by Jules Stockwood. She'd purchased them at Jules's gallery, and she loved them. "They look all innocent and black and white until you realize they're nudes. And it smells like Tahiti in here, all warm and tropical."

"It's the passion fruit candles."

"See?" He lifted an eyebrow. "Passion fruit."

Well. She nibbled her bottom lip. "I still don't…oh never mind."

"Yeah, you *are* like that, Brooke. I saw it in Tahiti. You showed up all stiff in your business clothes, and the next thing I know you're wearing a hot little sundress and seducing me."

"I did not seduce you!" Then she took in the twinkle in his eye and shook her head. How could she stay angry at this guy? But she had to keep her distance. "What did you want to talk to me about?"

"Oh yeah." His smile faded a bit. "About earlier. You seemed all…pissed off or something." His eyes searched her face. "You okay?"

"Of course! This is a busy week. Stressful for everyone. But not as much as you, I'm sure."

"Yeah. I guess. Okay."

"We should go. Matt and Corey will be there soon."

He nodded and they left.

They drove to the bar in his rental car. She opened her mouth to say something about drinking and driving then closed it. She didn't need to be that much of a babysitter. Dylan knew better than that, and now the competition had started he wouldn't be drinking much. She trusted him.

A lineup stretched from the front door of Aura down the sidewalk, but Dylan led her to a side door where the bouncer immediately let them in with a grin and a slap on his shoulder. Inside, music throbbed around them in the darkness, colored lights pulsing above the dance floor. People moved around, talking, laughing, flirting.

Once people had seen Dylan, that was it, he was the center of attention. Brooke went to step aside, but he slid his hand down her arm in a warm caress that made her shiver and clasped her hand, keeping her close. She kept a smile firmly in place as she listened to the conversations that didn't include her. When someone asked Dylan what he wanted to drink, he looked at her first. "What would you like?"

"Um. White wine."

He requested her wine and a San Pellegrino, which she guessed was for him. More people came up to talk to him and wish him well, other surfers there as well as fans. Dylan introduced her to people as much as he could, when the noise level permitted.

Matt and Corey arrived, further testing Brooke's acting abilities as she continued to smile and laugh and respond appropriately to the conversation.

This was a part of the Pro that a lot of people lived for, the partying and socializing that went on all night. There'd been years where she'd been partying all night too. The energy and enthusiasm and excitement of the crowd was contagious, and she found herself moving to the music as she stood there talking to people.

"Hey Brooke!"

She turned to see Josh Busher, one of San Amaro's police officers, now off duty, and smiled. "Hi Josh!"

He moved up closer, smiling back at her. They'd had an off-and-on flirtation for years but had never actually gone out together. When she was free, he was dating someone, and if he was free she was seeing someone. She really liked him though, and he was super attractive, a tanned athletic blond guy who looked great in his police uniform. "Haven't seen you for a while. Why aren't you working tonight? I'd think every police officer in San Amaro would be working this week."

He grinned. "We can't work twenty-four-seven. I'll be pulling some long shifts this weekend. Gotta keep those rowdy surfing fans under control."

"And the rowdy surfers," Dylan said from behind her, his hand tugging on hers.

She turned her head. "That too." She grinned. "Josh, this is Dylan Schell. Dylan, Josh Busher. Josh is a police officer."

The two men shook hands with narrow-eyed appraisal of each other. "Good to meet you, Dylan," Josh said. "We're all cheering for our hometown guy to win this week."

"Thanks," Dylan drawled. "I'll see what I can do."

Josh turned his attention back to Brooke. "So how's your sister? Last time I saw her, her car'd been broken into."

"Oh that's right! That was awful. But she's fine."

They started chatting about other people they knew, and Brooke tried to separate herself slightly from the crowd of people around Dylan so she could have a conversation with Josh, although she had to give her hand a tug from Dylan's to do so.

"Are you and Dylan going out?" Josh asked in her ear a little while later.

She shook her head. "No. I mean, not really. I mean…" She closed her eyes. "He's just here for this week. Jackson Cole is one of his sponsors, so we've been working together on a few projects while he's here." And keeping him out of trouble.

Which hadn't actually been that hard. Although who knew what kind of antics he'd have gotten up to if she hadn't gotten involved.

She and Josh chatted and drifted away from the rest of the group. "Hey, you need another drink." He gestured at her empty glass. "Come on. Let's see if we can shove our way through to the bar."

"It's a female bartender," she yelled over the loud music and voices. "You better try. She'll never pay any attention to me."

He laughed and shouldered his way through the crowd at the bar. Easy for him, standing over six feet tall and with football-player shoulders. He caught the bartender's eye and sure enough, the sexy brunette was right there in front of him with a flirty smile. In no time, they had their drinks.

"Thanks!" Brooke held up her wine glass to give a little clink against his beer glass.

"So. If you and Dylan aren't together, maybe we could go out some time."

"You and Jasmine aren't going out any more?"

He shook his head. "Nah. Long story."

"I'm sorry. I really like her." Jasmine owned the White Jasmine Bed and Breakfast in town.

"No hard feelings." He shrugged.

She sank her teeth into her bottom lip, unsure what to say to his invitation. She didn't want to go out with Josh. But why not? There'd always been a little spark of attraction between them. Somehow that had disappeared. And the little spark was nothing compared to the inferno of heat and lust she felt around Dylan. But what she'd said was true—they weren't together. And he was leaving next week. And here was Josh, single at the same time as she was. So why the hell not?

"Well, you know. Maybe after this crazy event is done, we could go for a drink or something. This week's really busy."

"I hear you."

"There you are."

Brooke turned to see Dylan standing there. "I thought you got lost somewhere."

"Not lost. Just got another drink." She held up her glass.

His eyebrows drew together and his mouth went tight. He shot Josh a sharp look.

Whoa. Was he jealous?

Brooke tipped her head to one side. Frack.

"Can I talk to you?" Dylan gripped her arm and drew her away.

"Sure. Excuse us," she said to Josh with a smile. "Catch up with you later."

"No you won't," Dylan said in her ear.

She eyed him. "What's your problem?"

"You're with me."

She lowered her chin. "Well, we came together. But you know as well as I do that we really only have a business relationship."

"Business?" He laughed. "*That's* what that was in your bed the other night? Business?"

His words were an uncomfortable echo of Barrett's earlier that day, and her insides twisted. She really didn't appreciate those insinuations. She gave Dylan a cool look. "No. That wasn't business. But *this* is. I'm here with you, keeping an eye on you so you stay out of trouble, and helping you out so your friends don't know you're still lusting after your best friend's new wife."

Flerkinshmidt! She shouldn't have said that. Any of it.

She caught a flash of something in his eyes that might have been anger—or pain—before his eyes narrowed and his lips tightened even more. "Right. Pardon me. This *is* business. And you can go back and talk to your friend and let him buy you drinks all night if that's what you want."

"You're leaving next week." Oh, *why* did she keep saying these things?

He gave her a long look. "Yeah. I am."

And he turned and shoved his way through the crowd to the bar.

20

Dylan ordered another San Pellegrino at the bar from a hot bartender who gave him a long sexy look. He smiled back at her as he took it then turned around to face the crowd. For the first time since he'd walked in, he was alone. And yeah, you could be totally fucking alone in a crowd.

His eyes sought out Brooke and found her, way across the room talking to…nope, not that cop guy, but two other guys, who stood there looking at her with foolish grins. Fuck.

She was so goddamn pretty. She laughed and tossed her hair behind her shoulder then sipped from her wine glass. And then she batted her eyelashes at one of the guys. Batted her eyelashes!

Something churned inside Dylan, hot and unpleasant. He gripped the bottle of water tighter. What. The. Fuck.

Then she was following one of the guys onto the dance floor. And dancing with him.

Dylan nearly crushed the bottle.

"Hi, hon," a cute blonde said to him. "You're Dylan Schell, right?"

He sucked in a long breath. With barely a glance at her, he said, "Yeah."

"You're an awesome surfer."

"Thanks." He turned his gaze toward her. She leaned on the bar next to him, and another girl beside her also smiled at him. They were both wearing skimpy tops that showed off a lot of tanned skin, short shorts and killer heels. He lifted an eyebrow. "What's your name?"

"Carly. And this is Stephanie."

"Hey girls. Can I buy you a drink?"

"Sure!" Their eyes went wide and their smiles beamed.

Dylan lifted a hand and caught the attention of the bartender, who gave the two girls a pursed-lipped look when he ordered.

Business. It was just business. Brooke was just there keeping him out of trouble, she'd said. And then she'd made that crack about him lusting after Corey. That was utter bullshit.

It hurt that she thought so little of him. Which was a weird experience for him. He didn't give a shit what people thought about him. Why did he care about her?

His lips twisted as he looked down at the floor.

He did care about her. And that made sweat pop out on his forehead and his breathing stop. Christ.

He was a stupid idiot. He should never have told her about Matt and Corey. That had been a messed up time of his life and she didn't understand. For her to say that was just wrong. He'd trusted her, thought she really cared about him and he could be honest about that, but this was just business for her, which she'd made crystal clear.

Shit.

He wanted to punch something, maybe drive his fist through a wall. Or maybe into the face of that guy Brooke was dancing with.

He forced himself to keep from looking at Brooke, keeping his gaze focused on the two chicks in front of him who were rambling on about the competition and the parties and how drunk they'd gotten the night before.

Sounded like a plan to him.

Brooke flirted and laughed and danced, studiously avoiding Dylan, but with a stone-cold feeling in her stomach because of what she'd said to him. Partly because she'd hurt him. Partly because she'd said out loud what was really bothering her—the feeling that he still cared about Corey.

She never should have slept with him. In Tahiti, yeah, but especially here at home. She should have known better. She was a professional. What was she thinking?

He'd bought those girls drinks. After he'd been pissed at her for talking to another guy. And there was *nothing* between them.

Nothing. So why was she all agitated? Why was she all hyper and flirty with guys she had no interest in? How long did she have to stay here, anyway? Dylan was the one who'd wanted to come.

It was nearing midnight and she had to get home to bed. Dylan's heat wasn't until later in the day, so maybe he didn't need to sleep, but she did. She located him across the bar, once more the center of attention in a crowd of mostly women.

She crossed over to him and slipped through the crowd, then went up on her toes to speak to him. "I need to go home. Are you ready?"

He gave her a toothy smile that chilled her. "Not really."

She frowned. "I think we should go, Dylan."

He lifted an eyebrow. "Yeah, no doubt you do. But I'm tired of being told what to do."

A quick little stab in the heart took her breath away. Yeah, no doubt he was. "It's my job," she said quietly.

He gave her a long look. "I know. Fine. I'll drive you home."

She nodded. "Good. Thanks."

The drive home was painfully silent. She searched around in her head for something to say but came up empty. Thick tension filled the car and she found herself rubbing at the cuticle on her thumb. He pulled up in front of her apartment building and got out to walk her in.

She had to close her eyes against the wave of longing that swept over her, remembering the last time he'd brought her home, the night of the wedding, and how he'd stayed all night. That wasn't going to happen tonight, not with this icy tension between them. This time he merely made sure she was safely inside and then lifted a hand in a curt good night. "Later, Brooke."

She bit her lip as she watched him stride back to his car, suddenly on the edge of tears. Holy guacamole. She was such an idiot.

Her bed felt very empty without him and that was even crazier.

The next morning she felt like crap. She'd drunk too much wine, stayed out too late and her sleep had been restless and filled with frustrating dreams about Dylan. Her head throbbed, her neck and shoulders ached and her stomach roiled. Great. It was going to be a good day.

She went into the office to get some things done before she headed back to the beach for more schmoozing with media people. The office was quiet. This week was never a normal work week, and today she was grateful for the quiet.

She'd been checking emails on her cell phone the day before, but there were things she couldn't attend to from her phone and other matters to follow up on. She still had a lot of work to do on the marketing strategy for Jolt. She popped a couple of painkillers and drank a big cup of coffee she'd picked up at the Black Bean on her way to work. Caffeine was supposed to help a headache.

Focusing on work took her mind off her aching head and also took her mind off Dylan Schell, and she'd made good headway on her list of tasks when Tim poked his red-headed, freckled face in her door. "Hey. I wasn't sure if you'd be in today."

"Of course I'm in." She tried to keep the irritation out of her tone. "Why wouldn't I be?"

"Heard you were out partying it up at Aura last night."

"I was there for a while. Didn't stay that late. How'd you hear that?"

"There are a bunch of pictures online on various blogs and Facebook."

She frowned. "Pictures of me?"

"You're in a couple. You and Dylan. But most of them are of him. Guess he had quite the night. Uh…not sure Barrett's going to be impressed."

She tilted her head. "Why? Nothing happened." Other than she and Dylan pretending to ignore each other all night.

"Really? You better have a look. Check out Joe Cosner's blog." He named a well-known surfing blogger.

She reached for her mouse and opened her Internet browser. In moments she was staring at pictures of Dylan and herself that she recognized as having been taken at Aura last night. Must have been early in the evening, when he had his arm around her shoulder and was looking down at her with a warm smile. She paused and stared at that image for a long moment then closed her eyes. Damn. It looked like…well, never mind.

She scrolled down through more images, other people who'd been at the party, more of Dylan…and then even more of Dylan, with girls she didn't recognize, another of him smiling, his arm around a girl's neck while she kissed him. And another with him standing with a girl on either side of him…both girls topless.

When the hell had *that* been taken?

Her stomach contracted into a tight ball. She scanned the blog article. The party had apparently lasted all night and had gotten a tad rowdy. And raunchy. Good God. Dylan must have gone back there after he'd dropped her off.

A wave of heat washed over her and for a moment she couldn't even see the computer monitor. Her stomach cramped and she thought she might throw up. Seeing this on top of being tired and a bit hungover was not good.

Her chest ached too, at the thought that Dylan had driven her home, dumped her, then gone back to party without her. And once again she had to remind herself that there wasn't anything real between them. They'd slept together, had hot sex together, pretended to date for the sake of Corey and Matt. No, the real reason she was so twisted up about this was because he was supposed to be behaving this week.

Holy floating jellyfish! If Barrett saw this…that was what Tim had been talking about.

She lifted a shaky hand and rubbed her forehead. God. Oh God. She was supposed to be keeping him out of trouble and… she'd failed.

Her eyes flew open and she continued reading and viewing the pictures, torturing herself, punishing herself maybe.

Dylan had left the party at about five in the morning with three hot girls, after an orgy had apparently broken out in the closed-to-the-public nightclub.

"Fuck, fuck, fuck." She lowered her head to her desk.

Was there any way she could keep this from going viral? Was there any way she could keep Barrett from seeing this? Or any of the executive management team, who'd been all twitchy about Dylan's antics, prompting her rescue mission to Tahiti?

Probably not.

Unless she could hack into that blog and…but that was beyond her tech abilities, and besides, it was illegal.

She sat like that for a while, head on her arms, thoughts swirling around inside her aching head. She had to come up with some kind of damage control plan, but she had no idea what that would be at that moment. The hard evidence of her failure was posted online for the world to see.

"Brooke?" Tammy's voice made her lift her head. "Barrett wants to see you in his office."

She sucked briefly on her bottom lip then nodded and shoved her hair back from her face with both hands.

How bad was this going to be? He could be such an asshole. He might fire her. He'd threatened that when they were making her go to Tahiti. But come on—how bad was it? Apart from the fact that she felt like her insides had been shredded, what Dylan had done hadn't been that bad. Just a little drunken, naked partying.

She pressed a hand to her heaving stomach and forced her legs to walk down the hall. She knocked on Barrett's open door to alert him she was there. He turned to face her from behind his desk. The corners of his mouth tipped down and a crease marred his forehead. Yeah, he was pissed.

"Come in, Brooke."

She advanced into the office. It was much larger than hers, sunshine pouring in the floor-to-ceiling windows that overlooked the intense green of Torrey Pines Park.

"Have a seat." He gestured at the chair.

She sank into the chair.

"I know you've seen the blogs," Barrett said. "I talked to Tim about them already."

She nodded. "I'm so sorry. I don't know how that happened."

"You don't know how that happened." He nodded, his jaw tight. "You don't know how that *happened?*"

She sighed. "Yes, I know how that sounds. I was at that party last night. I stayed until midnight. Dylan and I left together. I assumed he was going back to his hotel. I never thought he'd go back without me, and…" Her voice trailed off.

He nodded. "You assumed he was going back to his hotel." He inclined his head. "I had the impression that you two were sleeping together."

She kept her mouth from dropping open at his bluntness. "I don't even know what to say to that. That's not the issue here. And not your business."

"If you'd slept with him last night this wouldn't have happened."

She fought down a blaze of anger. "You do realize you sound like a pimp?"

"What?" His eyes widened, then narrowed and a vein throbbed in his temple.

God, she shouldn't have said that to her boss. "I really don't want to think that my job depends on me sleeping with certain people. I think there are laws against that kind of thing."

"Are you threatening us with a lawsuit?"

"Are you firing me?"

He glared at her. "No. But I am taking you off this project."

Her throat constricted. She was about to remind him that she was the one who'd suggested sponsoring Dylan Schell, but that might not be the best move at this point. "What about Dylan?" she asked quietly, stomach tensing. "Are you going to withdraw his sponsorship?"

"I haven't decided that yet."

"He's in the middle of an important competition. At least wait until it's over."

"I'll think about it. Tim will take over working with him. And maybe he'll do a better job of keeping Dylan from making a fool of himself in the press."

She knew there was no point in arguing with him and at least she had her job. For now. But inside, she burned.

She rose to her feet. "Tim probably won't sleep with him either," she muttered under her breath as she moved to the door.

"What was that?"

"Nothing." She paused. "Once again, I apologize, Barrett."

He gave a curt nod. "We'll reassess things after the Pro." And he turned to his computer.

Back in her office, she slumped in her chair. Flerkinshmidt! She took a long deep breath and let it out slowly, her head falling back against her chair.

Okay. This was probably just as well. She had a lot of work to do and now she had no reason to go to the Pro this afternoon and do all that schmoozing. That would be up to Tim now.

Also she needed to stay away from Dylan. For her own sanity and safety.

She checked the time on her computer. It was nearly noon and she was meeting Fraya at a little place near the Pier for lunch.

Somewhere away from the craziness that was happening at Breaker Beach. She grabbed her purse.

Fraya was already there, sitting in a booth next to a window in the diner-style restaurant. Brooke's heels clicked across the black-and-white tiled floor as she made her way to the booth.

"Hi Fray." She slid onto the purple vinyl seat in front of the hot pink and chrome table.

"Hey, you're here." Fraya looked up from the menu with a smile. "Tell me not to order the chili fries."

"I think we should get a double order. And onion rings. And milkshakes."

Fraya lowered her chin and gave Brooke a look. "Oy. Hungry today?"

"No. I'm pissed. And…well, pissed."

"What's wrong?" Fraya set down the menu, concern shadowing her eyes.

"Oh man. Long story. They don't serve booze here, do they?"

Fraya's lips quirked. "No. But we can go somewhere else if you want."

Brooke sighed. "That's okay. I have to go back to work."

"Me too. Client meeting at one thirty. But hey, milkshakes!"

A reluctant smile tugged at Brooke's lips. "Okay."

They ordered chili fries, onion rings and milkshakes. Fraya talked her out of adding a basket of sweet potato fries to the order.

"Okay, what's going on?" Fraya asked when milkshakes topped with whipped cream sat in front of them.

Brooke dipped her straw in and out of her milkshake. "Okay. You met Dylan when he came for dinner that night."

Fraya's eyebrows shot up. "Oooh. This has to do with Dylan Schell?"

"Yes." She stared hard at her whipped cream. "When I went to Tahiti…my boss sent me there to get him." She looked up at Fraya. "This is just between us, right?"

Fraya bit her lip. "Can't I tell Kevin?"

"No."

"Huh. Okay. Go on."

"Okay. Jackson Cole was getting upset about the things Dylan was doing. They didn't think it was in line with the company image, and they wanted me to go bring him home and help clean up his behavior. So I went all the way to Tahiti to get him."

"Even though you're afraid of flying," Fraya murmured.

Brooke waved a hand. "I can do it. I just…anyway. I got there and I convinced him to come back with me, basically threatening him that he'd lose his sponsorship from Jackson Cole if he didn't clean up his act. He wasn't very happy, but he agreed." She hesitated, not sure how much she should share with Fraya, so she skipped ahead. "So we come back, and he's been actually pretty cooperative, getting involved with a couple of charities and staying out of trouble."

Fraya nodded.

"So." Brooke dropped her eyes to her milkshake again. "We've been seeing a lot of each other since we got back."

"Mmmhmm."

"I was doing my job," Brooke said defensively. "And it was working. Everything was going great until last night. We went to the party at Aura, and damn him, he took me home at midnight and then went back to the party. Apparently he stayed all night and it turned into a drunken, debauched orgy or something. There are pictures all over the Internet and everyone's talking about it."

"Oh." Fraya pursed her lips around her straw.

Brooke cleared her throat. Her voice had gotten a little unsteady there, with all the emotion rising up inside her at telling the story. "My boss called me into his office this morning, all pissed off because I'd fallen down on the job, basically. This wasn't the first time, but he pretty much told me he expected me to sleep with Dylan if I had to, to keep him out of trouble."

"Whaaaat!" Fraya choked on her milkshake. "Are you serious?"

Brooke's mouth twisted. "Yeah. Serious as Tropical Storm Joyce."

"They can't expect you to do that. That's just…good God, what kind of place is it you work for?"

"It's not the place. It's Barrett." She scowled. She'd complained about Barrett before to Fraya.

"Asshole."

"Yeah. That about sums it up."

"We're gonna sue his ass for sexual harassment. He can't talk to you like that! That's just outrageous."

Brooke held up a hand. "I don't want to sue anyone. At least, I don't think I do. I handled it, although I may have said a few things that'll come back to bite me. I told him he sounded like a pimp."

Fraya covered her smile with her hand. "Good for you." She shook her head. "I've said it before, Brooke. You don't have to stay there. You're smart and talented and educated. There are lots of places you can get another job."

Brooke sighed and sat back against the purple vinyl. "Yeah, you say that, but realistically there aren't many big companies like Jackson Cole that close to home. I do like the company. But man, he makes it hard. I really don't want to give up this job though."

Fraya's mouth drooped as she studied her. "You don't have to put up with that. You *shouldn't* put up with that."

"Well. There's a good chance I'll be fired. He took me off the project because of what happened last night and said we'd re-evaluate everything after the competition. I made him promise not to yank Dylan's sponsorship right now, when he's trying to win this competition."

Fraya tipped her head to one side. "You stuck up for him? After what he did?"

Brooke frowned and played with her straw again. "Well. Yeah."

"Dylan knew your job was on the line. Right?"

"Well. No. I never really told him that."

"Oh. Okay. So throwing you under the bus was just an accident then."

Brooke's stomach tightened. Just then the waitress appeared with all their food, lifting it from her big tray to the table. Brooke gazed at it, her desire to eat having vanished. "Why'd we order all this?" She reached for a napkin.

"He did throw you under a bus," Fraya insisted. "He should have known that doing something like that was going to reflect on you."

"This isn't about me."

"Like hell it isn't! You're my sister. I don't care about Dylan Schell. I mean, I do, but…you know what I mean."

"I know. And thank you." Her heart softened and she smiled at her big sister. "Yeah, he was acting stupid and selfish. He does tend to be a bit self-involved. But as he once pointed out to me, that's how he got where he is." An ache settled behind her breastbone. "But he's done a lot of good things since we've been back. He really charmed people at the charities we got him working with. The kids love him, and he's genuinely interested in the oceans and doing what he can to help protect them now. He works so hard at his sport, he really does, and he deserves to win."

"Oh no. Oh no no no."

"What?"

"You *were* sleeping with him!" Fraya leaned across the table to whisper the words. "Weren't you? Are you falling for him?"

"Don't be silly!" She tried a laugh, but her face was tight and it came out sounding like a choked sob.

"Oh no! Brooke! What happened?"

Brooke dropped her head into her hand, ignoring the food. "Okay, yes. We slept together. It started in Tahiti. We were trapped in the hotel during that storm, and there wasn't much else to do."

Fraya burst out laughing and Brooke looked up and caught her eye.

Amusement tugged her lips too. "That sounded kind of lame, didn't it?"

Fraya nodded, eyes dancing.

"He's really hot." She sighed. "And actually really, really nice. And we were hot for each other. And it happened. And then…we came back here, and he wanted me to be a date at his friends' wedding—which is a whole other long and crazy story—and so I did because I'd said I'd do anything to make it easier for him to come back to San Amaro. He didn't want to come," she added. "I forgot that part."

Fraya shook her head slowly. "Whoa."

"So I met his friends and went to the wedding and we slept together again and it was really…amazing." She swallowed, her throat tight. "But it turns out he's actually still hung up on this friend…" Okay there were some things she wasn't going to share with Fraya. Not that she didn't trust her, but private things about Corey and Matt and Dylan were…private. "And he just wanted me there so she'd think he's over her. Which is when I realized what a mistake it had been to sleep with him, and then my boss said he *wanted* me to sleep with him, and I felt like he was pimping me out or something, and then there was *no way* I was going to sleep with him again, and Dylan and I kind of argued and I was flirting with Josh and Dylan was jealous and…that's what happened last night."

"Oh holy shitballs." Fraya sat back and gazed at her wide-eyed.

"I know, I know. I'm an idiot. I knew what he's like—a charming playboy who travels the world surfing big waves, partying and drinking and sexing girls." She paused and added a touch bitterly, "Sometimes more than one at a time."

Fraya made another choking sound.

"I have no idea why I thought I could sleep with him and come out of it unscathed. I know I was all kinds of crazy for doing that." She caught Fraya's eye again and held up a hand. "Don't judge me."

"I'm not."

But then memories flooded back like waves onto the shore—the warm admiration in Dylan's eyes when he looked at her, when he touched her, when he told her she was beautiful. When he'd made her face herself in the mirror as they made love so she could see herself, and how sexy and beautiful she'd felt after that.

And not just sexy memories taunted her, but also memories of him laughing and teasing the kids from Daytrippers, so generous with them of his time and experience. Him sitting there seriously discussing the perils of the oceans with people. Him at the wedding, flirting with old ladies and making them blush, him at her parents' place talking to her dad and brother and nephews about the physics of surfing and jumping into the pool with all his clothes on.

And then last night, when she'd made those awful comments to him about not being over Corey, and the flash of hurt she'd seen in his beautiful eyes. Pain shafted through her thinking of that. Because she'd hurt him. And also because—she was so afraid it was true.

Frack. Her head thunked down onto the diner table. She wasn't just falling in love with him. She was already there.

21

The phone woke him. Dylan reached out a hand and slapped it around, found his cell phone and closed his fingers around it.

He peered at it in the dim hotel room, found the talk button and punched it. "Yeah."

"Dylan. It's Holden."

He grunted and rubbed his eyes. "What?"

"Where are you?"

"In bed."

"Are you alone?"

"Sadly, yes."

"Not sadly, jerkoff. What the fuck were you doing last night?"

"Last night?" Dylan closed his eyes. "Went to Aura."

"Yeah. So I heard. So the whole world heard."

"What? What's wrong with that?"

"You stayed out all fucking night, the party turned into a fucking orgy and your pictures are all over the Internet with two naked chicks."

Dylan processed that. "Oh." Oh yeah.

"I've already had a call from Jackson Cole. They want a meeting."

Dylan rolled his eyes. "Of course they do." Brooke. Pissed as usual. Well, good. Because he was pissed at her. "But shit, man, I'm really busy. This is a crazy time."

"They're your sponsor," Holden bit out. "Make time."

"Okay, okay. Let me think." He closed his eyes and envisioned his day and all that he had to do. "If we can meet at the beach, how's three o'clock?"

"Fine. They'll make it work. See you then." He ended the call.

Shit. Holden sounded really pissed. This wasn't that big a deal, was it?

He knew it was.

Whatever.

He stretched in the bed, the sheets working their way down his naked body. Once more he lifted the phone in front of his face to check the time. Holy crap! It was almost one o'clock!

Not a big surprise since he'd been out until after five. But he'd had a good solid five hours of sleep and he was ready to go. He threw back the covers and bounded out of bed. Sunlight poured in when he tossed back the curtains. He checked the sky then the palm trees nearby to judge how windy it was. The trees swayed then tossed more. Awesome. Could be some good waves.

He needed to shower and then get down to Elroy's place. He and Brett were meeting there to watch video from the heats the day before. Then he had some yoga and visualization exercises to do. And then he had to surf. Yeah.

But before that, he'd see Brooke.

He cranked on the shower and after letting it warm he stepped inside.

Fuck, she'd pissed him off last night. Yeah, he knew her job was to keep him out of trouble but Christ, he wanted to think that she was there with him last night because she wanted to be, not because she *had* to be. When she'd said the only reason she was there was because of her job and then also because she thought he was still using her as a cover since he was still in love with Corey… well shit. That wasn't true.

Okay, it had been true at first. Not the part about him being in love with Corey. Coming back and seeing her after all this time had proved to him he was over her. In fact, he was pretty sure there'd been nothing to get over. He'd been messed up last year and thought he had feelings for her that now seemed…huh. But it was true that he'd used Brooke to make sure Corey and Matt knew he'd moved on. At first.

He turned his face into the shower stream. It made him so goddamn happy that he could do that without panicking like he had for months after the accident.

What were his feelings for Corey? He searched around inside himself for the answer. He felt affection for Corey. Friendship. Yeah, they'd had sex, but that had been a lifetime ago. He'd always have a soft spot for her in his heart, but he wasn't in love with her and he never had been. He knew that now, because…

Fuck.

He swallowed and bent his head, hands flat on the shower wall as water streamed down his back.

He knew that now because now he knew what love really felt like. Because he was in love with Brooke.

That's why her comments had pissed him off so much last night.

Well, this was pretty crappy. Last time he'd thought he was in love, he'd been rejected for another guy and because he hadn't been in a very good place, he'd been kinda down about that for a while. But it hadn't taken him long to get over that. He'd been focused pretty intensely on his surfing and getting over the crazy fears that had kept him out of the water and out of the sport he loved so much.

But now…fuck. The idea that Brooke didn't return his feelings, the idea that she viewed him as an irresponsible, immature jerk, nothing but a business obligation, fucking tore up his insides. He felt like sinking to the floor of the shower and just sitting there.

He cranked off the water, yanked the shower curtain aside and grabbed a plush hotel towel.

He'd be seeing her this afternoon. He could talk to her then. Did he have the guts to tell her how he felt, knowing that she didn't feel the same?

She'd sure seemed into him when they'd been in bed. His mouth twisted as he toweled off. Was that wishful thinking? Sex with her had been pretty special.

Pretty special. That was just stupid. Sex with her had been… not to get all sappy, but it had been fucking stupendous.

He walked naked from the bathroom into the hotel room. Okay. He'd see her later and play that by ear, but he had his own "business" to concentrate on too. He was in the middle of a competition he was determined to win. He had to focus on that. People were counting on him to do well in this competition and that was how he could show Brooke he was good enough.

After spending some time working on his boards and talking to Brett about some strategy for his heat, he went to a yoga class to get centered and limbered up. Then he headed to the beach to meet with Brooke and Holden. On the way there, he remembered what Holden had said about last night's party being all over the Internet. How it had turned into an orgy.

Well, it had been a bit raunchy, but he wouldn't call it an orgy.

But yeah, chicks had been taking their clothes off.

And then his gut cramped as he thought about taking Brooke home and then going back to the bar. He'd been pissed off and hurting. He hadn't thought she'd ever know about that though. Now he was realizing she probably did.

He found Holden in the VIP tent, schmoozing as usual. They greeted each other and Dylan looked around. "Okay, where's Brooke? Where do we want to have this meeting?"

"Brooke's not coming." Another guy stepped forward, dark red hair, friendly smile, lots of freckles. Dylan recognized him from the meeting at Jackson Cole. What was his name? Oh yeah, Tim.

"Hey." Dylan forced a smile. "She's not coming? Why not?"

He could only hope this meant they didn't have to meet about this and everything was copacetic, but somehow the crawly feeling on the back of his neck told him that wasn't the case.

"She's been taken off this project," Tim said. "I'm replacing her. Let's go somewhere we can talk."

Dylan's jaw went slack. "Off the project? You mean, my sponsorship deal?"

"Yeah. That's right."

He stood there staring at the guy. Then he gave his head a shake. "I don't get it."

"Hey, not your concern." Tim slapped a hand on Dylan's back. "You need to be worrying about your surfing right now. Come on, let's go sit at that table in the corner."

Tim led the way to a small table and they all sat down. Holden and Tim. No Brooke.

"First of all, don't worry," Tim said. "Your sponsorship deal isn't at risk right now. Nobody wants to stir things up right in the middle of a competition. Everyone wants you to do well this week."

"Yeah." Dylan licked dry lips. "Me too." He forced a smile.

Tim smiled too. "Great. Now, I'm not gonna lie to you. The execs at Jackson Cole weren't too happy about that party last night."

"It was just a party," Dylan muttered. "I didn't break any laws."

"Yeah, well, that's good. Because we might be having a different conversation if that was the case."

Dylan couldn't even think straight. "I don't understand why they took Brooke off this project."

"Well," Tim said. "She was given the job of bringing you back from Tahiti, getting things cleaned up and keeping you out of trouble. And last night she didn't do it."

"What the fuck?" Dylan stared at him. "They blame *her* for last night?"

"Uh…yeah."

His head spun. "I don't get it."

"Brooke was the one who suggested Jackson Cole should sponsor you," Tim explained. "Then you had that accident and broke your foot last year. Kinda looked like we were throwing money away, but she went to bat for you and convinced them that you'd be back and better than ever and still had a great future. So they kept the deal, but when you started acting up they were getting concerned again. Someone had to get things under control, and they figured it should be Brooke, since it was her idea to sponsor you. The executive team wasn't too happy about it all. Brooke wasn't either, but she knew she had to do it to save the deal. And her job, for that matter."

Dylan nodded slowly. Yeah, that was basically what Brooke had told him. But she hadn't told him it had been her idea to sponsor him. She hadn't told him she'd gone to bat for him. To save his sponsorship. And she hadn't told him her job was on the line. Fuck! "Brooke didn't get fired, did she?" he demanded.

"Hey, don't worry about her."

"*Did she get fired?*" He leaned forward and fixed his gaze on Tim. "Just answer my question."

"Uh. I don't think so. Not yet, anyway."

"Fuck!" He glared at Tim. "I'm calling her." He reached for his cell phone.

"You don't need to do that," Tim began, but Dylan had already punched the button for Brooke's cell phone. She didn't answer. He scowled.

"She's off the project," Tim said. "That's probably why she's not answering. It's not her job to deal with you anymore. It's mine." He gave what was probably supposed to be a reassuring smile, but Dylan didn't feel reassured. He felt pissed. And…sick.

"Fuck." He rubbed his forehead.

"So," Tim continued cheerfully. "The folks at Daytrippers apparently were a little concerned about the media coverage from that party last night. That wasn't a really wholesome image to present."

Dylan stared at him. "Oh Christ."

"But like I said, don't worry about that now. Nobody wants to stir things up at this point, right? We just want you to go out there this weekend and do your best. We'll talk more after; I've set up a meeting at the office for Monday afternoon."

Dylan continued to stare at him. "Monday." That would be after the Pro. "Okay."

"I'm here to make sure you have everything you need and liaise with the media for the next few days." Tim smiled.

Dylan could barely hear the man talk above the crazy thoughts that were crowding his head. They better not have fired Brooke. What if they had? What if she'd lost her job over this? And fuck, he didn't want anyone else looking after him! He wanted her. He had to talk to her.

But that wasn't going to happen. Despite his numerous attempts to call her, she wasn't answering. His schedule was crazy busy for the next few days but he managed to go by her apartment a few times, only she was never there. He stopped at her office once in a lame attempt to see her, but she wasn't there either. He even called her parents' home and talked to her mom, who coolly told him she'd pass a message on to Brooke, and when he bumped into her brother Anthony just after an interview, Anthony too was polite but distant. Her family was looking out for her.

She didn't show up at the beach, not at all, and that made him crazy too. He'd been so pumped to have her watching that first heat, to share his triumph with her.

The competition had to take priority, even though now it seemed pathetically unimportant, but when he was out in the water it took all his effort to concentrate on surfing and not on the fact that Brooke wasn't there. He needed to put all that other shit out of his head and focus. Even though his heart ached and he had this antsy urgent need to chuck his surfboard into the waves and run to find Brooke, this had to be done now. Surfing was everything to him.

Well. Maybe not quite everything.

Weird how priorities and goals could change.

And he did win, somehow pulling off decent scores, despite his fucked up head and heart, moving through the heats. Corey and Matt showed up after a heat he'd won to congratulate him. And he got even more annoyed that they were there for him like that when he totally didn't deserve it.

"What's wrong?" Corey asked him when he'd snarled a response to their congratulations. "You just won. You should be happy."

"I am happy."

"You don't look like it." Corey paused, studying him. "Did something happen with you and Brooke?"

"Why would you ask that?" he snapped. "Jesus, the whole world doesn't revolve around relationships."

"Um. Yeah, it kinda does." She and Matt divided a look between them. "What happened?"

"Nothing happened."

"Why isn't she here?"

Fuck. He closed his eyes. "Okay, here's the deal. Brooke and I weren't really dating. She came to Tahiti on business, and our whole relationship was business. She agreed to come to the wedding with me because…" Again, fuck. "Part of her job was keeping me out of trouble, so she agreed. But her boss took her off my sponsorship deal a few days ago, so she has no reason to be here now."

Corey's eyebrows flew up. "Oh." He watched her eyes flicker as she thought through what he'd said. "But—"

"Don't worry about it," Dylan interrupted. "It's none of your business anyway."

Her face fell. Matt frowned. "Hey, man, we're just trying to—"

"Don't bother." Dylan lifted a hand. "It is what it is. And I have stuff to do. Gotta go." He turned and left.

His stomach tight, his teeth gritted, he strode across the sand away from them, ignoring everyone else. He had to stay focused on one thing, and that was surfing. Thinking about anything else, caring about anything else, or any*one* else, wasn't an option right then. If he started going there, he was going to lose it and he needed to keep his shit together to get through this competition.

Then it was Sunday and time for the men's final. It was him and Heath, in the final heat. Just like he'd hoped for. Just like so many had predicted.

He had a pretty simple routine before he competed. He didn't like to eat, he just had some water and listened to some tunes on his iPod. He liked to be the last one at the water's edge when the heat was about to start, then he paddled out, surrounded by the Pacific Ocean rising and dipping beneath him, swelling and undulating. The sun sparkled off the water all around him and he was surrounded by blue. He tried to get a grip on his thoughts and emotions. This was it. This was the moment.

But he couldn't let that take over. He couldn't let that make him nervous. He had to control the adrenaline and use it to his advantage. He knew how to do that. He worked through some of the exercises he'd been taught to help him focus.

His frustration with not being able to get hold of Brooke, his frustration with her, started pushing up inside him. That weird feeling that this *wasn't* the most important thing in the world returned. He needed that hunger, that edge if he was going to win. Didn't he? Or did it even matter? Win, lose, whatever. If he didn't have Brooke, it didn't really matter.

Once more he reminded himself how long he'd been working toward this.

The stillness of the ocean, rocking him gently, the quiet out there, away from the hyper noise of the beach, sank inside him. He sat there, waiting, watching for that perfect wave.

For a moment, all that he'd learned about the ocean recently and all that he'd learned about the ocean through his life came back to him. The power and beauty of it. The world's greatest wilderness, the mysteries of her depths, the beauty of her unpredictability.

The waves developed slowly, like patient lovemaking, taking their time to build and crest. The building pressure grew, and grew…and then crashed in an explosion of vitality. The waves didn't last long, only moments, precious and fragile, yet powerful and magnificent. You had to take advantage of those moments, make the most of them.

Like life.

He watched the water swell toward him, eyeing it critically. Adrenaline flashed heat through his veins. This was it. He was going to catch this wave and do this.

Brooke watched the senior men's final from the bleachers on the beach, sitting among the crowd of half-naked tanned bodies, the scent of coconut sunscreen and the ocean floating in the warm air. The beach was packed with people including television cameramen and photographers with giant long lenses. The booming voice of the announcer echoed up and down the beach.

She stared out at the ocean, watching, waiting for Dylan to catch a wave. God, he had to do this. Heath had just done an amazing run and the crowd was going wild, the announcer winding them up. She picked at the ragged cuticle on her left thumb as she gazed out at the sparkling blue ocean. She watched Dylan turn. This was it. The crowd surged to their feet and she had to stand too if she wanted to see anything. Beside her, Fraya grabbed her husband's arm in a tight hold and bounced up and down a little. The boys watched from the other side of Brooke, caught up in the excitement.

Dylan caught the wave and began to ride it, twisting and turning his way along it, his body in a low crouch, also twisting and turning with apparent ease.

"It's a good wave," she murmured.

"Yeah!" Fraya agreed.

It looked like his feet were superglued to the surfboard, he stuck to it so well as he surfed, and then he caught some air and rotated a full three hundred and sixty degrees in the air. Brooke's breath caught and held as she waited for him to land, momentarily losing sight of him in the rushing white water, but there he was, still standing, still surfing. The crowd went wild.

"Look at that!" the announcer yelled. "*Are you kidding me?* Dylan Schell has got the groove today! Look at him just sitting in that wave forever! Holy barrel of monkeys! He is riding the heck-balls out of that wave!"

Brooke let out her breath and grinned. "Yes!" God, he was so good at that. But so was Heath and their last scores were close. She grabbed hold of Fraya's arm and the three of them held on to each other watching him finish, doing another spin, another jump, and then as the wave flattened, a series of tiny hops across the surface of the water. As he finished and sank into the water, both arms pumped up in the air.

"God, that was good!" Brooke cried above the roar of the crowd.

"It was! So good! He has to win!"

Along with the thousands of other spectators, they anxiously awaited the score. Brooke vibrated and bobbed, nibbling her bottom lip.

Finally, after some inane chit chat that had everyone nearly bursting out of their skin with anticipation, the announcer said, "All right ladies and gentlemen! Here are the results. With a final combined score of nine point five-seven…" He paused. "Dylan Schell has won his first Jackson Cole Pro title!"

The crowd cheered again and people rushed the beach, running out to greet Dylan as he waded out of the ocean, carrying his board.

What would it be like to be one of those down there, rushing to congratulate him? Brooke's smile turned wistful as she watched people lifting Dylan up and carrying him across the beach. Photographers crouched and snapped photos, television cameramen stumbled backward through the sand, carrying their heavy cameras, filming his triumph.

Something expanded in her chest, warm and soft, admiration and happiness for him. He'd done it. He'd won. Oh God, he'd won. She pressed a hand between her breasts, closed her eyes and tipped her head back for a moment.

Eventually he made it to the stage area to receive his trophy. It was hard to see from that far away, but on the Jumbotron Brooke caught his beaming smile and sparkling silver eyes. It was so awesome to see him that happy.

Someone opened a champagne bottle and sprayed him with it, and he laughed. The announcer with the microphone introduced him and the crowd went crazy again. "Hometown boy Dylan Schell comes out on top in the Jackson Cole Pro," he cried into the microphone. "How're you feeling, Dylan?"

"I feel great." Dylan waved to the crowd, still grinning. "I want to thank Heath for a great heat, he really made me have to bring it."

"And bring it you did! You are straight up the hometown hero right now! How did it feel out there?"

"It felt amazing. I saw that wave coming and I knew that was it, and as soon as I was up I felt like I was flying. The wind is good and I was really hoping to catch some air and show everyone here a few tricks..." Another roar erupted from the crowd at his words. "Heath had such a big dig out there. He charged so hard and I knew I had to really go for it."

Fraya squeezed Brooke's arm again. "You were so nervous for him, weren't you?"

Brooke made a face. "I guess I was." Relief made her legs wobble a little.

"Too bad you're not down there with him." Fraya eyed her.

Brooke shook her head, keeping her smile firmly in place. "Nah. He doesn't need any more people down there."

Fraya gave her a chiding look.

"I'm not working with him anymore," she reminded her sister.

"I know."

They watched him get his trophy and the announcer wrapped up the event as people started to make their way out of the bleachers and event officials came in off the water.

"Let's go," Brooke said.

"You sure you don't want to go find him?" They stepped down the bleachers, Fraya holding Jonathan's hand and Brooke holding James's.

"Why can't we go see Dylan?" James asked. "I wanna go see him! We know him."

"Yes, we know him," Brooke said. "But he has lots of people down there with him right now."

"He's going to teach us to surf like that!" Jonathan cried.

Brooke and Fraya exchanged glances.

So her job and her relationship with Barrett were on shaky ground. Dylan had accomplished what he'd wanted to, and now everybody should be happy including Jackson Cole management and the people from Daytrippers and Oceans Alive and all Dylan's other sponsors. Not to mention his team, his agent, Corey and Matt, and all those girls in bikinis mobbing him. But most importantly he should be happy. He'd done it.

It was bittersweet, happiness for him mingling with her own disappointment and aching heart. The competition was done and he'd be leaving for the next event, and she'd figure out what to do about her career. She wasn't sure she could continue to work for Barrett, after he'd all but told her to sleep with Dylan to ensure he behaved the way they wanted him to.

And then that whole mess with the party that night. Brooke had been upset about that for her own reasons, but professionally, she hoped Dylan wasn't going to lose his sponsorship because of it. That didn't seem fair after everything he'd done the last couple of weeks. But she did understand the concern of the people at Daytrippers, since Dylan had gotten involved with some of the kids. Lingering anger at him for being so thoughtless curled inside her.

"Hey Brooke!" She looked up as she and Fraya made their way through the throng of people, and saw Cam from Daytrippers. Like everyone there, he wore a huge smile. "Awesome event, huh? So thrilled for Dylan!"

"Yeah." She paused to speak to him. "He did great. I hope he can continue to work with your organization."

"Oh, definitely! He's done a great job for us!"

"I hope you won't let that one night of partying stop him from continuing to work with you. He really enjoyed working with the kids. And believe me, even though he partied that one night, the entire rest of the time he was here in San Amaro, his behavior was perfect. He's really serious about his sport. He works hard at it."

Cam smiled. "That's true. Don't worry, Brooke, we know the big picture."

Why was she defending him, for God's sake? She and Cam chatted for a couple of minutes, but Fraya and Kevin and the kids were waiting for her, so she said goodbye. But as she again started making her way across the beach, she ran into Corey and Matt.

Her stomach clutched and she pasted on a smile. "Hey! He won!"

"Yeah, he did." Corey gave her a worried look.

"You guys should be with him." Brooke looked back and forth between Corey and Matt.

"I don't think he wants us with him," Corey said.

Brooke's mouth fell open. "What? Of course he does. You're his friends." *More* than friends, she reminded herself with a little stab in her heart.

Corey nibbled her bottom lip and gave her another unhappy look. What? What was wrong?

"He told us you two weren't ever really together," Corey said.

Brooke's mouth dropped open. "He did?"

"Yes. He did." Corey's eyebrows drew down. "I found that hard to believe, after seeing you together."

"Yeah," Matt added. "That night at the wedding…"

His voice trailed off and heat flooded down through Brooke, remembering him walking in on her and Dylan…shnippits.

Matt cleared his throat. "It really seemed like you two were into each other."

Brooke's mind scrambled. She opened her mouth to say something, but no words came to her. "It was business," she finally mumbled. "Not the…I mean…"

"It's amazing that he won." Corey filled the awkward silence. "Considering how pissed off he was. At something. It almost seemed like it was at us." She shot Matt a glance. "I was afraid he wasn't going to be able to focus on his surfing. But he did it."

"Pissed off?" Brooke ran her tongue over her teeth. "I haven't talked to him for a few days. If anyone should be pissed off, it should be me."

"And are you?" Matt asked.

Brooke hesitated. "I don't know. I was. He…" She bent her head and looked briefly at the sand. "He took me home and went back to the party."

Hell, that wasn't what she'd meant to say. This wasn't about her and her hurt feelings.

"I mean, he caused a lot of trouble by going back to that party. My job's at risk. So's his sponsorship. Although winning probably helped that."

"Your job's at risk?" Corey's eyes widened. "And his sponsorship?"

"Yes." Brooke bit her lip. "It was my job to keep him out of trouble while he's here." She made a little face at them. "He'd been in a bit of trouble in the media and Jackson Cole execs weren't too impressed by that. They were considering cancelling his sponsorship deal."

"He never told us that," Matt said slowly, folding his arms across his broad chest. "He said you came with him to the wedding because it was part of your job to keep an eye on him, but I didn't realize it was that serious."

"Well, I don't suppose it's something he wanted to talk about much. And I probably shouldn't be telling you this now either. In fact, I have no idea why we're having this conversation."

"Dylan's our friend." Corey slipped her hand through Matt's arm and hugged it. "We care about him. If he's hurting, we want to help."

"Yeah, he told me about your *friendship*." The words slipped out before she could stop them.

Corey lips parted and she looked up at her husband. Her cheeks went faintly pink. "Oh really."

"It's none of my business." Brooke's own face heated. She should never have brought that up.

"Well. If Dylan told you about that…that doesn't really sound like a 'business' discussion." Corey tilted her head and gave Matt another questioning look. He gave a tiny nod. Corey looked back at Brooke and met her eyes steadily. "That bothers you, doesn't it?"

Brooke swallowed. "What? You and Dylan…being together? No."

"Bullshit." Corey smiled. "Brooke, I love my husband. Not Dylan. Dylan's a friend and nothing more."

"Maybe we should go somewhere else to have this conversation," Matt said.

"I'm just on my way home." Brooke took a step back. "My sister and her husband are waiting for me." The crowd had thinned out. "There's not really anything to talk about."

"I think you should know what happened with Dylan last year."

"I know what happened."

"Do you? Do you know that he almost died in that accident he had?"

"Um." She blinked. "Yes. It was in the news. He had a broken foot."

"It was more than that. He was trapped under water and couldn't get free. He lost consciousness before they could get him out and they had to resuscitate him on the beach."

She remembered him talking about being slammed by the wave, his leash caught, holding him underwater. Her stomach clenched and a shiver worked over her skin.

"He nearly died. He was a little messed up after that," Corey said. "Okay, a lot messed up. He came here to do some rehab while he was recovering. We didn't realize at first what was wrong. He was having nightmares. Flashbacks. Panic attacks. He was afraid to go in the water. He was talking about giving up his surfing career."

A muted buzzing noise sounded in Brooke's ears, beneath Corey's soft voice. She remembered the nightmare he'd had that night in Tahiti, how he'd woken up sweating. "He said he asked you to go on the tour with him. That doesn't sound like he was thinking of giving it up."

"Asking me to go with him just shows how confused he was." Corey shook her head. "Yes, he thought he had feelings for me, but even then, he knew he really didn't love me. Not like that. He didn't really want me to go with him. He was just terrified. I think he was terrified of losing the one thing that's been important in his life. His surfing. He has this idea that that's all he can do. And if he couldn't do that, who would he be?"

Brooke let Corey's words sink in, her brain trying to make sense of it all. "I know he was having nightmares. Did he have PTSD?"

Corey shrugged. "I'm not a psychologist, but he definitely had some symptoms. But he was keeping it all inside him. He didn't tell us about any of this, we found out by accident. Sort of. He needed help to get through it, and we're so, so glad he did. But when we talked to him the other day…it was like he was back in that bad place again. I was worried for him, worried he wasn't going to be able to do it."

"But he did." Brooke looked away from Corey and focused on a nearby palm tree. "Obviously he was able to focus on his surfing. That's one thing he's good at. Focusing on himself."

"Well. I guess it takes a certain amount of that to become the best surfer in the world," Matt said quietly. "But I don't think it's fair to say that he doesn't care about anything but himself."

"That's for damn sure," Corey added. "When he wanted me to go with him last year and I turned him down, he knew right away why that was. It was because I was in love with Matt, even though *I* didn't realize it. I mean, we all know Dylan wasn't really in love with me, but what he did was the most unselfish thing possible—he stepped aside so Matt and I could be together. That's not a guy who only thinks about himself."

Brooke shook her head and rubbed her forehead. "No. I know that. I didn't mean that."

"Brooke." Corey spoke gently and Brooke met her eyes. The softness there made her throat tighten. "Clearly this wasn't all business between you."

Brooke sighed. "Fine. We did kind of get involved. But that was a mistake. Because even though I..." She swallowed. "Even though I care about him, he made his choice. I'm happy for him, I'm so happy that he won, and his dream came true. I know how hard he's worked for this. But to me...you can't have real happiness without thinking of others, and he only thinks about himself. He made that clear the night of the party. He knew how important it was to be a team player, to keep out of trouble, for the sake of his sponsors, the charities he worked with..." She gave a bitter laugh. "And I even had some crazy idea he cared about me. But obviously he didn't. So I wish him well."

Corey and Matt shared another concerned look.

"Hey, it's okay." She pasted on a tight smile. "I'm okay, Dylan's okay. He won! He's probably on top of the world right now!"

22

Dylan was the center of attention, people congratulating him, hugging him, slapping him on the back, crowding around him. It was what he'd dreamed of and imagined, everything he'd always wanted. He'd won! Hot fuck, he'd done it!

Before he could do anything else, he was dragged off to pee in a cup for the drug testing that the winners and random other surfers had to undergo. Once that was done, he moved on to hours of interviews and photographs and autograph signings. It was surreal. It was what he'd been waiting his whole life for. He'd just won a hundred grand! He smiled until his face hurt, laughed and gave the media all the sound bites they needed, but it was like he was moving through a dream.

When he posed for pictures with some of the kids from Daytrippers who'd been given prime viewing spots, the joy on their faces was as great as his own, which gave him pause. Wow. They were happy for him! Damn, that felt good, knowing that he'd done something good for them and that Daytrippers would continue to benefit from his involvement. He wanted to do more.

Much as he was enjoying this, much as he'd waited his whole life for this moment, hours later he found himself wanting to get away from the crowds of people and all the noise and hype, and be alone for a few minutes. His empty hotel room didn't appeal to him. No, where he really wanted to be was back out there on the water. Floating on the swelling ocean, surrounded by water, made small and insignificant by the immensity and power of it. That was where he wanted to be. Just him and the ocean.

Tempting as it was to ditch everything, he had a new watchdog keeping track of his every move. He was pretty sure Tim wouldn't let him make a run for it. Neither would Brooke have, if she'd been there. But if she'd been there, he wouldn't *want* to make a run for it.

Christ.

"Congratulations, Dylan," Tim said with a huge smile and a slap on the shoulder. "You rocked out there."

"Yeah, thanks man."

Maybe now he'd won and the competition was over, the dude would leave him alone. But no. Tim was stuck like glue. Dylan started to feel pressure building up inside him, more pressure even than before the competition. Or maybe it was just different. He had to get away. He had to be alone. He needed time.

Finally, finally he'd done every interview he needed to, talked to every sports reporter and surfing blogger, every bigwig from ICON Entertainment, the ASP, Jackson Cole and his other sponsors. He thanked them all sincerely for their part in giving him a chance to achieve his dream. He expressed his desire to continue to work with them, again sincerely, hoping he hadn't completely blown everything at the exact time he'd finally won.

He wanted to mention Brooke, to make sure she was okay, but it was hard to work that into the conversation without seeming weird.

Wondering if Tim was going to accompany him to his hotel room and spend the night, he made a break for it when the guy got sidetracked talking to the guys from ICON. He slipped out through the crowd that had gathered around the stage for the last concert. Out of his wetsuit, now dressed in board shorts and a T-shirt, sunglasses and a ball cap, he headed for his car with one of his boards.

Breaker Beach had a lot of good memories for him, and now even more so. Returning to the beach where he'd learned to surf as a kid to win the Jackson Cole Pro was like a dream come true. He drove back up into town, along Shore Drive, past Corey's new chocolate shop that he hadn't even checked out yet. Damn. He'd like to see it. But not now. He also passed Matt's brew pub and all the other little businesses that lined the streets, the sidewalks still full of tourists in town for the event as people wound down their weekend.

He was supposed to be out celebrating and partying, which is what he usually did after any competition, never mind one that he'd won. He snorted as he drove to the very end of Shore Drive and pulled into the parking lot near Cave Road. This end of the beach was quieter, the water calmer here, not good for surfing at all. It was more of a family beach and there were still a few people out enjoying the late afternoon sunshine. He parked in another lot where sand spilled from the beach onto the pavement, grabbed his board and headed toward the water. He just wanted to paddle out and sit there and think for a while.

So he did.

Drifting on the gently rocking water, straddling the board, the wind in his ears, he gazed around him at the expanse of water that seemed to go on forever. He'd sat on this ocean in so many places—Tahiti was right over there. Well, a long ways over there. He imagined what would happen if he kept paddling toward it. How long would it take him to get there?

Then he laughed at himself. He'd never get there alive. He was thinking crazy thoughts.

He tipped his head up to the sky, so bright blue it was almost painful, the sun now lower in the sky lighting up the puffy clouds in stark white and palest peach. Awesome.

He let out a long, long breath. Alone. He was alone. He usually didn't want to be alone, hadn't wanted to be alone much since his accident last year. Any time he was alone, he started getting scared and that made him want to do crazy things like drink a lot and smoke dope and sleep with as many girls as he could.

What an idiot.

So he'd won. But at what cost? What had he lost?

Possibly his sponsorship. Possibly his work with the charities that he'd surprisingly enjoyed. His friends. And Brooke.

He didn't know if she'd ever been his to lose.

With a heavy ache in his chest, he closed his eyes and turned his face into the ocean breeze. A moment later, he opened his eyes and barked out a short laugh. Last time he'd been here in San Amaro, he hadn't wanted to leave. He'd been afraid to get back in the water, afraid of failing, mostly. And he'd made the mistake of thinking he needed a woman—Corey—to help him through that.

Now once again he didn't want to leave San Amaro but for a completely different reason. He wasn't going to make the mistake of asking Brooke to go with him. That was laughable. She hated his guts right now and besides, her life was here. She'd told him how much she loved her home, the city, her friends, the family she was so close to. That close family he'd envied.

He wanted those things that were so important to Brooke. He wanted a home. He wanted friends. He wanted family. He wanted Brooke.

He returned to his hotel room, alone, and for the first time in a long time, he was okay with that. He turned off his cell phone and the phone in the room and tried to sleep. It took a while, he was still so jacked up on adrenaline and excitement. His mind wandered to Brooke and having her in his bed, remembering touching her and tasting her and being inside her. And he got hard. Maybe a fast hand job would relieve some stress and help him sleep.

And maybe it did help, because he fell asleep. All night long he dreamed of Brooke, but the dreams turned frustrating. They were in the water, floating on surfboards, and he was trying to get to her, paddling, paddling, but he couldn't get closer; she kept drifting just beyond his reach.

He awoke in the morning feeling tired, irritable and out of sorts. He dressed for his meeting with Holden and the people at Jackson Cole and went down to the hotel restaurant for some breakfast. There he ran into Brooke's sister Fraya.

"Oh hi." He attempted a smile.

"Dylan. Congratulations." She gave him a narrow-eyed, cool look.

"Uh. Thanks."

They eyed each other.

"I was there yesterday watching you win. With Brooke."

His gut clenched. "She was there?"

"Of course she was there."

He shook his head. "She didn't have to be. I guess she probably told you we're not working together anymore."

"Yeah, she told me." She rolled her eyes. "She told me you threw her under a bus."

"What the f—under a *bus*?"

"Not literally, for God's sake. I meant that night you took her home and then went back to party. Didn't you know you were putting her job on the line? Maybe her entire career? Did you even think that you might be hurting her feelings? Have you ever thought of anyone but yourself?"

He took a step back, blinking. She might as well have poked him in the chest with her finger, she was so pissed. "Whoa." He held up his hands. "Hold on here." He glanced around the lobby of the hotel to see who was paying attention. Yeah, only everyone in the room. "You got some kind of problem with me?"

"Yeah, I do." She followed his retreat, like an angry mama bear defending her cub. And he remembered that Brooke was the baby of the family and as she put it, they never let her forget it. Big sister here was on the warpath. Damn. That was sweet that Brooke had people sticking up for her like that. Nobody'd ever done that for him. He grinned.

Fraya scowled at him. "What's so funny?"

"It's not funny." He looked around again. "Look, if you want to talk, let's go have coffee or something, where we're not putting on a big show."

She too cast her eyes around and grimaced. "Shit. Sorry."

"Come on. I was about to have breakfast."

"I don't have long. I have a breakfast meeting with a client in…" She glanced at her watch. "Ten minutes."

"Okay. Ten minutes." He led the way into the restaurant and they were seated at a booth.

"Okay, obviously you're angry at me." He picked up his cup of coffee. "I know I screwed up going back to that party, but I didn't know it was going to be such a big deal." He rolled his eyes.

Fraya nodded at the waitress to pour coffee into her cup too.

"Ready to order?" the girl asked cheerily.

"Cheese omelet with a side of fruit," he said.

"Toast?"

"No, thanks."

The girl looked at Fraya who shook her head. "Just coffee."

"All righty." The girl scooped up the menus and left.

"Nothing happened that night. I wasn't even drinking, and I went home alone."

Fraya lifted her chin and looked down her nose at him. "Uh huh."

His shoulders tensed. "It's the truth. You can ask Brooke, but whatever my faults are, and I know I have lots, I don't lie."

She nodded. "Still. It was a douchey move to drop her off and then go back to the party."

He pursed his lips. "It wasn't as if we were on a date. It was all business. She made that pretty damn clear."

"Yeah, and you know why?" She leaned across the table.

"Yeah, I know why. Because getting involved with someone like me would be stupid. I'm not worth it."

Fraya opened her mouth then closed it. She sat back in her seat and regarded him thoughtfully.

"What? It's true. I know she realized she'd screwed up by… well, never mind."

"I know you two slept together."

"Oh. Well. We never should have done that. For some twisted reason, I thought she actually cared about me. Like I said, she made it clear that night she didn't."

"Oh for God's sake." Fraya stared at him, shaking her head. "This is priceless."

"What?" He frowned and took a sip of his hot coffee, hoping some caffeine would clear his head and put him in a better mood. Because this conversation sure as hell wasn't doing it.

"Don't you get why she was making it all business?"

"Uh…"

"She was protecting herself." She leaned forward. "She thought you were in love with someone else. She thought you were using her. And on top of that, her asshole boss was telling her to sleep with you to keep you out of trouble."

Dylan's jaw went slack and he almost dropped the cup of coffee he held. "Huh?"

"I guess she never told you the things he said to her. She also never told you that her job was on the line and that if she didn't succeed in getting you back to San Amaro and cleaning up your act, she could lose her job."

"Uh. No. She didn't tell me, but Tim did." He sat there gaping at her. "*Her boss sent her to Tahiti to sleep with me?*"

"No! He sent her there to bring you home. It wasn't until later that he suggested doing that. Which was long after it had already happened, I understand."

Heat slid up into his face. "Well."

"After he said that, she was determined to stay away from you. She was so angry that her boss thought she would do something like that. Angry and hurt. And she was angry and hurt when you took her home and then went back to the party without her."

He was having a hard time making sense of all this. "I'm not in love with someone else."

Fraya smiled. "You were hurt when she backed off, weren't you?"

He frowned.

"Yeah, you were." She grinned. "I really think you two need to talk."

His eyes widened. "Tell me about it! I've tried to get hold of her for days! Not that I had much time, but shit, she wouldn't take my calls, I couldn't find her anywhere, and nobody would help me get hold of her."

"Really? You tried?"

"Yes! They took her away and replaced her with that dumbass Tim. Sorry." He rubbed his forehead. "He's not really a dumbass, but he's not Brooke. You know? I know I screwed up and I really didn't mean to make her lose her job. Fuck!" He stared down at his coffee. "She doesn't have to put up with a boss who talks to her like that! Did he really expect that she would do something like that?"

She shrugged. "I guess he did. She loves her job. Not her boss, but she likes working for Jackson Cole. I told her she should sue him for sexual harassment. Or quit."

"She doesn't want to quit."

"Nope." She glanced at her watch. "I have to go." She slid out of the booth.

"Fraya."

"Yes?" She turned back.

"Brooke's lucky to have a sister like you. Family like you."

Her eyes softened. "Thanks. I thought you might want to punch me."

He shook his head. "I'm the one who should be punched."

She gave him a slow smile. "There might be hope for you, Dylan Schell."

Then she walked out of the restaurant. He watched her, struck by how much the way she moved was like Brooke. From the back, if her hair was longer, it could be Brooke.

The waitress returned with his breakfast. He ate mindlessly, forking up scrambled eggs and melted cheese, stabbing the tines into pieces of melon and strawberries.

Jesus Christ. What kind of douchebag was Brooke working for? No wonder she'd been so adamant she had to get him home to San Amaro. And keep him out of trouble.

Once again, he had to wonder if she'd slept with him for the sake of keeping her job. But he didn't have to think very hard about it. What had happened in Tahiti hadn't been planned, he was certain of it, and she'd tried so hard to keep things businesslike between them when they got back.

The food in his stomach turned to a rock. He'd gotten her in trouble; he'd known when Tim had told him he'd be working with him instead of Brooke. Now it was driven home to him even more that in that thoughtless, careless night of partying, trying to distract himself from the fact that Brooke had wised up to the fact that he was not someone worth caring about, trying to pretend he wasn't jealous of those other guys she'd been flirting with and dancing with, he'd hurt her. He'd hurt her career. He was an asshole.

He'd been hurt, but he'd also been thoughtless and selfish and stupid that night, going back to that party without Brooke. He hadn't even thought of the impact his actions would have on her. He hadn't been thinking about himself either, but whatever the consequences of that were for him, he'd deal with it. But the consequences for her…fuck.

He called himself all kinds of names. He'd fucking let her down and all she'd done was be loyal and generous and caring. Trying to do the right thing. Flying all the way to Tahiti to drag his sorry ass back home to California, even though she was afraid of flying. Going to the wedding with him so he didn't look like a big loser to his friends. Setting up all those charity events, not only for him but for the kids and the oceans. All she was doing was trying to live a life that mattered, and all he was doing was pissing his life away.

No wonder he'd been all alone when he'd won the damn competition. He deserved to be alone.

He checked his cell phone for the time. He was supposed to be at that meeting at Jackson Cole in less than half an hour. Great. Good times.

23

Brooke knew Dylan was in the building. She knew the big meeting had been scheduled and her stomach cramped with nerves at the thought that they might end the sponsorship deal with him. She'd talked to Tim earlier that day, and he didn't think it would happen since Dylan had just won the Jackson Cole Pro. But still. They were dealing with Barrett there, and, well, he was a jerk.

Her gaze fell on her desk calendar and the little circle she'd drawn around last Friday's date. She closed her eyes briefly, once more counting back the days to Tahiti, pressing a hand to her stomach, wondering…damn. What would she do if… She shook her head and got up from her desk.

She walked through the office to where she could peek from behind a cubicle partition and see into the conference room through the glass wall. She watched Dylan walk into the room and seeing him made her heart constrict. He smiled that white sexy smile, his face tanned, his dark hair hanging onto his forehead. His loose shirt hung from his broad shoulders, and he moved with that easy athletic grace she now knew so well.

She opened her eyes and watched them all take their seats and begin talking. She couldn't hear a word, but she watched Dylan. He didn't smile again once they began talking. He leaned forward to say something and she wished she could read lips.

Then someone came up behind her and said, "What are you doing, Brooke?"

With a jump, she made an excuse and fled back to her office, where she tried hard to distract herself with work. But that wasn't so easily done.

Tim appeared in her door long before she thought the meeting would end. She frowned at him. "Hey. Done already?"

"Yeah." He shook his head and lowered himself into a chair. "Okay. That didn't go like I'd expected."

Her nerves leaped. "What happened?" She bit her lip and curled her fingers around a pen.

"Dylan dumped us."

She blinked. "What?"

"He dumped us. He told us he didn't want to accept sponsorship money from a company that would treat one of its employees like they treated you."

She could only stare at him, a buzzing noise in her ears. His words replayed in her head and still didn't make sense. "Me?"

A smile ghosted across his mouth. "Yeah. You. Somehow he knew some things Barrett said to you."

Her jaw dropped. "How? I haven't even talked to him since then."

"I don't know how. But apparently it was true because Barrett just about had a stroke. I've never seen his face so red."

"But…oh my God. Pierson was in that meeting too." The VP of Marketing.

"Yep."

"Oh my God," she said again, still processing it all. "So we're not sponsoring him anymore?"

"Nope."

"Because of *me*?" She stood, adrenaline rushing through her veins. "Oh my God, no!"

"Yep."

"But…but…he can't do that."

"He did."

"He's crazy!"

Tim laughed. "You know what? I don't think so. He might be a little rash, but not crazy. And frankly…" He shrugged. "I was impressed. He also told them that he was the one who'd screwed up by going to that party that night, not you. He told them it wasn't your fault, that he'd taken you home and dropped you off and he'd gone back to the party."

She sank back into her chair again. She rubbed her temples. "Barrett must be so furious."

"Yeah. That's an understatement. He started talking about suing Dylan for breach of contract."

"Ack!"

"I know."

"I'm going to be fired for sure."

"Doubtful. Dylan told them if they sued him or fired you, he'd go public with the things Barrett said to you. That was when I thought Pierson was going to have a stroke, and we were going to have to call an ambulance for both of them."

She felt as if she was choking. She lifted a hand to her throat. "Arghrahg," she began. She cleared her throat. She nibbled her bottom lip. Her eyes darted around the room. "What should I do?"

"Go for lunch? It's noon."

"Lunch? Are you kidding me?"

He grinned. "Yeah, you're right. This has been quite the morning. We'll go for drinks instead."

"I can't go out drinking! I'm about to lose my job! And what about Dylan? Oh my God. What's he going to do?"

"He just won the Jackson Cole Pro. Pretty sure he can pick and choose from the sponsors lined up at his door now."

"Oh." She pressed her lips together, gazing at him. "Yeah. Maybe. Oh. Wow." She let out a long breath and leaned back into the chair. "You know, I think I'm gonna take you up on that liquid lunch offer. Let's go."

Tim laughed and led the way out. They took his car.

"Where to?" he asked. "Laguna Dorada?"

"No!"

"Oookay. Breaker Café?"

"Sure."

But when it came time to order, she hesitated. "I think I'll have a crantini," she said. "But without the vodka."

"That would be cranberry juice," the server said.

"Right."

Tim shook his head and ordered a Bloody Mary. "*With* the vodka," he added. "Make it a double."

"I have to talk to Dylan," Brooke said.

Tim pointed at her cell phone sitting on the table. "Call him. He was upset because you weren't answering his calls."

"Really?"

"What's with you two, anyway?" He leaned his elbows on the table.

"Nothing."

He lifted an eyebrow but said nothing.

She picked up her phone, found Dylan in her contacts and pushed the button to call him. Fully expecting him to not answer, when he did, her stomach did a little flip. "Dylan. Hi. It's Brooke."

"Brooke. Hi." His low deep voice made her close her eyes.

"Why did you do that?" she whispered.

Silence. Did he know what she was talking about?

"Because you're worth it," he finally said. "And I'm not."

"What are you talking about?"

Another pause. "I know they wanted to fire me. I know I screwed up. But it wasn't your fault and I didn't want you to pay the price for my mistake."

"Oh Dylan." She closed her eyes and the noise of the bar she and Tim sat in faded away. Her throat constricted. "You shouldn't have done that. We were your biggest sponsor."

"Yeah. I know. But I had to."

"How did you know?"

"That doesn't matter. I'm glad you called. I wanted to talk to you before I go."

Her throat closed up. "You're leaving?"

"Yeah. I fly out tomorrow. I just wanted to say thank you for everything you did. I know you put your job on the line for me. I know it was your idea to sponsor me, and I feel like crap that I made that so painful for you. Before I'd even met you, I was acting like a spoiled selfish jerk and you were trying to save my butt. So thank you, for that, and for introducing me to those great charities. It felt good helping them."

"You still can." Her voice thickened, her eyes burning. She covered her eyes with her hand, her elbow on the table.

"Yeah, I know. I think I will."

Her throat ached so much she couldn't talk. Her lips pushed out helplessly. He was leaving. She tried to swallow. Tried again. "Dylan."

"Don't let them treat you like that. Stand up for yourself. Like I said, you're worth it. You hear me?"

She nodded, which was ridiculous because he couldn't see her. A tear dropped onto the polished wood table.

"'Bye, Brooke." And then the phone went dead.

She stayed like that for long moments, the phone to her ear, her hand over her eyes, trying to get her emotions under control. She hadn't congratulated him on winning. She hadn't told him that her period was late. And that made her throat hurt even more.

When she could get air into her constricted esophagus and down into her lungs, she licked her lips and lowered her hand. She clicked off her phone and gave Tim a smile.

"You okay?" He leaned forward, eyebrows drawn together above his nose.

"Oh yeah. Of course. Well, not really. But yeah."

His eyebrows lifted. "It's good you're sure."

"Let's go. We'd better get back to the office."

Back in Tim's car heading toward the office, she reached for the knob of the radio and turned it on, wanting some music to drown out the silence and the ache throbbing in her chest. Then she leaned her head back into the seat and listened to Maroon 5 while she stared out the window at passing traffic.

What had Dylan done? He'd killed her, that was what. God. What kind of crazy gesture had that been, going into that meeting and taking a stand like that? She pressed a hand to her chest where it ached.

But he was leaving.

Of course he was leaving. She'd known all along he would leave. That was his life. But dammit, once more she was reminded that deep inside he was a good man. And her words to Corey and Matt returned to her, how he was so self-absorbed he didn't even realize he'd done something wrong. God. He sure knew how to make up for it when he screwed up.

He may have saved her job. Maybe not. Who knew how Barrett was going to take to being humiliated like that. But Dylan's threat was real, and after what he'd done that morning, giving up such a lucrative deal on principle, there couldn't be anyone who thought he wouldn't make good on that threat.

Another tear slid down her cheek.

She'd have to give some serious thought to whether she wanted to stay at Jackson Cole. God, if Dylan could take a stand like that, she should be able to too. Those things Barrett had said to her were unacceptable.

Maybe Dylan had saved her job for nothing. Maybe she'd quit. Wouldn't that be funny? A hysterical sob rose in the back of her throat.

Quit and do what, exactly?

Don't be hasty. She swiped fingertips across her wet cheek. God, Tim probably thought she was a nutbar, crying like this.

"And in breakings news," the radio announcer spoke, Adam Levine done singing, "there are unconfirmed reports that drug tests have revealed ASP champion surfer Dylan Schell may have consumed banned substances prior to competing and winning yesterday's Jackson Cole Pro."

Brooke lurched forward in her seat. Her head whipped around to look at Tim. "Did you hear that?"

"Yeah."

She stared at his frowning profile. "Did they just say what I think they said?"

"They did say *unconfirmed* reports."

"Oh holy hobbling Christ on a crutch."

Sitting in his hotel room, Dylan ended the call with Brooke. His face felt tight, his belly muscles rigid, a feeling of pressure building inside him. He was glad she'd called so he'd had the chance to say thank you, but he was kind of embarrassed she'd found out about what he'd done so quickly. He'd thought maybe he'd be gone before she found out.

She'd probably give him shit and call him crazy for throwing in the towel on the sponsorship deal that she'd worked so hard to salvage. Now it was all for nothing. He still wasn't sure if he'd done anything good, or if it had just been another stupid screw up. But he felt better. So it had to be kinda good. Maybe. Sort of.

He tossed the phone on the bed, but as it landed, it rang. He frowned and reached for it. Brooke calling back maybe?

But no. It was Holden. Jesus, what now?

He hadn't told Holden what he was going to do, and although Holden had sat there nodding and supportive during the meeting, afterward the guy had been irate that he hadn't known. How could Dylan have told him though, when he'd had no idea until he sat in that meeting what he had to do? He'd tried to explain things to Holden after the meeting. Holden had nodded stiffly and told him he'd have to think about whether he could continue to represent him. Fuck it. Now he was really on his own. The only people he hadn't alienated were Elroy and Brett.

So what was Holden calling about? To finish things off? He answered the call.

"Where are you?" Holden immediately demanded.

"I'm in the middle of a drunken orgy," Dylan said. "With twenty-seven girls."

"Shut the fuck up, this is no time for jokes. Where are you?"

Jesus. "In my hotel room."

"Alone?"

Dylan sighed and shoved his hair back. "Yes. Alone." Hadn't he just been reflecting that he was pretty much alone in the world? Boo hoo.

"I'm on my way. Don't move."

Ooookay. Dylan gave the phone a look and tossed it back onto the bed. Guess this was happening now.

The banging on the door moments later told him Holden hadn't been very far away when he'd called. He opened the door and Holden burst in. His hair was loose from its usual ponytail as if he'd run his hands through it, and his eyes blazed. "Sit down. You're going to want to be sitting for this."

Dylan made a face and sat on the side of the bed. He held his arms out at his side. "I'm sitting."

"Were you smoking dope this week?"

Dylan's head jerked back. "What? No. I've barely even had a beer all week."

"Are you sure? Are you being honest with me?"

"What's going on, Holden?" Dylan's heart started thudding against his ribs.

"Positive drug test. TCP. Lionel Collier just notified me." The Rules & Discipline Judge from the ASP.

Dylan could only stare blankly at Holden. "No. That's not right."

"They're not usually wrong, Dylan. Come on."

"I swear to you Holden, I wasn't smoking. I haven't touched the stuff in…well months actually. Since before Tahiti. There's no way it would stay in my body that long."

Holden gave him a long, hard look then nodded. "Okay. We have to figure out what we're going to do about this."

Dylan's blood ran cold. "I'm gonna lose my title, aren't I?"

"Yeah. And probably be suspended for a year. Unless we prove it's a mistake."

"Shit." Dylan's body went numb.

Jesus Christ. Jesus fucking Christ. Could things get any worse, for fuck's sake?

He bowed his head and stared at the carpet. It was too much. He lifted his head and looked at Holden. "Just forget it. I give up. Just take a gun and shoot me."

Holden's lips twitched. "A little while ago I would have, if I'd had a gun."

"I know. I promise you, Holden, I didn't do it. But fuck, man. I'm losing my title. I've lost my biggest sponsor."

"You didn't lose them. You dumped them. Your choice."

"Whatever. I figured I'd lost my agent. I've lost my friends. And I've lost…the woman I love. Fuck, that sounds sappy."

Holden's eyebrows lifted. "You? In love?"

Dylan's lips twisted. "Hard to believe, huh?"

"Brooke Lowry."

"Yeah."

"Nice gesture for her today. Stupid, but nice."

"Thanks. I'm trying to reform so I'm not just stupid, but both stupid *and* nice."

"Shit, Dylan." Their eyes met and they both gave rueful smiles.

"I know." Dylan rubbed his forehead. "What happens now?"

"They do an investigation. You have the opportunity to have Sample B tested. That's the second sample they take."

Dylan nodded. He was well familiar with the testing protocol.

"You can also present a defense in writing to the Rules & Discipline Judge with an explanation of any mitigating circumstances, any physical or medical reasons for the positive drug test, and any supporting evidence."

"Like what?"

"I don't know. Witnesses, doctors' notes."

"As if I'm going to have a witness who *didn't* see me smoke dope. That would be….oh, everybody."

Holden paced back and forth across the carpet. "You don't seriously just want to accept this, do you?"

Dylan thought about that. "I don't know. I don't fucking know. Right now, it doesn't matter. I'll probably regret saying that at some point."

"Yeah. You will. Come on, buddy. This is your life. Don't throw it away."

Another knock on the door startled him. Dylan glanced at Holden but rose to his feet and crossed to the door. When he opened it, Corey and Matt stood there.

"Whoa." He stared at them. "What are you doing here?"

"We heard the news," Matt said. "Is it true?"

"No, it's not fucking true."

"So there wasn't a positive drug test? They said on the news it was unconfirmed."

Dylan sighed. "Yeah, there was a positive drug test. Apparently. Come in."

He stepped aside so they could enter the room. They both wore identical expressions of concern. "Why are you here?" he asked again.

"Because we're your friends and we came to support you, asshole," Matt said.

Dylan nodded. "I *was* an asshole to you guys the other day."

"Yeah. You were. But it wasn't the first time and probably won't be the last. Christ only knows why we still care."

Dylan's heart clenched and he swallowed. "What if it's true? What if I did do drugs?"

"Did you?"

"No."

Matt nodded. "Okay. I believe you. What are we going to do about it?"

We? Dylan stared at him. His gaze shifted to Corey, standing there with her arm linked through Matt's, and she nodded. "What can we do?"

The silence stretched out. Dylan's heart bumped and his muscles jumped and twitched. His throat felt raw when he swallowed. "I don't know," he finally said, his voice hoarse. "We were just talking about options."

Matt nodded and grabbed a chair. He held it for Corey then pulled another one out from the small table. "Okay. Let's hear 'em."

Holden repeated what he'd told Dylan and told them more about the rules and appeal procedures. Dylan knew about this, although he'd never been involved in this kind of situation before. But it happened. To other people. Not to him.

Corey and Matt were there for him. That thought kept going around and around in his head. He didn't deserve it. He didn't deserve them. But fuck, he was glad they were there and he wasn't all alone in this mess.

The next knock at the door was so quiet he almost didn't hear it over their voices as they talked. He listened and didn't hear anything, but curious, he got up and moved to the door even as he still listened to Holden. He cracked open the door, almost expecting to see nothing, but he froze at seeing Brooke.

24

Brooke stood there with nerves fluttering in her stomach as Dylan opened the door and stared at her. "Brooke."

She nodded.

"What are *you* doing here?"

"I heard on the radio. About the drug test."

He rubbed the back of his head. "You and the whole world, apparently."

"Are you okay?"

He looked at her for a long moment. She felt as if a magnetic force was tugging her nearer to him and her body moved toward him. She tried to read the expression on his face, the emotions playing over his features as his eyes darkened and his mouth softened. "Yeah," he finally said softly. "I'm okay." He reached out a hand and touched her hair.

Again her body shifted closer to his, close enough to feel his body heat, to breathe in his scent. The door swung shut behind her with a click as she moved into the hotel room.

"What happened?" she asked, her voice husky.

"One of my samples tested positive for TCP."

"Marijuana?"

He nodded. And waited.

"You haven't been smoking it," she said firmly. "Unless…that night…" She looked into his eyes.

He met her gaze steadily. "Do you think I would do that? When I'm in a competition and I know I could be tested at any time?"

She didn't even hesitate. "No."

He closed his eyes briefly and slid his hand around the nape of her neck. He drew her to him, against his chest, and she moved there effortlessly. He felt so good. His other arm slid around her and she wrapped her arms around his waist and held on.

"Nothing happened that night." He pressed his cheek to her hair. "I swear to you, Brooke. Yes, I went back to the party. I was pissed at you. I was tempted to get wasted and there were hot girls everywhere." She smiled against his chest. "But I did nothing with any of them except get my picture taken, which I didn't even know about until the next day, and I left alone."

She nodded. "Why?"

"Why what?"

"Why were you pissed at me?"

She felt his sigh against her hair. "Because you were pushing me away. Because you were insisting it was just business between us. And I…" He paused. "I thought there was more than that."

She squeezed her eyes closed. "How can we have more than that? You're leaving tomorrow."

He drew back and held her upper arms. He looked into her eyes. "We need to talk."

She gave him a hesitant nod then glanced over his shoulder and saw the hotel room full of people. "Oh, shnippits. I didn't know you had people here…"

His lips twitched at her curse. "Yeah. Come on in."

Brooke looked again and saw it was really just three other people. Corey, Matt and Holden. "Hi." She gave them a weak smile.

Corey smiled back. "Hi Brooke. Glad you came. We showed up to support Dylan and find out what we can do about this."

Brooke nodded. Holden was sitting at the desk with a laptop, clicking away at it. "What do we know?" She sat on the edge of the bed.

They told her about the positive test and how he could have a second sample tested.

"But that would only help if there really was a mistake." She frowned.

Dylan gave her a look. "Oh, there *was* a mistake."

"I'm just saying. If there's something in your urine that resulted in a positive test, it would probably also be there in the second sample."

"I didn't smoke anything though," Dylan objected. "So it can't be positive."

"What are the banned substances?" Brooke asked.

They read her the list.

"So there are some things it's okay to take," she said.

"I guess basically anything legal and that's not considered performance enhancing."

"I'm just researching the rules in the rule book," Holden said. "Because there are exemptions."

"Like what?" Matt asked.

"There are situations where a surfer can have an exemption if they have a physical or mental medical condition that requires prescription medication. Here it is."

Brooke stared at Holden. Her vision blurred and she saw herself standing in the bathroom at L'Auberge Pacifique in Papeete, poking into Dylan's toiletry bag, checking out his medications. She'd been concerned about him taking drugs and so she'd snooped. What had she seen? There'd been two bottles and she'd meant to Google the names of the drugs, but then she'd completely forgotten about it in the days following when they'd had no Internet access.

She rose to her feet and walked into the bathroom of Dylan's hotel room. There was the same black toiletry bag sitting on the marble counter. She unzipped it and peered inside, but then had to dig around under a few things to find the two small, white-capped bottles. She pulled them out. Pantoloc and Effexor.

She dropped the bag and carried the bottles into the room. She stopped in front of Dylan, who sat in an armchair, and held them out. He looked at them, then back at her. His mouth twisted as he took them from her. "I told you about the Pantoloc," he said quietly. "But not the Effexor."

"What is it?"

His lips pursed. "It's an anti-depressant medication."

Her heart squeezed. "Oh." She remembered what Corey had told her. Frack. He really had had a rough time. She went to her knees on the carpet in front of him and set her hands on his hard thighs. "It's okay, Dylan. It's okay to need that."

"I don't need it. Not anymore. I haven't taken that stuff for a long time."

"We're going to talk about that too. Okay, what about the Pantoloc?"

"I take it every day."

She shifted and looked at Holden. "Can I use the laptop?"

"Sure." He stood so she could have the chair. Dylan helped her to her feet and she sat in front of the desk and started Googling. She clicked in and out of various medical sites, not finding what she wanted. She typed in another search using different terms. She tapped her fingers on the desk…waiting… and…there! There it was. She clicked to the site. "Oh. My. God."

"What?" everyone in the room asked.

"Pantoloc—or pantoprazole—can result in a false positive for TCP."

"Shut the fuck up." Holden leaped to his feet. "Seriously?"

She slanted him an amused glance and looked at Dylan. "Seriously. Read for yourself." She turned the laptop so he could see the screen.

He read. He looked at her. He read again."Jesus Christ."

"Why the fuck didn't you tell the ASP about that?" Holden shouted. "They make exceptions, but you're supposed to tell them ahead of time!"

"I never thought." Dylan looked as if someone had hit him in the head with a longboard. "I never even thought. A doctor prescribed it and it's not performance enhancing. In fact, it's kind of embarrassing. But I had this stomach acid problem and I was tired of having heartburn all the time."

"Goddamn," Matt said.

Corey blew out a long breath.

"What do we do now?" Brooke asked. "Can you tell them? Surely an appeal on that basis would work."

"We have to try," Holden said. "We need a good lawyer. I know a few."

"My sister," Brooke said. "She's an attorney." She looked questioningly at Dylan. "Want me to call her?"

He gave her a crooked smile. "I don't know if she'll want to help me."

Brooke smiled back at him. "I'll convince her."

"Go for it, babe." He sat there, still looking stunned.

Brooke called her sister. Fraya came to the hotel right away. When they told her what was going on, she leveled Dylan with a long, hard stare. Brooke watched Dylan hold her gaze steadily and then Fraya nodded. "Have you two talked yet?"

"No."

Brooke frowned. "What—?"

"But you're going to," Fraya said. "Right?"

"Right."

And Brooke's mouth fell open a little when Fraya smiled at him. With frightening efficiency and impressive skill, she obtained all the details, including the name of the doctor who had prescribed the medication for Dylan, then left to go back to her office to begin the appeal process. "I'll keep you in the loop," she told Dylan and Holden, having programmed their cell phone numbers into her phone.

When she'd gone, everyone looked at each other.

"What do you think?" Corey asked. "Will it work? Will he get to keep his title?"

"And not get suspended for a year." Dylan rubbed his face.

Brooke was afraid to feel hopeful, but she had utmost faith in her sister's abilities. "Fraya's good. I know that doesn't guarantee anything. Rules have been broken."

"Sort of."

"Sort of." She nodded. "I don't have any idea how the organization will look at this. They could say you should have told them before and it's too late now. Or maybe they'll agree that the drug didn't make any difference in the outcome of the competition."

She looked at Dylan, the lines of strain around his mouth and eyes, the way the corners of his mouth dipped down, and her heart turned over in her chest. God. He'd worked so hard for this, his whole life, and when he finally won, a stupid, innocent screw up could rob him of his title. He'd been so happy and she'd been so happy for him, and she did *not* want this taken away from him. She knew what it meant to him.

"I'm sorry, Dylan. Maybe if I'd said something when I saw those medications in Tahiti—" She paused and heat flooded her cheeks. "Um, yeah, I did snoop a little. I was worried about what drugs you were taking, but when I saw they were a prescription, I never even thought that there could be problems with drug testing."

"Christ, Brooke, this isn't your fault. It's my fault, and only my fault."

"Your doctor should have said something," Matt interjected. "He knew you were a pro surfer, didn't he?"

Dylan shook his head. "Nah. I mean, he did, I mentioned it in passing, but he wouldn't be familiar with pro sports and rules and drug testing. I can't blame anyone else." He looked around the room, meeting everyone's eyes unflinchingly. "I take full responsibility for this."

"It'll be okay," Corey said softly. "I know it will."

"Thanks, Cor." He smiled at her and Brooke watched the interaction, seeing the affection between them, and also seeing the complete lack of anything…more. No attraction, no sexual sparks, no heat. Just friendship, pretty much the same as when he looked at Matt.

She bit her lip and looked down at the carpet. Maybe she'd overreacted to that whole revelation about what had happened between them. She shifted in the chair. It still made her a little uncomfortable. But that was in the past.

"Okay." Matt stood. "I guess there's not much more we can do right now. Fraya's on it. Let us know if you hear anything."

Corey stood too, slinging her purse over her shoulder. She looked at Dylan. "Will you still leave tomorrow?"

He shook his head. "No. I guess I better stay in case there's a hearing. There's lots of time before the next event, and anyway, I don't even know if I'll be able to surf in it."

"You will." Corey smiled at him. "If you want to come over later, have dinner with us, hang out…just come on by. We're there."

"Thanks." Dylan rose too and shoved his hands into the pockets of his loose shorts. He followed them to the door, and Brooke watched and listened. "Thanks guys, for coming. You have no idea how much it means to me."

They smiled, all of them embracing, then left.

Dylan turned back and looked at Holden.

Holden looked back at him. Then he looked at Brooke. "Ah! Brooke!" He jumped to his feet again. "Right! I have to go too."

Brooke lifted an eyebrow.

"We'll talk more later," Holden said. "Listen, Dylan. What I said earlier. I'm here for you too. We'll get through this."

Dylan nodded, his eyes crinkling at the corners. He slapped a hand on Holden's shoulder as he walked him to the door too. "Thanks, man. Appreciate it."

"I'll work on a media release. Talk to you later."

And then the door closed and she was alone with Dylan.

Dylan shoved a hand through his hair and let out a long, slow breath of pent up tension. "Well. This has been a crazy day."

"No kidding."

They looked at each other. He wasn't sure where to start. What to say.

He walked over to the window and braced one palm against the cool glass. Big mounds of white clouds floated across the blue sky.

His friends had come when he was in deep shit. Matt. Corey. Brooke. All the people he cared most about in the world, the people he'd pushed away. The people who easily could have believed the worst of him and left him to clean up this mess on his own. He wanted to deserve their faith in him. He wanted to be the man they all seemed to think he was. Especially Brooke. She'd believed in him. Defended him. Put her job on the line for him.

He'd won that championship fair and square and he was proud of it. If he lost the title because of this screw up…well, it would suck. Definitely. But it wouldn't be the end of the world. Because it wasn't the most important thing in the world. Surfing didn't make him the man he wanted to be. The man he wanted to be was honest and honorable and generous and selfless. He had a long way to go before anyone would call him selfless, but he thought he'd made progress these last few weeks with the work he'd done, and even more that morning when he'd gone in to the Jackson Cole offices and gone to bat for Brooke.

He turned to look at her. She sat on the bed, watching him, her silky brown hair falling over her shoulders, her eyes big and warm.

He didn't want to leave her. He didn't want to leave San Amaro. And then it hit him that, yeah, his feelings were kind of the same as the last time he'd been there. Yeah, he was afraid to leave—but not because he was afraid of surfing. Not even because he was afraid of failing, because he'd just showed himself and the whole world he could win. What he was really afraid of—was being alone.

His selfish existence all these years, traveling from one place to another with no real home, partying with people he called friends but who really didn't give a shit about him, seemed meaningless. The only people who really cared about him were right here in San Amaro. Corey and Matt, and why he was lucky enough to have their friendship he had no fucking idea, after what he'd done. And Brooke.

Amid all the excitement about winning, all the attention and adulation and celebration, he'd really been alone. No Brooke. No Corey and Matt. He didn't really have any family. Despite all the throngs of people around him, hoisting him onto their shoulders, spraying him with champagne, hugging him and slapping his back and yes, coming on to him, he'd been alone. More alone than he'd ever been in his life.

So if he lost that title, he'd be okay—but only if he still had the things that really mattered. His friends. And Brooke.

"Are you okay?"

He pressed a hand to the faint ache in his chest. "I think so."

"Tell me about your accident." She scooted over on the bed and sat cross-legged, tucking her knee-length cotton skirt between her legs.

He sat on the bed, mimicking her pose, facing her. "I did tell you about it."

"Not everything. Corey and Matt told me a little. Did you have PTSD?"

"No." She gave him a look and he shook his head, leaning forward a little. "I didn't have an official PTSD diagnosis. I had some of the symptoms but not enough of them to say it was PTSD."

"Oh."

"It was bad enough." He gave her a rueful smile. "For a while I was afraid I was never going to be able to get back in the water and surf again."

"But you did."

"I did. I got some counseling, and as you saw, the doctor prescribed the Effexor. I took it a few times. Then I kind of tried other ways of medicating myself. Booze. Weed. Sex."

He watched her reaction for signs of disgust or judgment. But she just nodded. "Corey said that was why you wanted her to go with you, last year when you were here. Because you were afraid."

He tipped his head back and looked at the ceiling, took in a breath and let it out. "Yeah. She's right. She knew that then. I was terrified but I didn't want to admit it to anyone."

"So you weren't really in love with her?"

"No." He met her eyes and shook his head slowly. "No, Brooke. There was attraction between us, back then, but she's my best friend's girl and they love each other, and once I realized that, there was no way I would ever touch her again. I liked her, yeah. I mean, I still do. But just as friends." He paused. "That bothered you, didn't it?"

She pressed her lips together and bent her head, her hair sliding over her shoulders and over her face. "Yes. I was…jealous."

He smiled. He liked that. But he hated that he'd hurt her. "I'm sorry. I can't take it back. It was something that happened a long time ago before I met you. I mean, met you again. But it really means nothing in my life."

"Really?" She lifted her head and gazed at him. "Wasn't that why you didn't want to come back to San Amaro? You said it was because they were bugging you about being single, but that wasn't the real reason, was it?"

He grimaced. "No. You're right. I kinda fudged that a bit. Fuck." He closed his eyes briefly as his gut tightened. "You're gonna think I'm the biggest pussy in the world. But the truth is, I was scared to come back and face both of them. I had this idea in my head that Matt had gotten the girl we both wanted. Not to mention, it was totally awkward seeing them after what had happened and now they're together and getting married. But most of all, I didn't want them to feel sorry for me. I wanted them to know I'd moved on and I figured that was a good way to show them I had." He opened his eyes and made himself meet her gaze head-on. "When I got here, I almost started having another panic attack. It brought back memories of last time I was here and how fucked up I was. But here's the truth: Once I saw Matt and Corey…it was okay."

She watched him with big eyes, her face serious, her pretty lips parted as she listened intently.

"It was okay," he repeated. "I was happy for them. Matt and I are okay. Corey's still a friend. I was over it and it wasn't long before I realized I'd never really loved her. Because…" He swallowed. Damn. People thought he was brave and fearless going out on the ocean and surfing crazy big waves, taking risks and doing dangerous things. But that was nowhere near as scary as what he was about to do. "Because I love *you*, Brooke. And that was when I knew I never loved Corey. Not like that."

She rolled her lips inward and her eyes got all shiny. Shit. She was going to cry. He wanted to haul her across the bed and onto his lap and squeeze the breath out of her. But he waited.

"I don't want to leave, Brooke."

She gazed at him with those luminous eyes. "But you have to."

"Well, I guess we'll see about that. If I end up suspended for a year, I won't need to. But even if I do…I want to have a home. I want somewhere to come home to. I want some*one* to come to. I want come home to…you."

A tear rolled down her cheek, a narrow silvery trail.

"Come here." He held out his arms to her.

She shifted onto her knees and crawled toward him, curling onto his lap, and he wrapped his arms around her and held on tight. She felt perfect and right and lovely there in his arms, so small and soft. And yet he knew she was strong and dependable. Someone you could count on, to be there, to do the right thing. He so did not deserve her.

"I love you, Dylan," she whispered into his chest. But he heard her. His eyes stung at the corners and he squeezed them shut and tightened his arms around her.

"I love you too, babe. So much." He found her chin and tipped her head up, then bent to kiss her mouth, a soft, long, clinging kiss. She slid her arms around his neck and shifted closer still, her soft breasts pressing against his chest, and the kiss went deeper, hotter. Their tongues rubbed together as their mouths opened to each other. Blood rushed hot through his veins and his heart picked up a rapid percussion against his ribs. His dick hardened against her hip.

"Hey, would you look at that," he said, long moments later, their foreheads pressed together, both of them breathing fast. "We're on a bed."

"How convenient."

"I thought so too."

They shared a smile.

He opened the three buttons of her loose top then slipped his fingers inside to stroke the soft skin over her collarbone, up to the side of her neck, then lower where her breast began to swell. His whole hand slid inside the top and cupped her shoulder, and he kissed her again, gently pushing her down to the bed. He moved over her, still kissing her, licking into her mouth, tasting her sweetness.

"I wanted to tell you." He brushed his lips over her cheek. "After that night when I went back to the party."

"Tell me what?" She turned her face so he could kiss her cheek and nuzzle her ear, and her body shivered against his.

"That I love you. I realized I was so fucking jealous of you flirting and dancing with those other guys. I wanted to tell you. And then everything went to shit. They took you away and sent Tim instead, and you wouldn't answer my calls."

"You were jealous?"

He nipped her jaw and she gasped. "Hell yeah. That cop guy better not ever fucking look at you again."

She huffed out a laugh as he took her earlobe between his lips and tugged. "I guess I won't go out with him this week after all."

"What!" He drew back and scowled at her. "You were going to go out with him?"

"Well, we didn't make an actual date, but he asked me out and I said maybe after the Pro was done. You were leaving and…"

He growled. "Fuck that."

She laughed softly and twined her arms around his neck. "I didn't want to go out with him, Dylan. I only wanted you." She sucked briefly on her bottom lip. "I'm sorry I tried to make you jealous. I thought you were still all hung up on Corey."

He let out a sigh. "Hell, Brooke. And I thought you'd realized what a mistake it was sleeping with me because I'm such an asshole."

"Oh Dylan. I already told you." She kissed his jaw, his cheek, beside his eye. "You're not an asshole. I may have thought that when we met up in Tahiti, but it didn't take me long to see what you're really like inside."

He buried his face in the side of her neck and breathed in her warm female scent. It filled his head, and warmth spread through his body, centering in the heavy ache at his groin. "Brooke, God, Brooke, I love you so much."

The kiss went deeper, hotter, and he sank into it, sank into her, like he was drowning and only she could save him. He pressed her down into the mattress, his cock throbbing against her soft body, his hands buried in her hair, his thumbs on her cheeks. Her arms wrapped around his shoulders and she parted her legs so they fit together even closer, his hardness at her center where she was warm and damp. When her heels dug into his ass, heat raced through his veins and he groaned.

Reluctantly he eased away from her to remove her clothing, then his own, and then they were both naked, skin to skin, her body soft curves and smooth skin against his. Her soft sounds of pleasure surrounded him as he kissed her again, tongues sliding together. He touched her everywhere, her soft breasts with hard little tips, the dip of her waist, the smooth line of her hip and thigh. Her kissed her and kissed her and kissed her until they were both panting and inside out with need.

He reached between them for his cock to find his way inside her body, desperate need pulsing through his body, centered there where he was so hard and aching. And then…*shit.*

"I need a condom." He leaned his forehead against hers.

She went very still, her hands holding his shoulders. "It's okay. I think."

"Really?" He lifted his head to look down at her. He should have asked more, but the blood pounding through his veins and the urgent need to have her, to be inside her now, took over his body and with sweet, delicious relief he pushed inside her. Scalding hot around him, so tight, so wet, he moved inside her in one long slide of pleasure.

They rocked together in a haze of heat and arousal, love and lust, relief and hope. Murmured words and soft sighs passed their lips between long kisses. As Brooke's body tightened beneath him and her fingers dug into him, he lifted his head to watch her face, to absorb her cries of pleasure and whimpers of delight, her body tightening around him. He couldn't hold it off any more and he let the powerful orgasm crash over him, holding himself deep, deep inside her. "Never," he muttered. "Never wanna leave you. Love you."

They might have dozed off for a while. A pinging noise filled Dylan's ears and he floated back to awareness and lifted his head.

"My cell phone," Brooke murmured. "Maybe it's Fraya."

Both immediately more alert, Brooke scrambled out of the bed and found her phone in her purse. But she'd missed the call. She studied the screen. "Not Fraya. Tim."

"Huh."

"I am supposed to be at work right now." She tapped the button to call him back. She shoved her hair back and held the phone to her ear.

She stood there naked and gorgeous, her skin smooth and

lightly tanned with the paler outline of a bikini over her breasts and hips. Her tousled hair gleamed in the sun shining in the big window. "Hey Tim. What's up?" She paused. "I'm still at the Hilton. Yeah." Another pause. "Okay." This time she listened for longer. Her eyes went wide. Her forehead creased. Her pretty mouth fell open. "Are you serious? Shut the front door!"

What the hell was going on? Dylan pushed himself to sitting, dragging the sheet over his lap.

She turned to look at him, still wide-eyed. "Whoa, that's unbelievable. Yeah. Yeah, I'll be in tomorrow. Holy guacamole! Okay. Yeah. Thanks, Tim."

She clicked off the phone and shook her head, a dazed expression on her face.

"Everything okay?" Dylan asked.

"Um. Yeah." She dropped the phone back in her purse and walked back toward the bed. He took in the excellent view. She slid in beside him and pulled the covers up over her sweet breasts. "They fired Barrett."

"Whoa! Seriously?"

"Seriously. I can't believe it. Pierson was furious at him for how he talked to me." She met Dylan's eyes. "And Tim says Pierson wants to meet with me tomorrow morning." She tipped her head to one side. "I still don't know how you knew about that." Her eyebrows flew up. "Oh. My. God. Fraya. It was her, wasn't it?"

"Yeah."

She bit her lip. "Damn." Then she peeked at him through her eyelashes. "Look what you've done."

Was she upset about that? He thought she hated Barrett. That was what Fraya had said…

She smiled. "Frack, I hated working for that guy. I guess I don't need to quit now." And she leaned over and gave him a big smooch on the lips. "Thank you."

He grinned and pushed her down into the pillows to kiss her properly.

When they came up for air, she said, a little breathlessly, "I have something I have to tell you. But I don't want you to freak out."

Dylan propped himself on an elbow. "Uh…Jesus. When you say something like that to a guy, you could give him a heart attack."

"I know. I'm sorry. But this is kind of…big."

His heart stopped then lurched into heavy thuds. "Are you pregnant?"

She stared up at him with those big, glowing eyes, her lips parted. She blinked. "My period is late. How the hell did you know that?"

"We had sex five hundred times with no condom. It wouldn't exactly be a surprise."

"Five hundred times. In your dreams, buddy."

He grinned, something soft and warm unfurling in his chest. "Oh yeah. Definitely in my dreams. I should be freaking out right now, shouldn't I?"

"Lots of guys would." She stared at him searchingly.

"I probably would have too, a few months ago. I mean, the idea of being a father *is* kind of terrifying. But Christ, Brooke. I love you. I want a family. I want a home."

"I don't know if I'm pregnant." She sank her teeth into her soft bottom lip and made him want to lick it.

"Right. Right. Okay. We'll deal with whatever happens. It's not like I didn't think about it, after what we did. But I love you and we're going to get married anyway."

"We are?" Her eyes narrowed. "What the heck kind of proposal is that?"

"Oops. Not good, huh? Okay, forget I said that. Just wipe it from your hard drive. I can do better."

Her lips curved into a sexy smile. "Too late. You can't put the toothpaste back in the tube."

He burst out laughing and hugged her to him. "Christ, I love you."

"I love you too."

"Our lives are a big mess right now."

"Yep."

"But I don't care. I mean I care. But I realized earlier…none of it matters. What matters is, I have you."

"What matters is, we have each other."

EPILOGUE

Four months later...

Brooke sat on the deck of the Surf Sisters' beach house. Little white lights twinkled everywhere, including on the Christmas tree in the corner, lining the deck railing and wrapping around the trunks of the palm trees swaying in the night breeze next to the deck. A bonfire on the beach flickered toward the dark sky, people sitting on the sand around it. The rush of ocean waves washing onto the sand was a distant murmur beneath the music pouring from the big speakers, currently My Chemical Romance singing "All I Want for Christmas is You". People all around her were having fun, drinking Laguna Dorada beer that Matt had brought, eating all the food laid out on the big table just inside the sliding doors, dancing and laughing.

Brooke sighed, lifted her drink and took a sip, watching Corey and Matt across the deck, their heads leaning close together. Matt lifted a hand and slid it around the nape of Corey's neck and her eyes drifted closed. He kissed her temple. Brooke smiled, her chest warming, but she also felt a pinch of envy and yearning.

"Hey Brooke, how's it going?"

Brooke looked at Jules Stockwood who dropped into the chair beside her. "Good. How about you? Are you all moved in? Moved out? Both?"

Jules laughed. "Yes. I know you aren't supposed to move into my old place until January first, but you can have the house sooner if you want."

Brooke smiled. "That might work. But Christmas is such a busy time. We'll see."

"Just let me know."

"You're a brave woman. Living with two guys."

"I know." Jules rolled her eyes and took a drink of the red wine in her glass. "There are some advantages, mind you…two guys to fix things, cut the grass, change the oil in my car…double the orgasms."

Brooke choked on a laugh. She'd gotten to know Jules better since they'd agreed that Brooke would take over the lease on Jules's small beach cottage, which helped Jules out so she could move in with Mike and Carlos. "But how about double the laundry." Brooke grinned. "Double the socks lying on the bedroom floor. Double the towels in the bathroom. Two guys not cleaning up after themselves in the kitchen."

"Uh uh." Jules' eyes danced. "Mike is a neat freak. No worries there."

"I'm not a neat freak." Mike appeared beside Jules's chair and laid a hand on her shoulder.

"Course not, babe." Jules laid her hand on top of his and winked at Brooke.

"Come on down to the fire," Mike said. "It's cold tonight."

"Okay. Coming, Brooke?"

"Sure." They all rose, but just then Brooke's cell phone buzzed in the pocket of her jeans. She pulled it out to see "Dylan".

Her heart bumped and a smile broke across her face. "Dylan," she said to the others. "You go on, I'll be right there."

She hit the button to talk. "Hi hon!"

"Babe. Where are you? Sounds noisy."

"Surf Sisters are having a Christmas party." She paused. "Wish you were here."

"Me too."

"How's Hawaii?"

"Done. Be home soon."

"As the Kahakai Pro champ." She grinned, turning away from the party and facing the dark beach.

"Yeah." She heard the satisfaction in his voice. "Just wish you could've been there to see me win."

"I know. Me too."

"You're coming with me to Australia in March."

She made a face that he couldn't see. Australia was a twelve-hour flight away. But hey. She'd made it to Tahiti a few months ago. She could do Australia.

"Happy to be coming home for a few months. Gonna be so good to stay in one place for a while."

"I know. Miss you so much, hon."

The song on the speakers changed to U2 singing "Baby Please Come Home". With a grin she moved to one speaker and held her phone to it.

When she returned it to her ear, Dylan was laughing. "On my way, babe."

She laughed softly too. "Good."

"Are you on the beach? Or the deck?"

"The deck. I was just going to go down to the fire. Jules and Mike and Carlos are here, and Corey and Matt. Neve's here somewhere."

And then she frowned as she heard U2 singing in her ear. Through her phone.

She turned around. Dylan stood across the deck. His smile

was white in his tanned face, and he swept his dark hair back out of his eyes with one hand, his other holding his phone to his ear. "It's fucking cold here compared to Hawaii," he said into the phone.

Her heart expanded so much she felt like she was going to burst. She looked at him for a long moment and then she started to cry. Smiling, she shook her head and shoved her phone into her pocket, then launched herself at him. He dropped his phone to a chair and braced himself, and she jumped him, wrapping her legs around his hips, her arms around his neck. He caught her by her ass and then one arm slid higher up to hold her tight. "Babe," he murmured into her hair.

"Dylan. God, Dylan." She sobbed and held on tighter.

"Hey. Hey, I'm back. It's okay."

She nodded, her throat too clogged with tears to talk. Then she shifted in his arms so she could kiss him. Their mouths joined hungrily. She couldn't get close enough to him, fisting his hair in one hand. His tongue licked into her mouth and she gave another half-moan, half-sob.

"You weren't supposed to be here until tomorrow."

"Caught an earlier flight."

"It's hard," she said, still crying. "So hard to be away from you."

"I know, babe, I know, me too. But I'm here now and I'm not going anywhere until March. And we're moving in together next month—"

"Jules said we can move in right away. She's all moved out."

"Whatever. As long as we're together."

She nodded and squeezed him again. He lowered her so her feet touched the deck and Brooke became aware of people standing around them wearing big smiles. She gave a shaky smile back and swiped at her wet face with one hand.

Then Corey was there, her hand rubbing Brooke's back, leaning in to kiss Dylan's cheek. "Welcome home, champ."

Dylan grinned.

Matt was there too, slapping his back. Dylan tucked Brooke under one arm to greet everyone and accept their congratulations.

Then Jules pressed something cold into Brooke's hand. "If you want some privacy for a few minutes," she whispered to Brooke.

Brooke looked down at the key. She met Jules's eyes. "Thanks." She smiled.

If she could drag Dylan away from his adoring fans, maybe they could have a few minutes to themselves.

Someone put a beer in Dylan's hand, people kept talking to him, but he never let go of her and she stayed like that, her front pressed to his side, arms wrapped around his waist. Finally things calmed down a little and she manoeuvred him away from the crowd.

"Come on." She showed him the key. "Let's go look at our new house."

The cottage Jules had been living in was just up the street. Jules was moving to the house next door, where Mike and Carlos lived. Matt and Corey lived on this street too. It was going to be awesome to live so close to their friends.

Matt and Corey had been amazing. They'd stood by Dylan after he'd failed the drug test and all the resulting craziness. And they'd been awesome to her when Dylan had been away. Matt was such a great guy, looking out for her, and Corey was so positive and encouraging when Brooke was sad and missing Dylan.

They followed the stone sidewalk around the side of the Surf Sisters' house and then walked down the narrow road, the music and voices fading away behind them. Colored lights and decorations twinkled on every house.

"It's small." She handed Dylan the key to unlock the front door. "But it's close to the beach. And it'll be ours."

"We'll need a bigger place soon." He led her into the dark house.

"What for?"

"For all the kids we're gonna have."

"Aw. Are you still disappointed I wasn't pregnant?"

He stopped in the middle of the empty living room. Hardwood floors gleamed in the faint light coming in the big front window. She moved to him and he slid his arms around her and pulled her up against him, pelvis to pelvis. She laid her hands on his chest, big and strong, and they looked at each other. "Yeah. You know I am." He touched his lips to her nose.

"It worked out for the best." She gazed up at him. "Since I got promoted and took over Barrett's job, it wouldn't have been a great time to tell them I was going on maternity leave. Plus…" She sighed. "I don't know if I can be a mom when you're away traveling so much. It's hard enough without you when it's just me, never mind a baby."

"I know." His hands slid down to her butt. "One more year. Now I'm winning, I can make some serious cake."

She laughed. After his positive drug test, he'd been allowed to keep his championship but he *had* been suspended for a month for not telling the ASP that he was taking the Pantoloc, which meant he hadn't been able to compete in France this year. But after that, he'd won again in Portugal and just now, Hawaii.

"I've got bigger sponsorship deals. The prize money is good. We can buy a bigger house and be set financially. And I'll figure out what I want to do after that."

"Mike and Carlos offered you a job teaching surfing. And the Surf Sisters would probably hire you too."

"Yeah. I feel like I need more than that though. Just haven't figured it all out yet. But I'm going to like having a home base to come back to between competitions. I'm going to like having you to come back to between competitions." He glanced over his shoulder. "I don't suppose Jules left a bed here?"

Brooke giggled. "I don't think so. I bought a king-sized one the other day, but it's not going to be delivered until after Christmas."

"Gonna be a good Christmas."

"My family can be a little crazy."

"Bring it. I can do crazy." He kissed her mouth. "I'm stoked to have a big family Christmas here."

"Me too. It'll be full-on derelict. Gnarly, even."

He threw his head back and laughed. "Dudette. God I love you."

She grinned and kissed his chin. "Love you too, surfer dude."

AUTHOR NOTE

Thank you so much for reading Slammed! Make sure you're on my mailing list for news about my next releases. If you enjoyed Slammed, please consider leaving a review at the retailer of your choice or at Goodreads to help other readers find my books. You can also contact me at info@kellyjamieson.com to tell me what you thought of it or ask me any questions!

OTHER BOOKS BY KELLY JAMIESON

Heller Brothers Hockey

Breakaway

Faceoff

One Man Advantage

Hat Trick

Offside

Love Me

Friends with Benefits

Love Me More

2 Hot 2 Handle

Lost and Found

One Wicked Night

Sweet Deal

Hot Ride

Crazy Ever After

All I Want for Christmas

Sexpresso Night

Irish Sex Fairy

Conference Call

Rigger

You Really Got Me

How Sweet It Is

Power Series

Power Struggle

Taming Tara

Power Shift

Rule of Three Series

Rule of Three

Rhythm of Three

Reward of Three

San Amaro Singles

With Strings Attached

How to Love

Slammed

Windy City Kink

Sweet Obsession

All Messed Up

Playing Dirty

Three of Hearts

Loving Maddie from A to Z

Brew Crew

Limited Time Offer

No Obligation Required

Aces Hockey

Major Misconduct

Off Limits

Icing

Top Shelf

Back Check

Slap Shot

Last Shot

Body Shot

Hot Shot

Bayard Hockey

Shut Out

Cross Check

Dancing in the Rain

ABOUT THE AUTHOR

Kelly Jamieson is a best-selling author of over forty romance novels and novellas. Her writing has been described as "emotionally complex", "sweet and satisfying" and "blisteringly sexy." She likes coffee (black), wine (mostly white), shoes (high heels) and hockey!

Subscribe to her newsletter for updates about her new books and what's coming up, follow her on Twitter @KellyJamieson or on Facebook, visit her website at www.kellyjamieson.com or contact her at info@kellyjamieson.com

Printed in Dunstable, United Kingdom

63988455R00171